"Gentleman, the silver spike is loose in the world. It's not the Dominator. He's dead. But the undying black essence that drove him remains. And that could be used by an adept to summon, coerce, and shape powers even I cannot begin to fathom. That spike could become a conduit to the very heart of darkness, an opener of the way that would confer upon its possessor powers perhaps exceeding even those the Dominator possessed.

"Our mission, our *holy* mission, given the White Rose by Old Father Tree himself, is to recover the silver spike and deliver it for safekeeping, at whatever cost to ourselves, before someone of power seizes upon it and shapes it to his own dark purposes and is, in his turn, shaped—perhaps into a shadow so deep there would be no chance ever for the world to win free."

Also by Glen Cook from Tor Books

GLEN COOK

THE SILVER SPIKE

TOR®
fantasy

A TOM DOHERTY ASSOCIATES BOOK
NEW YORK

THE SILVER SPIKE

A Tor Book
Published by Tom Doherty Associates, LLC
175 Fifth Avenue
New York, NY 10010

www.tor.com

Tor® is a registered trademark of Tom Doherty Associates, LLC.

ISBN: 0-812-50220-5

First edition: September 1989

Printed in the United States of America

0 9 8 7 6 5

I

This here journal is Raven's idea but I got me a feeling he won't be so proud of it if he ever gets to reading it because most of the time I'm going to tell the truth. Even if he is my best buddy.

Talk about your feet of clay. He's got them run all the way up to his noogies, and then some. But he's a right guy even if he is a homicidal, suicidal maniac half the time. Raven decides he's your friend you got a friend for life, with a knife in all three hands.

My name is Case. Philodendron Case. Thanks to my Ma. I've never even told Raven about that. That's why I joined the army. To get away from the kind of potato diggers that would stick a name like that on a kid. I had seven sisters and four brothers last time I got a head count. Every one is named after some damned flower.

A girl named Iris or Rose, what the hell, hey? But I got a brother named Violet and another brother named Petunia. What kind of people do that do their kids? Where the hell are the Butches and Spikes?

Potato diggers.

People that spend their whole lives grubbing in the dirt, sunup to sundown, to root out potatoes, cabbages, onions, parsnips, rootabagas. Turnips. I still hate turnips. I wouldn't wish them on a hog. I joined the army as soon as I could sneak off.

They tried to stop me. My father and uncles and brothers and cousins. They didn't get away with it. I'm still amazed how that one old sergeant managed to look so bad the whole clan backed down.

That's what I wanted to be when I grew up. Somebody who could just stand there and look so bad people dribbled down their legs. But I think you got to be born with it.

Raven's got it. He just looks at somebody trying to jack him around and the guy turns white.

So I joined up and went through the training and went out soldiering, sometimes with Feather and Journey, sometimes with Whisper, mostly here in the north. And I found out soldiering wasn't what I thought it would be. I found out I didn't like it a whole lot better than digging potatoes. But I was good at it, even if I kept doing something to get busted every time I made sergeant. I finally got posted to the Guards at the Barrowland. That was supposed to be a big honor but I never believed it.

That's where I met Raven. Only he went by the name of Corbie then. I didn't know he was a spy for the White Rose. 'Course, nobody did or he would have been dead. He was just this quiet old crippled guy who said he used to soldier with the Limper but had to get out after he got his leg hurt so bad. He hung out in an abandoned house he fixed up. He made his living doing things for guys that didn't want to do them for themselves. The Guards got paid good and the Barrowland was a hundred miles into the Great Forest where there wasn't nothing else to spend it on but booze. Corbie got plenty of work polishing boots and swabbing floors and currying horses. He used to come in and do the colonel's office and then play chess with him, which is where I ran into him the first time.

He smelled odd right from the start. Not White Rose odd but you knew he wasn't no runaway farm boy like me or some city kid from the slums that signed up because there wasn't nothing else to do with his life. He had some class when he wanted to show it. He was educated. He talked maybe five or six languages and he could read and I heard him talk with the old man about things that I didn't have a rooster's notion what they meant.

So I got me this idea. I'd get to be his buddy and then get him to teach me how to read and write.

It was the same old thing, see. Join the army and get off

the farm and go on adventures and life would be great. Learn to read and write, I could get out of the army and go off on adventures and everything would be great.

Sure.

I don't know if everybody is that way. I'm not the kind that can ask guys about things like that. But I know me enough to know that there ain't nothing ever going to turn out to be exactly what I want and nothing is ever going to satisfy me. I'm the guy with so much ambition I'm living here in a one room walk-up with a wino whose big talent seems to be puking his guts up after scarfing down about three gallons of the cheapest wine he can find.

So anyway I got Raven to start teaching me and we ended up buddies, even if he was weird. And that didn't do me no good when the shit storm hit and he turned out to be a spy. Lucky for me, my bosses and his bosses had to get together to gang up on the monster in the ground up there, that us Guards was getting paid so good to watch.

That's when I found out he was really Raven, the guy that used to run with the Black Company, that took the White Rose away from the Limper when she was a little kid and hid her out and raised her up till she was ready to take on her destiny.

I thought he was dead. So did everybody else, on both sides. Especially the White Rose, who had loved him, and not like a brother or father. Which is why he turned himself into a dead man and ran away. He couldn't handle what it means to have somebody in love with you. Running away was the only thing he knew how to do.

But he was some in love with her, too, and the only way he had to show it was turn himself into Corbie and go spying and hope he could find her some big weapon she could use when she came to her final confrontation with the Lady. My big boss.

So what happens? Fate sticks an oar in and stirs everything up and when we look around what do we find? The Dominator, the old monster buried in the Barrowland, the blackest evil this old world ever knew, was awake and trying to get out, and the only way to stop him was for everybody to drop their old fights and gang up. So the Lady came to the Barrowland with all her double-ugly champions, and the White Rose came with the Black Company, and things started getting interesting.

And damnfool Raven mooned around in the middle of it all thinking he could just walk over and take up with Darling like he hadn't walked out on her and let her think he was dead for a bunch of years.

The damn fool. I know more about sorcery than he'll ever know about women.

So they let the old evil come up out of the ground, then they jumped all over it. It was so big and black they couldn't kill its spirit, only its flesh, so they burned that flesh to ash and scattered the ash and imprisoned its soul in a silver spike. They drove the spike into the trunk of a sapling that was the son of some kind of god that would live forever and grow around it and keep it from ever causing any more grief. Then they all went away. Even Darling, with some guy named Silent.

There were tears in her eyes when she went. Some of that feeling for Raven was still there inside her. But she was not going to open up and let him do it to her again.

And he stood there watching her go, dumbstruck. He couldn't figure out why she would do that to him.

Damn fool.

II

It was weird that nobody else thought of it right away. But maybe that was because people were more taken with what had happened between the Lady and the White Rose and were wondering what that would mean to the empire and the rebellion. For a while it looked like half the world was up for grabs. Everybody who was the sort to do some grabbing was eyeballing his or her chances and scouting around to see if they might get turned into eunuchs if they tried.

So it was up to some second-rate hustlers from Oar's north side to take first whack at stealing the silver spike.

The news from the Barrowland was still in the shithouse rumor stage when Tully Stahl came pounding on the door of the room where his cousin Smeds Stahl stayed.

The room Smeds lived in had no furnishings except roaches and dirt, half a dozen mildewed, stolen blankets, and half a gross of empty clay wine jugs that he never got around to taking back. They made him pay deposit at the Thorn and Crown. Smeds called the jugs his life savings. If times got really tough he could trade eight empties for a full.

Tully said that was a dumb way to do things. Whenever Smeds got ripped and pissed he started throwing things around. He wasted his savings.

The shards never got picked up, either, just kicked against one wall, where they formed a dusty badland.

When Tully got on him Smeds figured he was just putting on airs because he was flush. Tully had two married women giving him presents for helping out around the

5

house when the old man was gone. And he was living with a widow he was going to clean out as soon as he found some other woman to take him in. He thought being a success gave him the right to dish out advice.

Tully pounded on the door. Smeds ignored him. The Kinbro girls from upstairs, Marti and Sheena, eleven and twelve, were there for their "music lessons." The three of them were naked and tumbling around on the ratty blankets. The only instrument in sight was a skin flute.

Smeds made the girls stop bouncing and giggling. There was people who wouldn't appreciate how he was preparing them for later life.

Pound. Pound. Pound. "Come on, Smeds. Open up. It's me. Tully."

"I'm busy."

"Open up. I got a deal I got to talk about."

Sighing, Smeds untangled himself from skinny young limbs and trudged to the door. "It's my cousin. He's all right."

The girls had been into the wine. They didn't care. They didn't cover themselves. They just sat there grinning when Smeds let Tully in.

"Some friends," Smeds explained. "You want in? They don't mind."

"Some other time. Get them out."

Smeds glared at his cousin. Getting too damned pushy. "Come on, girls. Get your clothes on. Papa has to talk business."

Tully and Smeds watched while they got into ragged clothing. It didn't occur to Smeds to dress. Sheena gave old Hank the Shank a playful slap as she went by. "See you later."

The door closed. "You're going to get your ass in a sling," Tully said.

"No more than you. You ought to meet their mother."

"She got any money?"

"No. But she blows a mean horn. Got a thing about it. She gets going she just can't quit."

"When you going to clean this pigsty?"

"Soon as the maid gets back from holiday. So what's so important you have to break in on my party?"

"You heard about what happened up in the Barrowland?"

"I heard some stories. I didn't pay no attention. What do I care? Won't make no difference to me."

"It might. You hear the part about the silver spike?"

Smeds thought. "Yeah. They stuck it in a tree. I thought that would be handy to glom on to. Then I thought some more and figured there wouldn't be enough silver in it to make it worth the trip."

"It isn't the silver, cousin. It's what's in the silver."

Smeds turned it around in his mind some. He couldn't find Tully's angle. "You better lay it out by the numbers." Smeds Stahl was not known for his keen mind.

"That big nail has the soul of the Dominator trapped in it. That means it's one bad hunk of metal. You take some big wazoo of a sorcerer, I bet he could pound it into some kind of all-time mean amulet. You know, like in stories."

Smeds frowned. "We aren't sorcerers."

Tully got impatient. "We'd be the middlemen. We go up there and dig it out of that tree and hide it out till word gets around that it's gone. Then we let it out that it's for sale. To the highest bidder."

Smeds frowned some more and put his whole brain to work. He was no genius but he had plenty of low, mean cunning and he had learned how to stay alive. "Sounds damned dangerous to me. Something we'd need help on if we wanted to come out of it in one piece."

"Right. Even the easy part, going up there and liberating the damned thing, would be more than a two-man job. The Great Forest might be a pretty rough place for guys who don't know anything about the woods. I figured we'd need two more guys, one of them who knows about the woods."

"Already we're talking a four-way split here, Tully. On how much?"

"I don't know. Give them time to bid it up, I think we'd be set for life. And I ain't talking no four-way split, neither, Smeds. Two ways. All in the family."

They looked at each other. Smeds said, "You got the plan. Tell me."

"You know Timmy Locan? Was in the army for a while?"

"About long enough to figure out how to go over the hill. Yeah. He's all right."

"He was in long enough to learn how it works. We might run into soldiers up there. Would your heart be broken if they found him in an alley with his head bashed in?"

That was an easy one. "No." His heart would be fine as long as it wasn't Smeds Stahl they found.

"How about Old Man Fish? He used to trap in the Great Forest."

"Couple of straight arrows."

"That's what we need. Honest crooks. Not some guys who might try to do us out of our share. What do you say? Want to go for it?"

"Tell me how much is in it again."

"Enough to live like princes. We going to go talk to those guys?"

Smeds shrugged. "Why not? What have I got better to do?" He looked at the ceiling.

"You better get some clothes on."

Heading down the stairs, Smeds said, "You'd better do the talking."

"Good idea."

Heading up the street, Smeds asked, "You ever killed anybody?"

"No. I never needed to. I don't see where I'd have any problem."

"I had to once. Cut a guy's throat. It ain't like you think. They spray blood all over the place and make weird noises. And they take a long time to croak. And they keep trying to come after you. I still get nightmares about that guy trying to take me with him."

Tully looked at him and made a face. "Then do it some other way next time."

III

Each night there was moonlight enough, a thing came down out of the northern Great Forest, quiet as a limping shadow, into the lorn and trammeled place of death called the Barrowland. That place was heavy with the fetor of corruption. A great many corpses lay rotting in shallow graves.

Limping on three legs, the thing cautiously circled the uncorrupted carcass of a dragon, settled on its haunches in the hole it was digging so patiently, night after night, with a single paw. While it worked it cast frequent glances toward the ruins of a town and military compound several hundred yards to the west.

The garrison had existed to shield the Barrowland from trespassers with evil intentions and to watch for signs that the old darkness in the ground was stirring. Those reasons no longer existed. The battle in which the digging beast had been crippled, in which the dragon had perished, in which the town and compound had been devastated, had put an end to the need for a military stewardship.

Except that it had not occurred to anyone in authority to give the surviving Guards new assignments. Some had stayed, not knowing what else to do or where else to go.

Those men were sworn enemies of the beast.

Had it been healthy, the thing would not have been concerned. It could have dealt with those men easily. Healthy, it was a match for any company of soldiers. Crippled and still suffering from a dozen unhealed wounds, it would not be able to outrun a man let alone outfight those it would have to get through before it could pursue the messenger the Guards were sure to send flying to their masters if they discovered it.

Those masters were cruel and deadly and the beast stood no chance against them even when in the best of health.

Its master could protect it no more. Its master had been hacked to pieces and the pieces burned. Its master's soul had been imprisoned in a silver spike that had been driven into his skull.

The beast was doglike in appearance but rather uncertain in size. It had a protean nature. At times it could be as small as a large dog. At other times it might be the size of a small elephant. It was most comfortable being about twice the size of a war-horse. In the great battle it had slain many of its master's enemies before overpowering sorceries had driven it from the field.

It came stealthily, again and again, despite the fear of exposure, the pain of its wounds, and its frustration. Sometimes the wall of its excavation collapsed. Sometimes rainwater would fill the hole. And always there was the inescapable vigilance of the only truly watchful guardian the victors had left.

A young tree stood among the bones, alone. It was near immortal and was far mightier than the night skulker. It was the child of a god. In time, each night, it wakened to the digger's presence. Its reaction was uniform and violent.

A blue nimbus formed among the tree's limbs. Pale lightning ripped toward the monster. It was a quiet sort of lightning, a sizzle instead of boom and crash, but it slapped the monster like an angry adult's swing at a small child.

The beast suffered no injury, only extreme pain. That it could not endure. Each time it was hit it fled, to await another night and that delay before the child of the god awakened.

The monster's work went slowly.

IV

Darling left Raven standing there. She rode off with that guy Silent and some other guys that were all that was left of the Black Company, a mercenary outfit that really wasn't anymore. A long time ago they was on the Lady's side but something happened to piss them off and they went over to the Rebel. For a long time they was almost the whole Rebel army.

Raven watched them go into the woods. I could tell he wanted to sit down and cry like a baby, maybe as much because he couldn't understand as because she did ride off on him. But he didn't.

In most ways he was the toughest, hardest bastard I ever saw, and not always in the best ways. When I first found out he was Raven and not Corbie I like to crapped my drawers. A long time ago there was a Raven that rode with the Black Company that was the baddest of the bad. He was with them only about a year before he deserted but he made himself a big rep while he was there. And this was the same guy.

He said, "We'll give them a couple hours' head start so it don't look like we're dogging them, then we'll get out of here."

"We?"

"You want to hang around here now?"

"That would be desertion."

"They don't know if you're dead or not. They haven't counted noses yet." He shrugged. "Up to you. Come or stay."

I could tell he wanted me to come. Right then I was the

11

only thing he had. But he wasn't going to make no special appeal. Not hard guy Raven.

I didn't have no future at the Barrowland and I sure as hell wasn't going back to ride herd on potatoes. And I didn't have anybody else in the world, either. "All right. I'm in."

He started walking into town. What was left after the fight. I tagged along. After a while, he said, "Croaker was about the closest thing to a friend I had when I was in the Company." He was still confused.

Croaker was the boss merc. He wasn't boss back when Raven was with them, but they had been through a few captains since the old days. Raven was confused because his old buddy and him had gotten in a fight after the Dominator got put down.

Probably to show off for Darling, Raven had decided he was going to round everything off and close the books by getting rid of the Lady, who lost her powers during the battle. And Croaker said no you don't and didn't back down. He put an arrow into Raven's hip just to show him he was serious.

"Is a friend somebody who just stands back and lets you do whatever you want whenever you want to do it?"

He gave me one of his puzzled looks.

"Maybe he was a whole lot more her friend than he was yours. Way I heard tell, they spent a lot of time together. They rode off into the sunset together. And you know the way those guys are about brotherhood, sticking together no matter what, the Company being their family, them against the whole world. You told me about it enough."

There was more I could have said. I could have given it to him by the numbers, how they felt about brothers who ran out on them, but he wouldn't have got it.

There wasn't nobody with more guts in a fight than Raven. He wouldn't back down from nobody or nothing. But in the emotional tight spots he was ready to pack up and run in a minute. He did it to the Company and he did it to Darling, but they could take care of themselves when he did.

I think maybe the worst stunt he ever pulled, and the one that still bugs him the most, is when he ran out on his kids.

He did that back when he enrolled in the Black Company. Maybe he had his reasons, and good ones at the time. He comes up with good excuses. But there's no getting around the fact that he left his kids when they were too young to take care of themselves. Without making any arrangements for them. He never even told anybody he had kids till he told me, sort of, when he was still being Corbie and started trying to find out what happened to them. They would be grown up now. If they survived.

He didn't find out anything.

I figured he would make finding them his quest now. He didn't have anything else going. And trudging through the forest headed south, he made noises like that was what he was planning to do.

We got as far as Oar. He went out on a drunk. And stayed on it.

I went on one, too. I went through me some bad girls. All the things a guys does when he's been out in the woods for a long time, then hits the city. Took me four days to work through that and another day to shake the hangover. Then I took a look at Raven and saw he was just getting started.

I went and found us a cheap place to stay. Then I got me a job protecting a rich man's family. That wasn't hard to do. There were all kinds of rumors about what happened in the Barrowland. The rich saw troubled times coming and wanted to get themselves covered.

Darling and her bunch were in the city somewhere, for a while. So were the bunch from the Black Company. We didn't run into any of them before they left out.

V

Smeds got sick of Tully's idea before they were four days out of Oar. Nights were cold in the forest. There was no place to hide from the rain. Whole hordes of bugs chewed on you and you couldn't get rid of them when you were sick of them like you could with lice and fleas and bedbugs. You could never get comfortable sleeping on the ground—if you could sleep at all with all the racket that went on at night. There were always sticks and stones and roots under you somewhere.

And there was that bastard Old Man Fish, hardly saying shit but always sneering at you because you didn't know a bunch of woodsy stuff. Like you needed to know that shit to stay alive on the North Side.

It was going to be a pleasure to cut his throat.

Timmy Locan wasn't much better. Little carrot-top runt never shut up. All right, so he was funny most of the time. So he knew every damned joke there ever was and knew how to tell them right and half of them were the kind you wanted to remember so bad it hurt, so you could crack up your friends. But they never came out right for you even when you did remember them. . . . Damn it, even funny got old after four days.

Worse than funny, the little prick never slowed down. He bounced up in the morning like he knew it was going to be the best damned day of his life and he went after every damned day like it was. Short people weren't supposed to be joyous, they were supposed to be cocky and obnoxious. Then you could thump on them and shut them up without feeling bad about it.

14

Worst thing of all was, Old Man Fish said they couldn't follow the road on account of they might run into somebody who would want to know what they were up to or somebody who might remember them after they did the job. It was important that nobody knew who did it. But busting through the tangle of the woods was awful, even with Old Man Fish finding the way.

Tully hated it worse than Smeds, but he backed the old man up.

Smeds had to admit they were right. What he didn't have to admit was that the expedition was worth the slapping branches, the stabbing, tearing briars, and the for gods' sake spiderwebs in the face.

Or maybe the worst was the blisters on his feet. Those started practically before they got out of sight of Oar. Even though he did everything Old Man Fish told him to do, they just kept getting worse. At least they didn't get infected. That jerk Timmy kept telling cheerful little tales about guys in the army who had had blisters that had gotten infected and they'd had to have their feet or legs chopped off. Dipshit.

Fourth night in the woods he had no trouble sleeping. In fact, he was getting to that point where he could sleep whenever he stopped moving. The old man observed, "You're starting to toughen up. We'll turn you into a man yet, Smeds."

Smeds could have killed him then, but it was too much work to get out of his pack straps and go over and do it.

Maybe the pack was the worst part of it. He had to lug eighty pounds of junk on his back, and what they had eaten of the food part hadn't lightened the load a bit.

They reached their destination shortly after noon eight days after they departed Oar. Smeds stood just inside the edge of the forest and looked out at the Barrowland. "That's what all the fuss was about? Don't look like shit to me." He sloughed his pack, plopped down on it, leaned against a tree, and closed his eyes.

"It ain't what it used to be," Old Man Fish agreed.

"You got a name besides Old Man?"

"Fish."

"I mean a front name."

"Fish is good."

Laconic bastard.

Timmy asked, "That our tree out there?"

Tully answered, "Got to be. It's the only one there is."

Timmy said, "I love you, little tree. You're going to make me rich."

Tully said, "Fish, I think we ought to rest up some before we go after it."

Smeds cracked an eyelid and glimmed his cousin. That was as close as his cousin had come to complaining since the expedition had started. But Tully was a big-time bitcher. Smeds had wondered how long he would hold out. Tully's silence so far had helped Smeds keep going. If Tully wanted it bad enough to take what he had been, then maybe it really was as good as he talked.

The big hit? The one they had been seeking all their lives? Could it be? For that reason alone Smeds would endure.

Fish agreed with Tully. "I wouldn't start before tomorrow night. At the earliest. Maybe the night after. We have a lot of scouting to do. We'll all have to learn the ground the way we learn the geography of a lover."

Smeds frowned. Was this no-talk Fish?

"We have to find a secure place to camp and establish a secondary base for emergencies."

Smeds could not keep quiet. "What the hell is all this shit? Why don't we just go out there and chop the damned thing down and get out of here?"

"Shut up, Smeds," Tully snapped. "Where the hell have you been for the last ten days? Get the shit out of your ears and use your head for something besides keeping them from banging together."

Smeds shut up. His ears were open, suddenly, and they had caught a very sinister undertone in Tully's voice. His cousin had begun to sound like he regretted letting him in on the deal. Like maybe he was thinking Smeds was too

dumb to be left to live. Right now he had on that same
contemptuous look Fish wore so often.

He closed his eyes, shut out his companions, let his
mind roll back over the past ten days, picking up things
that he had heard without really hearing because he had
been so busy feeling sorry for himself.

Of course they couldn't just strut out there and chop the
damned tree down. There were soldiers watching the
Barrowland. And even if there weren't any soldiers there
was the tree itself, that was supposed to be big mojo.
Sorcery there great enough to have survived the dark
struggle that had hammered the guts out of this killing
ground.

All right. It wasn't going to be easy. He would have to
work for it harder than he'd ever worked for anything in
his life. And he would have to be careful. He would have
to keep his eyes open and his brain working. He wasn't
going to give the Kimbro girls music lessons out here.

That day and night they rested. Even Old Man Fish said
he needed it. Next morning Fish went to scout for a
campsite. Tully said, "You got blisters up to your butt,
Smeds. You stay here. Take care of them the way Fish
said. You got to get in shape to move if we got to move.
Timmy, come on."

"Where you going?" Smeds asked.

"Gonna try getting close to that town. See what we can
find out." They went.

Fish came back an hour later.

"That was quick. Find a place?"

"Not a very good one. River's moved some since I was
up here. Banks two hundred yards over there. Not much
room to run. Let me look at them feet."

Smeds stuck them out. Fish squatted, grunted, touched a
couple of places. Smeds winced. "Bad?" he asked.

"Seen worse. Not often. Got some trenchfoot getting
started, too. Others probably got a touch, too." He looked
vacant for a moment. "My fault. I knew you was green
and Tully was as organized as a henhouse. Shoulda not let

him get in such a big hurry. You get in a hurry you always end up paying."

"Decided what you're going to do with your cut yet?"

"Nope. You get to my age you don't go looking that far ahead. Good chance you might not get there. One day at a time, boy. I'm going to get some stuff for a poultice."

Smeds watched the straight-backed, white-haired man fade into the forest silently. He tried to blank his mind. He did not want to be alone with his thoughts.

Fish returned with a load of weeds. "Chop these into little pieces and put them in this sack. Equal amounts of each kind." There were three kinds. "When the sack is stuffed close it up and pound on it with this stick. Roll it over once in a while. All the leaves got to get good and bruised."

"How long?"

"Give it a thousand, twelve hundred whacks. Then dump it in this pot. Put in a cup of water and stir it up."

"Then what?"

"Then do another sack. And stir the pot every couple minutes." The old man faded into the woods without saying where he was going.

Smeds was pounding his third sack when Fish returned. He sniffed. "Guess you can do a job right when you want." He settled, took the pot. "Good. That sack will be enough."

He turned Smeds's oldest shirt into bindings for his feet, packed them with soggy, mangled leaves. A cool tingle began soothing his pains.

Fish made the others treat their feet, too. He did his own.

Smeds leaned against his tree, troubled. He did not think he was hard enough or bad enough to kill the old man.

"There between sixty and eighty people still living over there," Tully said. "Mostly soldiers. But we heard them talking like a big bunch would be leaving in a couple days. Wouldn't hurt to wait them out on that. We could finish up our scouting."

• • •

Scouting the Barrowland started after sunset, by the light of a quarter moon. The village was dark and silent. It looked a good time to prowl the open ground.

Out the four went in a loose line abreast barely in sight of one another, Tully guiding on the tree. It was not much of a tree by Smeds's estimation. Right then it looked like a fat-trunked silver-bark poplar sapling about fifteen feet tall. He could not see anything remarkable there. Why the reputation?

He reached a point where the angle was right, caught a glint of moonlight off silver. It was real! And having gotten that one glance, he began to feel the throbbing dark power of it, like it was not metal at all but an icicle of pure hatred.

He shuddered, forced his gaze away.

It was real. The wealth was there to be had. If they could take it.

He hurried forward. A long, low, stony ridge barred his path. Odd that such a thing should be there, but he did not connect it with the dragon that was supposed to have devoured the infamous sorcerer Bomanz before being slain itself. Maybe if there had been more light to reveal what his hands and feet exposed as they disturbed the masking dirt . . .

He was near the top when he heard the sound. Like an animal snuffling. And another sound beneath it, like something scratching at the earth. He looked for the others. He could see no one but Tully, who was staring at the tree from ten feet away. There was something odd about the tree. The tops of its leaves glimmered with a faint bluish ghost light.

Maybe it was a trick of the rising moon.

He got up where the footing was good, stood, glanced at the tree again. Definitely something weird going on there. The whole thing was glowing.

He looked down in front of him. His heart stilled.

Something stared back at him from fifty feet away. It had a head the size of a bushel basket. Its eyes and teeth shown in the tree light. Especially its teeth. Never had he seen so many sharp teeth, or so big.

It started toward him.

His feet would not move.

He looked around wildly, saw Tully and Timmy headed away from the tree at a dead run.

He looked forward again as the monster began its leap, its jaws opening to snap at his head. He hurled himself backward. As the monster arced after him a blue bolt from the tree smacked it aside as a man's hand swats a flying insect.

Smeds landed hard, but hard did not slow him a step. He took off running and never looked back.

"I saw it, too," Old Man Fish said, and that put the quietus on Tully trying to make like Smeds was imagining things. "Like he said, it was as big as a house. Like a giant three-legged dog. The tree zapped it. It ran away."

"Three-legged dog? Come on. What was it doing?"

Smeds said, "It was trying to dig something up. It was sniffing and pawing the ground just like a dog trying to dig up a bone."

"Damn it to hell! Complications. Why does there always have to be complications? That for sure means it'll take longer than I thought. But we don't got no time to waste. Sooner or later somebody else is going to get the same idea I did."

"Don't get in no hurry," Fish said. "Take your time and do it right. That is, if you want to live long enough to enjoy being rich."

Tully grunted. Nobody suggested they give it up. Not even Smeds, who had felt the monster's breath on his face.

"Toadkiller Dog," Timmy Locan said.

"Say what?" Tully snapped back.

"Toadkiller Dog. There was a monster in the fight up here called Toadkiller Dog."

"Toadkiller Dog? What the hell kind of name is that?"

"How the hell should I know? He ain't my pup."

Stupid joke, but everybody laughed anyway. They needed to.

VI

Raven hardly sobered up for three weeks. One night I came back to our place, I'd had enough. I'd had to hurt a man bad that day, a nut who earned it trying to grab my boss's kids. Even so I felt bad. Somehow I worked it out that it was all Raven's fault I got in a position where I had to hurt somebody.

He was drunk on his ass. "Look at you, sucking on a wineskin like it was your mother's tit. The great and famous tough guy Raven, so bad he offed his old lady in the public gardens at Opal. So bad he went head-to-head with the Limper. Laying around feeling sorry for himself and whining like a three-year-old with a bellyache. Get up and do something with yourself, man. I'm sick of seeing you like this."

In a stumbling, slurred voice he told me to get stuffed, it wasn't any of my damned business.

"The hell it ain't! It's my damned money paying for the room here, dipshit. And I got to come home every day to the stink of old puke and spilled wine and a goddamn soil pot you ain't got time to empty yourself. When was the last time you bothered to change your clothes? When was the last time you had a bath?"

He cussed me in a cracked-voice scream.

"You're just about the most selfish, thoughtless bastard I ever seen. Won't even clean up after yourself."

I went on like that, louder and angrier. But he never really fought back, which made me think maybe he was about as disgusted with himself as I was with him. But who can go around admitting he's a hopeless, useless hunk of shit?

21

Finally he ran out of what little fight he had. He got up and staggered out, without any parting shot. He did not burn any bridges behind him.

A guy I worked with and I talked it over about what you do with drunks. His dad was a reformed drunk. He told me you got to stop trying to help them out. You got to stop making excuses for them and not take excuses from them. You got to put them on a spot where they can't do nothing but face the truth because they aren't going to change a bit till *they* decide to do it. *They* got to be the ones who believe they've turned into dregs and something has got to be changed.

I didn't know if I could wait around long enough for Raven to decide he was a real grown-up man and he was going to have to face reality. Darling was gone and that was that. There were kids to be found. That whole past, down in Opal, had to be hooked back out into the light and made peace with.

Actually, I was pretty sure he would come around, given time. The kind of guy he was being was the kind he held in deep contempt. That had to seep through. But it sure was frustrating, waiting him out.

He came back home four days later, sobered up and cleaned up and looking halfway like the Raven I remembered. He was all apologetic. He promised to get straight and to do better.

Sure. They do that, too.

I would believe it when I saw it.

I didn't make any big deal out of anything. I didn't preach. There wasn't no profit in that.

He hung on pretty good. He looked like he was getting somewhere. But then two days later I came home and found him so stinking he couldn't crawl.

Hell with him, I said.

VII

They were running shorthanded, what with Timmy laid up after getting caught in a blast of the tree's blue light, but Smeds did not see where it made any difference. They were not getting anywhere. They could not go out there in the daytime without being seen from the town. After dark that monster always came and dug in its hole. They could not go out there then. And for a long time after it chased the monster, the tree remained alert, laying for more intruders. Timmy had found that out the hard way.

It looked like there was maybe an hour each morning, just before dawn, when it might be possible to get something accomplished safely.

But what? Nobody had figured that out. They sure weren't going to get a chance to chop the sucker down. Ringing it wasn't worth squat, even if you could get close enough for long enough to do it. How long for a ringed tree to die? Especially this kind?

Somebody suggested poisoning it. That sounded so good that they talked it over, recalling things they had seen used to kill weeds and stuff. Only the method demanded that they have a poison. Which meant going back to Oar to buy it. With money they did not have. And it might take as long as ringing the son of a bitch. Time was not an ally. Tully was in a panic about time already. He thought it a miracle no competition had yet shown.

"We got to do it fast."

Timmy said, "We ain't going to get it done as long as that monster keeps coming around."

"So maybe we help him find what he wants."

"You better got a mouse in your pocket when you say 'we,' cousin," Smeds said. "Because I ain't going out there to help that thing do squat."

"We burn it," Fish said.

"Huh? What?"

"The tree, fool. We burn it down."

"But we can't go out there and . . ."

Fish yanked a stick out of their woodpile. It was a yard long and two inches in diameter. He sailed it off through the woods. "Take a while, but it'll pile up. Then in with a torch or two. *Whoosh.* Up in flames. Fire burns out, we go pick up our spike."

Smeds sneered. "You forgot the soldiers."

"Nope. But you're right. Got to come up with a diversion."

Tully said, "That's the best idea yet. We'll go with it till somebody thinks up something better."

Smeds grunted. "It'll beat sitting on our asses, that's for sure." He was used to the woods now. There was no adventure left in this. Not that there had been a lot before. He was bored.

They started pitching sticks immediately. The three younger men made it a game, betting from their shares. Sticks began to accumulate.

The tree did not like the game. Sometimes it sniped back.

They thought Smeds was crazy, sneaking out every couple nights to watch the monster dig. "You got more balls than brains," Tully told him.

"Better than sitting around."

It was not that dangerous. He just had to keep down. The beast never noticed a low profile. But if you got up and showed it a silhouette, look out!

The monster's labor was slow, but it worked as though obsessed. The nights came and went, came and went.

In time it unearthed what it sought.

Smeds Stahl was watching the night it came up with a grisly trophy, a horror, a human head.

That head had been too long in too many graves, and too often injured. The monster closed its jaws on ragged remnants of hair, lifted the gruesome object. Dodging bolts from the tree, it carried the head to a backwater in the nearby river.

Smeds tagged along behind. Carefully. *Very* carefully.

The beast laved the head with care and tenderness. The tree crackled and sputtered, unable to project its power that far.

Once the head was clean, the giant hound limped back the way it had come. Smeds stole along behind, amazing himself with his daring. The beast circled the dead dragon, which more than ever appeared to be an odd feature of the terrain. It stepped over a bit of tattered leather and stone almost invisible in the soggy earth, not noticing. Smeds spotted it, though. He picked it up and pocketed it without thinking.

On the other side of the dragon the tree continued to crackle and fuss, frustrated.

When Smeds pocketed that old fetish it twitched, proclaiming to anyone properly attuned the fact that it had been disturbed.

Smeds halted in a shadow, freezing. Moonlight had fallen upon that horrible head. He saw it clearly.

Its eyes were open. A grotesque smile stretched its ruined mouth.

It was alive.

Smeds almost lost sphincter control.

VIII

Oar is the city nearest the old battleground and burying place called the Barrowland. The alarm cried by the fetish there touched two residents.

One was an old, old man living incognito because he had contrived to stage his apparent death during the struggle that had devastated the Barrowland. The alarm struck him as he sat guzzling in a workingman's tavern with new cronies who thought him an astrologer. When it hit him he knew a moment of panic. Then, tears streaming, he rushed into the street.

A questioning babble arose behind him. When his comrades came out to learn what was wrong he had vanished.

IX

It was another of those damned days. Oar was a troubled city. There were scattered disturbances, conflict between Rebel and imperial partisans, and a lot of private crimes were getting committed under the guise of politics. My boss was talking about shutting up his city house and moving out to a place he owned near Deal. If he did that I'd have to decide whether or not to go along. I wanted to talk it over with Raven, but . . .

He was passed out when I got there.

"Over a goddamned woman you never even had," I grumbled, and kicked a tin plate across the room. The son of a bitch hadn't bothered to clean up after himself again. I thought about kicking him around the room. But I wasn't mad enough to try that yet.

Even drunk and wasted away, he was still Raven, the baddest man I'd ever met. I didn't need to get into it with him.

He woke up so sudden I jumped. He used the wall to pull himself up. He was pale and shaking and I never for a second took it for the effect of the wine. That old boy was scared shitless.

He couldn't hardly stand up without that wall to help, and he was probably seeing three of me and little blue men besides, but he gobbled out, "Case, get your stuff together."

"What?"

He was working his way along the wall toward his heap of stuff. "Something just broke out of the Barrowland. . . . Oh, god!" He went down on his knees, holding his stomach. He started puking. I handed him water to cleanse his mouth and a rag to wipe up with. He didn't argue. "Something got out. Something as dark as . . ."

Up came another load.

I asked, "You sure it wasn't just a nightmare? Or maybe the grape boogies?"

"It was real. It wasn't the wine. I don't know how I know. I know. I saw it as clear as if I was there. There was that beast everybody called Toadkiller Dog." He talked slow, trying not to slur. He slurred anyway. "Something was with it. Something greater. Something of the true darkness."

I didn't know what to say. He believed it even if I didn't. He had his mess cleaned and was starting to stuff his things into a bag. He asked, "Where did you stable the horses?"

He *was* serious. Unable to navigate and brain-pickled, but he was by-damned going to do something right now.

"Thulda's. Why? Where you going?"

"We got to get help."

"Help? We? You forgetting I got me a job here? I got responsibilities. I can't just mount up and ride off chasing lights you seen in the swamp because you got aholt of some doctored wine."

He got mad. I got mad right back. We yelled and screamed some. He threw things because he wasn't in good enough shape to run me down. I stomped his wineskin to death and watched its blood trickle across the floor.

The landlady kicked the door in. She weighed two hundred pounds and was as mean as a snake. "I told you bastards I wasn't going to put up with no more of this. . . ."

We rushed her. She was a liar and a cheat and a bully and she probably stole things from the rooms when she thought she wouldn't get caught. We threw her down the stairs and stood around laughing like a couple of kid vandals. She started screeching again down below. She wasn't hurt.

I stopped laughing. She wasn't hurt, but she might have been. And I didn't have the excuse of being drunk. "I take it you're headed out of town?"

"Yeah." The humor had fled him, too. His color was ghastly.

"How you going to get out of town? It's the middle of the night."

"Cash considerations. The magical key." He shouldered his bag. "You about ready?"

"Yeah." He knew I would come all the time.

"Hey, Loo!" the gateman called into the gatehouse while Raven clinked coins. "Get your ass up. We got us another customer." He grinned apologetically. "Loo, he's got a day job plucking chickens. Got too damned many kids. You would think a guy would learn how to stop after the first dozen. Not Loo." He kept on grinning.

"You'd figure," I admitted. "This that good a job? I don't see so many guys happy with their work like you."

"Pretty boring on the night watch, mostly. Been a profitable night tonight, though."

"Others have gone before us?" Raven asked.

"Only one guy. This old man about an hour ago. In such a big damned hurry he just scattered coins all over the place."

That was what you call your basic broad hint. Raven ignored it. I made small talk till Loo turned out with the keys and opened the small port through the big gate. Raven just stared straight ahead. When Loo opened up he tossed some silver.

"Why, thank you, yer grace. Come around anytime. Any time. You got a friend down here to South Gate."

Raven didn't say anything. He just grimaced and led his horse through the gateway onto the moon-washed road.

"Thanks," I told the gatemen. "See you guys around."

"Anytime, yer grace. Anytime. I'm yer man."

Raven must have paid them off good.

The grimace was familiar, though I hadn't seen it for a while. "Your hip bothering you again?"

"It'll be all right. I've traveled with worse."

Sour bastard. He'd shaken the wine, pretty well, but the hangover was hanging over. "Taking a long time to heal."

"What the hell you expect? I'm not so young anymore. And it was one of *her* arrows Croaker got me with."

Raven didn't seem to hold no grudge. He just couldn't figure it out.

He probably didn't *want* to figure it out. His idea of Raven was that Raven was a doer, not a thinker.

Sometimes I wondered how he could feed himself so much crap.

X

The old man, worn out, stood beside his ragged mount, stared at the dusty crossroads. To the east lay Lords. Southward the road led to Roses and beyond, to other great cities. The people he had come chasing had split here. He did not know who had gone which direction, though it seemed reasonable that the White Rose had turned east toward her fastness in the Plain of Fear. The Lady should have continued southward, toward her capital, the Tower at Charm.

With that parting, the armistice between them would have ended.

"Which way?" he asked the animal. The shaggy pony did not express an opinion. The old man could not decide which woman would be best equipped to act on his news. His impulse was to keep going south, but only because by turning east he would be headed into the rising sun.

"We're too old for this, horse."

The animal made a sound that, for a moment, he took to be a response. But the pony was looking back the way they had come.

Dust cloud. Fast riders coming down. Two, looked like. After a moment the old man recognized the wild-eyed style of the man in the lead. "Here comes our answer. Let's go." He hurried along the eastbound road, turned aside into a copse, found a spot where he could watch the riders. He would take the road they ignored.

Their mission had to be the same as his. That those two men should arrive here at this moment, hurrying like hell was yapping at their heels, for any other reason, strained credulity. The one called Raven could have heard the alarm. At some time in his life he had had some small training in the art, and his spirit had spent a long time snared in the coils of the Barrowland. He was sensitive enough.

The old man's eyelids drooped. He prepared an herbal draft that would help keep him alert long enough to see what those two men would do.

XI

Raven reined back to a walk. "We gave that old boy a fright."

"Probably figures we're bandits. We look it. You going to kill these horses today? Or can we string them along for a while?"

Raven grunted. "You're right, Case. No sense getting in so big a hurry we end up taking twice as long because we have to walk most of the way. Funny. That old boy reminded me of that wizard Bomanz that got eaten by the Barrowland dragon."

"All them old-timers look the same to me."

"Could be. Hold up." He studied the crossroads. I tried to spot the old man in the copse. I was sure he was watching us.

"Well?" I asked.

"They split up like they said they would."

Don't ask me how he knew. He knew. Unless he was just faking it. I've seen him do that.

"Darling went east. Croaker kept heading south."

I'd play his game. "How do you figure?"

"*She* was with him." He rubbed his hip. "*She* would be headed for the Tower."

"Oh. Yeah." Big deal. "Which way are we headed? Whichever, we got to rest soon."

"Yes. Soon. For the horses."

"Sure." I kept my face blank. Inside I was wishing I had balls enough to yell at him that he didn't have to go on being the iron man for me. He didn't have to prove anything to me but that he could stop sucking wine by the

33

gallon and could stop feeling sorry for himself. He wanted to show me how much guts he had, let him show me he had the kind it took to go find his kids and make up with them.

He didn't have to prove anything to that old man over there in the trees, did he?

I wished he would go ahead and announce the decision I knew he was going to make. I was getting uncomfortable, knowing I was being watched. "Come on. Which way?"

He responded by spurring his mount down the south road.

What the hell was this? I even started to turn east before I realized what he'd done.

I caught up. "Why south?"

Kind of hitting it sideways, he told me, "Croaker was always an understanding kind of guy. And forgiving."

The son of a bitch was crazy.

Or maybe he'd suddenly gone sane and didn't need to whimper over Darling anymore.

XII

The three-legged beast carried the head to the heart of the Great Forest, to the altar at the center of a ring of standing stones that had been in place for several thousand years. It could barely squeeze through the picket of ancient oaks surrounding that greatest of the holy places of the pitifully diminished forest savages.

The monster deposited the head and hobbled back into the dappled woods.

One by one the beast hunted down the shamans of the woodland tribes and compelled them to go to the head. In their terror those petty old witch doctors threw themselves upon their faces before it and worshiped it as a god. They swore oaths of fealty for fear of the jaws of the beast. Then they began tending to the head's needs.

Not once, to any, did it occur to take advantage of its powerlessness to destroy it. The fear of it was impressed too deeply into their kind. They could not imagine resistance.

And, always, there was that slavering monster to overawe them.

They went away from the holy place to collect willow withes, mystical herbs, rope grasses, leather both raw and tanned, blessed feathers, and stones known to possess magical properties. They gathered small animals appropriate for sacrifices, and even brought in a thief who was to be killed anyway. The man screamed and begged to be dispatched in the usual way, fearing the perpetual bondage and torment of a soul dedicated to a god.

Most of the stuff collected was junk. Most of the shamans' magic was mummery, but it proceeded from a deeper truth, from a fountain of genuine power. Power that was real enough to serve the head's immediate purpose.

In that oldest and most sacred of their holy places the shamans wove and built themselves a wicker man of willow and rope grasses and rawhide. They burned their herbs and slaughtered their sacrifices, christening and anointing the wicker man with blood. Their chanting invocations possessed the ring of stone for days.

Much of the chant was nonsense, but forgotten or only partly understood words of power lingered in its rhythms. Words enough to do.

When those old men finished the rite, they set the head on the wicker man's neck. Its eyes blinked three times.

One wooden hand snatched a staff from a shaman. The old man fell. Tottering, the amalgam moved to a patch of bare earth. With the foot of the staff it scratched out crude block letters.

Slowly the thing gave the old men their orders. They hurried off. In a week they were ready to make improvements on their handiwork.

The rites this time were more bloody and bizarre. They included the sacrifice of two men snatched from the ruined town beside the Barrowland. Those two were a long time dying.

When the rites were finished the wicker man and its corrupt burden possessed more freedom of movement, though no one would mistake the construct for a human body. The head could now speak in a soft, gravelly whisper.

It ordered, "Collect your fifty best warriors."

The old men balked. They had done their part. They had no taste for adventures.

The thing they had created whispered a chant in which there were no waste words. Three old men died screaming, devoured by worms that ate them from within.

"Gather your fifty best warriors."

The survivors did as they were told.

When the warriors came they hoisted the wicker man onto the back of the crippled monster. No woodland pony or ox would allow the amalgam to mount it. He then led the band down to the wreck of the town at the Barrowland. "Kill them all," he whispered.

As the massacre began the wicker man moved past, his ruined face fixed southward. His eyes smoldered with a poisonous, insane hatred.

XIII

Timmy came flying into camp moments after the racket started. He was so scared he could hardly talk. "We got to get out of here," he choked out, in one-word gasps. "That monster is back. Something is riding it. Some savages are killing them in the village."

Old Man Fish nodded once and dumped water on the fire. "Before it remembers us. Just like we rehearsed it."

"Oh, come on," Tully snarled. "Timmy's probably seeing things. . . ."

The tree cut loose with the granddaddy of all blue bolts. It filled the forest with its glow and banged like heavenly lightning.

"Holy shit," Tully whispered. He took off like a stampeded bear.

The others were not too far behind.

Smeds was thoughtful as he trotted along, his arms filled with gear. Fish's precautions had paid off. Maybe. Like the old boy said, they weren't out nothing getting away for a while.

From behind came a flare in a rosy peach shade answered by another blast of blue. Something yowled like the lost soul of a great cat.

Tully claimed Fish thought too much. But here was Fish turning out to do more and more of the leading while Tully eased into Smeds's old place as shirker and complainer. Timmy wasn't changing, though. He was still the handy runt with the thousand stories.

Fish and Timmy were putting more into this than Tully. Smeds didn't think he could cut them. Especially not if the payoff was as big as Tully expected. No need to be bloody greedy then.

Smeds squatted beside his log, placed his stuff in the nest of branches left to hold it. Tully was on the river already, splashing away. "Sshh!" Fish said. Everybody froze, except Tully out there, splashing away.

Old Man Fish listened.

All Smeds heard was a lot of silence. Nor was there any lightning anymore.

Fish relaxed. "Nothing moving. We got time to strip."

Smeds took the old man's word but he didn't waste any time getting naked and shoving off.

Lying on his chest on a log in the middle of a river in the middle of the night, Smeds felt the first nibbles of panic. He could not see the island for which they were headed, though Fish said there was no way they could miss it from where they had left the bank. The current would carry them right to it.

That was no reassurance. He could not swim. If he missed the island he would drift maybe all the way to the sea.

A sudden barrage of blue flares illuminated the river. He was surprised to see that Fish and Timmy were nearby. And for all his furious splashing Tully was only a hundred feet ahead.

He felt an urge to say something, anything, just to draw courage from the act of communication. But he had nothing to say. And silence was imperative. No point asking for trouble.

During the coming hour he relived every moment of fear he'd ever known, every instance of misfortune and disaster. He was very ragged when he spied the darker loom of the island dead ahead.

It wasn't much of an island. It was maybe thirty feet wide and two hundred yards long, a nail paring of a mudbank that had accumulated weeds and scrub brush. None of the brush was taller than a man. Smeds thought it a pretty pathetic hideout.

At the moment it looked like paradise.

A minute later Fish whispered, "It's shallow enough to touch bottom. Walk your way around to the far side so there won't be tracks coming out over here."

Smeds slid off his log, discovered the water was no deeper than his waist. He followed Fish and Timmy, his toes squishing in the bottom muck, his calves tangling in water plants. Timmy yipped as he stepped on something that wriggled.

Smeds glanced back. Nothing. There had been no fire-works since the exchange that had shown him his compan-ions on the river. The forest had begun to recall its night murmur.

"What took you guys so long?" Tully asked, with a touch of strain.

Smeds snapped, "We took time to pick up some stuff so we wouldn't starve to death out here. What're you going to munch, fireball?"

Smeds wondered if an occasional dose of stress wasn't good for the state of a guy's common sense. He'd dug up some useful memories during his helpless voyage.

Tully had run off on him before. When they were little, as a simple act of cruelty, and later, abandoning him to the mercies of bullies or leaving him to be beaten by a mer-chant when he, unwitting, had distracted the man while Tully had snatched a handful of coppers and run.

Tully bore watching.

Smeds could see the shadow of the future. Get Old Man Fish and Timmy Locan to kype the spike. Get dumb old Smeds to croak them when they do. Then take the loot and walk. Who is Smeds going to complain to when he has the blood of two men on his hands?

That would be just like Tully. Just like him.

They stayed on the island four days, feeding the gnats, broiling in the sun, waiting. It went hardest for Tully. He mooched food enough to get by, but he could not borrow dry clothing or a blanket to keep the sun off.

Smeds had a feeling Fish drew the wait out mainly for Tully's benefit.

Fish went over to the mainland the fourth afternoon. Walking. The channel between the island and bank was never more than chest-deep. He carried his necessaries atop his head.

He did not return till after dark.

"Well?" Tully demanded, the only one of them with any store of impatience left.

"They're gone. Before they left they found our camp and savaged it. They poisoned everything and left dozens of traps. We won't go back there. Maybe we can find what we need in the village. Those folks won't be needing anything anymore."

Smeds learned the truth of Fish's report next day, after a pass near their old camp to show Tully he was wasting his time whining for his stuff. The massacre had been complete, and had not spared the dogs, the fowl, the livestock. It was a warm morning and the air was still. The wings of a million flies filled the forest with an oppressive drone. Carrion eaters squawked and barked and chittered, arguing, as though there was not a feast great enough for ten times their number.

The stench was gut-wrenching even from a quarter mile away.

Smeds stopped. "I got no business to take care of over there. I'm going to go eyeball the tree."

"I'll give you a hand," Timmy said.

Tully looked at Smeds with a snarl. Old Man Fish shrugged, said, "We'll meet you there." The stink and horror didn't seem to bother him.

XIV

The wicker man strode through the streets of the shattered city like an avenging god, stepping stiffly over the legions of the dead. The survivors of his forest warriors followed, awed by the vastness of the city and aghast at what sorcery had wrought. Behind them came a few hundred stunned imperial soldiers from the Oar garrison. They had recognized the invader and had responded to his call to arms—mainly because to defy him was to join those whose blood painted the cobblestones and whose spilled entrails clogged the gutters.

Fires burned in a thousand places. The people of Oar sent a great lament up into the darkness. But not near the dread thing stamping the night.

Furtive things moved in the shadows, rushing away from their places of hiding. Their fear was so great they could not remain still while the old terror passed. He ignored them. The backbone of resistance had been broken.

He ignored everything but the fires. Fire he avoided.

Bowstrings yelped. Arrows zipped into the wicker man as if into an archery butt. Chunks of willow and bits of stone flew. The wicker man reeled. But for the woodland warriors he would have toppled. Breathy rage tore through the head's tortured lips.

Then words came, soft and bitter, chilling the hearts of those near enough to hear. More arrows ripped the fabric of the night, battered the wicker man, clipped one of his ears, felled one of the savages supporting him. He finished speaking.

Screams tore the shadows fifty yards away. They were

42

terrible screams. They brought moisture to the eyes of the soldiers who followed the wicker man.

Those soldiers stepped over the knotted, twitching, whining forms of men wearing uniforms exactly like their own, brothers in arms whose courage had been sufficient to buoy their loyalty. Some shuddered and averted their eyes. Some took mercy and ended the torment with quick spear thrusts. Some recognized old comrades among the fallen and quietly swore to even accounts when sweet opportunity presented itself.

The wicker man proved as unstoppable as a natural disaster. He passed through Oar, trailing death and destruction and accumulating followers, and came to the city's South Gate, where Loo and his sidekick vanished in a flurry of heels. The wicker man extended a hand, whispered secret words. The gate blasted to flinders and toothpicks. The wicker man stamped through and halted, staring down the darkened road.

The trail had grown confused. That of the prey was overlaid by other scents equally familiar, tantalizing, and hated. "As well," he whispered. "As well. Take them all and have done." He sniffed. "*Him!* And that accursed White Rose. And the one who thwarted me in Opal. And the wizard who set us free." Ruined lips quivered in momentary fear. Yes. Even he knew the meaning of fear. "*Her!*"

The beast called Toadkiller Dog believed that *she* had lost her powers. He wanted to believe that himself. That would be a justice beautiful beyond compare. He needed to believe it. But he dared not, not entirely, till he saw for himself. Toadkiller Dog operated from motives not his own. And she was as crafty and treacherous a being as ever any human had been.

Moreover, he had tried to disarm her himself, once, and his failure had reduced him to this.

Toadkiller Dog bulled through the gateway, shouldering soldiers aside. Gore dripped off him. For hours he had ravened through the city, feeding an ancient thirst for blood. He moved on four limbs now, though one was as artificial as the wicker man's body. He, too, peered down the road.

The forest warriors collapsed, falling asleep where they were. The wicker man was driven. He showed no inclination to baby his followers.

A tottering shaman, on his last legs, tried to speak to the wicker man, tried to make him understand that unalloyed flesh could not keep the pace he had set.

The head turned slightly. The expression that shown through the ruin was one of contempt. "Keep up or die," it whispered. It beckoned men to come lift it onto the back of the beast. It rode out, insane with a hunger for revenge.

XV

The folks we was chasing never did much to cover up which way they was headed. I don't guess they thought they had any reason. Anyway, Raven knew where the guy he was chasing was headed. Some place called Khatovar, all the way down on the southern edge of the world.

I knew the guy, Croaker. Him and his Black Company boys did a job on me at the Barrowland, though they never did me too bad. I got out alive. So I had mixed feelings about them. They were a hard bunch. I didn't feel like I really wanted to catch them.

The more we rode along, the more Raven dried out and turned back into the real Raven. And I don't mean into the Corbie that I got to know when I first met him, I mean the real bad-ass so tough and hard he was death on a stick. I don't think it ever occurred to him to take a drink after he made up his mind that he had something else to do.

We had practice sessions every morning before we rode out and every evening after we set camp. Even when he was at his weakest it was all I could do to handle him. When he really started coming back he beat me at everything but throwing rocks and running footraces.

His hip never let up on him.

He wouldn't never stop over at an inn or in a village. Putting away temptation, I guess.

You ain't never going to impress me with nothing if you think you're going to tell me tall tales and you ain't never see the Tower at Charm. There ain't nothing ought to be that big. It's got to be five hundred feet tall and as black as

a buzzard's heart. I never seen nothing like it before and I
don't expect I ever will again.

We never went too close. Raven said there wasn't no
sense getting those people's attention. Damned straight.
That was the heart of the empire, the home of the Lady
and all those old evils called the Ten Who Were Taken.

I went off a few miles and kept my head down while
Raven skulked around trying to find something out. I was
perfectly happy to get rested up from all those hundreds of
miles of riding.

He materialized out of a sunset that painted the horizon
with end-of-the-world fires. He sat down across from me.
"They're not in the Tower. They stopped there for a
couple weeks, but then they headed south again. *She*
followed them."

I got to admit I groaned. I never was a whiner in all my
soldiering days, but I never got put through anything like
this, either. A man ain't made for it.

"We're gaining on them, Case. Fast. If they fool around
in Opal like they did here we'll have them." He gave me a
fat smile. "You wanted to see the world."

"Not the whole damned thing in a week. I kind of
counted on enjoying the seeing."

"We don't get them turned around and headed toward
the trouble, there might not be much damned world left."

"You going to take time out to look for your kids while
we're down there?" I wanted to see the sea. I wanted that
since I was little. A traveling man come through and told
us kids lies about about the Jewel Cities and the Sea of
Torments. From then on I always thought about the sea
when I was digging potatoes or pulling weeds. I pretended
I was a sailor, holy-stoning a deck, but I was going to be a
ship's master someday.

What did I know?

More than the sea, now, I wanted to see Raven do right
and get right with himself and his kids.

He gave me a funny look, then just ducked the question
by not answering it.

•   •   •

We accumulated a fair arsenal here and there as we rode along. Just outside Opal we got a chance to show it off. Not that that done a lot of good.

This great big old hairy-ass black iron coach come roaring out of the city and straight up the road at us, them horses looking like they was breathing fire. I never saw anything like it.

Raven had. "That's the Lady's! Stop it!" He whipped out a bow and strung it.

"The Lady's coach? Stop it? Man, you're crazy! You got guano for brains." I got my bow out, too.

Raven threw up a hand in a signal for them to halt. We tried to look stand-and-deliver, your money or your life. Mean.

Them coachmen never even slowed down. It was like they never even saw us. I ended up going ass over appetite into a ditch with about a foot of muck and water in it. When I got up I saw Raven had ended up in some black-berry bushes on the other side. "Arrogant bastards!" he shouted after the coach.

"Yeah. Got no damned respect for a couple of honest highwaymen."

Raven looked at me and started laughing. I looked at him and went to laughing right back. After a minute, he said, "There wasn't anybody inside that coach." He sounded puzzled.

"When did you have time to look?"

"I think I know what's happening. Come on. We have to hurry. Catch your horse."

I caught her. She was too stupid to hold a grudge. But his kept leading him around, looking back like he was thinking, You ain't going to pull that crazy shit on me again, you son of a bitch. This game went on for a while. I finally stopped it by sneaking up on the beast from the other direction.

We blew about a half hour diddling around there.

The big black ship was about a half hour down the channel when we got to the waterfront. For a minute I thought Raven was going to chop that gelding of his into fish bait. But he just dismounted and stood there on the wharf, staring out to the sea. Whenever a local growled at us about being in the way he just gave them one of those looks that stilled the heart and quickened the feet.

He had it all back, whatever it was. Those weren't soft guys, there on that waterfront.

The black ship faded into the haze out on the water. Raven shuddered his way back to the racket and fish smells. "Guess we'll have to sell the horses and find a ship headed for Beryl."

"Hang on here, man. Enough is enough. Reasonable is reasonable. You figure on heading all the way to the end of the world? Look around here. This is Opal. Almost ever since I've known you I been hearing how you got to get back to Opal and find out about your kids. Look it! We're here! Let's do it."

The guy was my friend. But he had trouble hanging in. Before he was Raven he was Corbie, and before he was Corbie he was Raven. And sometime way back he was somebody else before he got to be Raven the first time. I don't know who, but I know he was somebody high-class and he came from Opal and he left two kids behind, twins, when he got on with Croaker and that bunch and headed north for the fighting in Forsberg.

He plain left those kids to the winds of fortune. He tortured himself because he didn't know what happened to them, because he wasn't shit as a father. Me, I figured it was high time he got that all straightened out.

He thought about it a long time. He kept looking down the coast, eastward, like the answer might be there. What I saw when I looked that way was the homes of rich people on top of cliffs, overlooking the sea. I always kind of suspected he was one of them.

"Maybe when we come back through," he said, finally. "When we're headed north again."

"Sure." Bullshit.

He heard me thinking. He sort of shrank into himself. He did not look at me.

Best ship we could get for Beryl was on some kind of fat scow leaving in two days. I got sick just looking at it.

Raven got good and polluted that night even though I never said another word about his kids. I guess he heard me thinking. Or he heard himself, which is worse.

I got up early. Raven would be nursing a hangover all day. He was one of those old farts had to tell you all about how he never got one when he was young. I went off to look around.

I did all right. I never got lost. And the city had so many different kinds in it after a couple generations being part of the empire that almost everywhere I could find somebody who spoke one of the languages that I did.

It wasn't a lot of fun rooting around in a friend's past. I didn't learn a whole lot, anyway. I couldn't find hardly anybody who remembered anything, and what they did remember mostly sounded like it was fairy tale. Good stories always get bigger. But I think I got some sense out of all the nonsense.

A long time back a character named the Limper was the governor of the province that included Opal. The Limper was one of the original Ten Who Were Taken, the undead sorcerer-devils who were the Lady's champions. They were called Taken because they had been great villains in their own right once, but they had been enslaved by a greater and darker power.

This one called the Limper was about as corrupt and rotten a governor as ever there was.

I knew the guy later. He had been up to the Barrowland for the last big battle, where he got his. All I can say is, there wasn't no one anywhere in this wide world who shed a tear when he went down. Of all the Taken he was the craziest and nastiest.

Anyway, he was the boss in Opal and him and his cronies was gutting the province, stealing the coppers off dead men's eyes. A certain Baronet Corvo, whose family had become allied with the empire when it first came into the area, went off on an assignment somewhere. While he was gone his old lady got to messing around with the

Limper's gang. To the point where she helped rob the baronet's family of most of its honors and titles and all its properties. She helped frame some uncles and cousins and brothers so they could be executed and their properties confiscated.

I couldn't find out much about her. The marriage was arranged and there never was any love in it. I got the impression it was set up to end a feud that had been going on for a hundred years. It didn't work.

She cleaned out and killed off Raven's family. Then he killed her and her whole gang except for the Limper himself. Maybe he could have gotten everything back if he had wanted. The Limper never was in good with the Lady. But Raven found Darling, the White Rose, who became the Lady's mortal enemy. . . .

Not a bad job of finding out, if I do say so myself. Even if I couldn't find out one thing about Raven's kids. I only run into two people who remembered there was kids. They didn't know what happened to them.

Nobody cared but me, it seemed.

We sold the horses. They didn't bring enough. They was pretty ragged after the beating they took coming south. Raven had a bad hangover and wasn't in no mood to argue. But I was getting brave in my old age.

I asked him, "What's the point in us chasing Croaker halfway across the world? Especially when the last time you ran into him he put an arrow into you? Say we do catch him. If he don't finish the job, if he even listens, what's he going to do about whatever happened up north?"

I got to admit I was plenty skeptical about what he claimed maybe happened up there. Even if he did study a little black sorcery way back when.

I guess you could call it nagging. I said, "I figure you got a lot more important business right here in Opal."

He gave me an ugly look. "I don't much care what you think about that, Case. Mind your own business."

"It is my business. It's me getting dragged halfway across the world and maybe ending up getting killed someplace I never heard of because you got problems inside your head.''

"You aren't a slave, Case. There's no one holding a knife to your throat.''

I couldn't say I owe you, man, but you wouldn't understand nothing about that. You taught me to read and write and believe I had a little value as human being before you went off the end. So I said, "If I drop out, who's going to clean you up when you puke all over yourself? Who's going to drag you out after you start a fight in some tavern and get your ass stomped?''

He'd done that last night and if I hadn't showed up when I did he maybe would've gotten himself killed.

This guy who was riding off to save the world.

He was in a rotten mood. His head ached with the hangover. His hip hurt. His body ached from the beating. But he could not find a way to answer me even in that humor. He just said, "I'm going to do what I'm going to do, Case, right or wrong. I'd like to have you along. If you can't make it, no hard feelings.''

"What the hell else I got to do with my life? I got nothing to tie me down.''

"Then why do you keep bitching?''

"Sometimes I like to have what I'm doing make some kind of sense.''

We got on the boat, which was a grain ship crossing over in ballast to collect a cargo, and we were off to a part of the world even Raven hadn't seen before. And before we got to the other side we was both damned sure we shouldn't have done it. But we did decide not to try walking back to Opal when the ship's master refused to turn her around.

Actually, the trip didn't start out all that bad. But then they had to go untie the mooring ropes.

A storm caught us halfway over. It wasn't supposed to blow at that time of year. "It never storms this season,'' the bosun promised us right after the wind split a sail the topmen didn't reef in time. For four more days it kept on not storming at that time of year. So we were four more days behind when we hit the dock in Beryl.

I didn't look back. Whatever I'd thought about Raven and his kids and obligations before, that wasn't interesting now. They were on the other side of the big water and I was cured of wanting to be a sailor. If Raven suddenly decided he had to go back and balance accounts I was going to tell him to go pick his nose with his elbow.

The bunch we were chasing had left a plain trail. Raven's buddy had gone through Beryl like thunder and lightning, pretending to be an imperial legate on a mystery mission.

"Croaker is in a big hurry now," Raven said. "It's going to be a long chase."

I gave him a look but I didn't say it.

We bought new horses and rounded up travel stuff. When we headed out what they called the Rubbish Gate we were seven days behind. Raven took off like he was going to catch up by tomorrow morning.

XVI

In the heart of the continent, far to the east of the Barrowland, Oar, the Tower, and Opal, beyond Lords and even that jagged desolation called the Windy Country, lies that vast, inhospitable, infertile, bizarre land called the Plain of Fear. There is sound reason for the name. It is a land terrible to men. Seldom are they welcomed there.

In the heart of the Plain of Fear there is a barren circle. At the circle's center stands a gnarly tree half as old as time. The tree is the sire of the sapling standing sentinel over the Barrowland.

The few scabrous, primitive nomads who live upon the Plain of Fear call it Old Father Tree and worship it as a god. And god that tree is, or as close as makes no difference. But it is a god whose powers are strictly circumscribed.

Old Father Tree was all a-rattle. Had he been human, he would have been in a screaming rage. After a long, long delay his son had communicated details of his lapse in the matter of the digging monster and the buried head and the wicker man's insane murder spree.

The tree's anger was not entirely inspired by the tardiness of his son. As much was directed at his own impotence and at the dread the news inspired.

An old devil had been put down forever and the world had relaxed, had turned to its smaller concerns. But evil had not missed a stride. It was back in the lists already. It was running free, unbridled, unchallenged, and looked like it could devour the world it hated.

He was a god. On the wispiest evidences he could

discern the shapes of potential tomorrows. And the tomorrows he saw were wastelands of blood and terror.

The failure of his offspring could be precursor to the greater failure of his own trust.

When his hot fury had spent itself he sent his creatures, the talking stones, into the farthest, the most hidden, the most shadowed reaches of the Plain, carrying his call for an assembly of the Peoples, the parliament of the forty-odd sentient species inhabiting that most bizarre part of the world.

Old Father Tree could not move himself, nor could he project his own power beyond certain limits, but he did have the capacity to fling out legates and janissaries in his stead.

XVII

The old man could barely keep himself upright in the saddle when he reached Lords. His life had been sedentary. He had nothing but will and the black arts with which to sustain himself against the hazards of travel and his own physical limits.

His will and skill were substantial but neither was inexhaustible nor indefatigable.

He learned that he was just five days behind his quarry now. The White Rose and her party were in no hurry, and were having no trouble getting around the imperial authorities. For all his desperation he took two days off to rest. It was an investment of time he was sure would pay dividends down the road.

When he left Lords he did so with a horse and pack mule selected for stamina and durability, not for speed and beauty. The long far leg of the next stage would take him through the Windy Country, a land with a bad reputation. He did not want to linger there.

As he passed through ever smaller, meaner, and more widely separated hamlets, approaching the Windy Country, he learned that he was gaining ground rapidly—if closing the gap by four days in as many weeks could be called rapid.

He entered the uninhabited land with little optimism for a quick success. There were no regular, fixed tracks through the Windy Country, which even the empire shunned as worthless. He would have to slow down and use his talent to find the trail.

Or would he? He knew where they were headed. Why worry about where they were now? Why not forget that and just head for the place where they would leave the Windy Country? If he kept pushing he might get there before they did.

He was three-quarters of the way across the desolation, into the worst badlands, a maze of barren and wildly eroded stone. He had made his camp and had fed himself and had lain back to watch the stars come out. Usually it took him only moments to fall asleep, but tonight something kept nagging at the edge of his consciousness. It took him a while to figure out what it was.

For the first time since entering the Windy Country he was not alone within that circle of awareness open to the unconscious scrutiny of his mystic sensibilities. There was a party somewhere about a mile east of him.

And something else was moving in the night, something huge and dangerous and alien that cruised the upper airs, hunting.

He extended his probing mind eastward, cautiously.

Them! The quarry! And alert, troubled, as he was. Certain something was about to happen.

He withdrew immediately, began breaking camp. He muttered all the while, cursing the aches and infirmities that were with him always. He kept probing the night for that hunting presence.

It came and went, slowly, still searching. Good. There might be time.

Night travel was more trouble here than he expected. And there was the thing above, which seemed able to spot him at times, despite his best efforts to make himself one with the land of stone. It kept his animals in a continuous state of terror. The going was painfully slow.

Dawn threatened when he topped a knife-edge ridge and spotted his quarry's camp down the canyon on the other side. He began the descent, feeling that even his hair hurt. The animals grew more difficult by the minute.

A great shadow rolled over him, and kept on rolling. He

looked up. A thing a thousand feet long was dropping toward the camp of those he sought.

The still stone echoed his shouted, "Wait!"

He anticipated the lethal prickle of steel arrowheads with every step. He anticipated the crushing, stinging embrace of windwhale tentacles. But neither dread overtook him.

A lean, dark man stepped into his path. He had eyes as hard and dark as chunks of obsidian. From somewhere nearby, behind him, another man said, "I'll be damned! It's that sorcerer Bomanz, that was supposed to have got et by the Barrowland dragon."

XVIII

A serpent of fire slithered southward, devouring castles and cities and towns, growing larger even as pieces of it fell away. Only fire black and bloody red lay behind it.

Toadkiller Dog and the wicker man were the serpent's deadly fangs.

Even the wicker man had physical limits. And periods of lucidity. At Roses, after the city's punishment, in a moment of rationality, he decided that neither he nor his soldiers could survive the present pace. Indeed, losses among his followers came more often from hardship than from enemy action.

He camped below the ruined city several days, recuperating, till wholesale desertions by plunder-laden troopers informed him that his soldiers were sufficiently rested.

Five thousand men followed him in his march toward Charm.

The Tower was sealed. They recognized him in there. They did not want him inside. They named him rebel, traitor, madman, scum, and worse. They mocked him. *She* was absent, but her lackeys remained faithful and defiant and insufficiently afraid.

They set worms of power snaking over stone already adamantine with spells set during the Tower's construction: writhing maggots of pastel green, pink, blue, that scurried to any point of attack to absorb the sorcerous energy applied from without. The wizards within the Tower were not as great as their attacker, but they had the advantage of being able to work from behind defenses erected by one who had been greater than he.

The wicker man spewed his fury till exhaustion overcame him. And the best of his efforts only left scars little more than stains on the face of the Tower.

They taunted and mocked him, those fools in there, but after a few days they tired of the game. Irked by his persistence, they began throwing things back at him. Things that burned.

He got back out of range.

His troops no longer believed him when he claimed that the Lady had lost her power. If she had, why were her captains so stubborn?

It must be true that she was not in the Tower. If she was not, then she might return anytime, summoned to its aid. In that instance it would not be smart to be found in the wicker man's camp.

His army began to evaporate. Whole companies vanished. Fewer than two thousand remained when the wicker man's sorceries finally breeched the Tower gate. They went inside without enthusiasm and found their pessimism justified. Most died in the Tower's traps before their master could stamp in behind them.

He fared little better.

He plunged back outside, rolled on the ground to extinguish the flames gnawing his body. Stones rained from the battlements, threatened to crush him. But he escaped, and quickly enough to prevent the defection of his few hundred remaining men.

Toadkiller Dog did not participate. And he did not hang around after that humiliation. Cursing every step, the wicker man followed him.

The Tower's defenders used their sorcery to keep their laughter hanging around him for days.

The cities between Charm and the sea paid, and Opal doubly. The wicker man's vengeance was so thorough he had to wait in the ruins six days before an incautious sea captain put in to investigate the disaster.

The wicker man's rage fed upon his frustration. The very fates seemed to conspire to thwart his revenge. For all his frenzied and indefatigable effort he was gaining no ground—except in the realm of madness, and that he did not recognize.

In Beryl he encountered wizardry almost the equal of that he had faced at the Tower. The city's defenders put up a ferocious fight rather than bend the knee to him.

His fury, his insanity, then, cowed even Toadkiller Dog.

XIX

Tully sat on a log and scratched and stared in the general direction of the tree. Smeds didn't think he was seeing anything. He was feeling sorry for himself again. Or still. "Shit," he muttered. And, "The hell with it."

"What?"

"I said the hell with it. I've had it. We're going home."

"Listen to this. What happened to the fancy houses and fancy horses and fancy women and being set for life?"

"Screw it. We been out here all damned spring and half the summer and we ain't got nowhere. I'm going to be a North Side bum all my life. I just got a big head for a while and thought I could get above myself."

Smeds looked out at the tree. Timmy Locan was out there throwing sticks, a mindless exercise that never bored him. He was tempting fate today, getting closer than ever before, policing up sticks that had flown wide before and chucking them onto the pile around the tree. That was less work than gleaning the woods for deadwood. The nearby forest was stripped as clean as parkland.

Smeds thought it looked like they could set the fire any day now. In places the woodpile was fifteen feet high and you couldn't see the tree at all.

What was Tully up to? This whining and giving up fit in with his behavior since their dip in the river, but the timing was suspect. "We'll be ready to do the burn any day now. Why not wait till then?"

"Screw it. It ain't going to work and you know it. Or if you don't you're fooling yourself."

"You want to go home, go ahead. I'm going to stick it out and see what happens."

"I said *we're* going home. All of us."

Right, Smeds thought. Tully was cranking up for a little screw your buddy. "What you want to bet you come up outvoted three to one, cousin? You want to go, go. Ain't nobody going to stop you."

Tully tried a little bluster, coming on like he thought he was some kind of general.

"Stuff it, Tully. I ain't no genius, but just how dumb do you think I am?"

Tully waited a little too long to say, "Huh? What do you mean?"

"That night you went chickenshit and run off to the river on us. I got to thinking about how you done that to me before. You ain't going to pull it on me this time, Tully. You ain't taking off with the spike and leaving old Smeds standing there with his thumb up his butt."

Tully started protesting his innocence of having entertained any such thoughts. Smeds watched Timmy Locan throw sticks. He ignored Tully. After a while he watched Fish approach from the direction of the town. The old man was carrying something over his shoulder. Smeds couldn't make out what it was. He hoped it was another of those dwarf deer like the old man had got a couple weeks back. That had been some good eating.

Timmy spotted Fish. He lost interest in his sticks, wandered over.

It wasn't a deer Fish had, it was some kind of bundle that clanked when he dropped it in front of the log. He said, "Smell's gone over there. Thought I'd poke around." He opened his bundle, which he had folded from a ragged blanket. "Those guys didn't take time out to loot when they went through over there."

Smeds gaped. There were pounds and pounds of coins, some of them even gold. There were rings and bracelets and earrings and broaches and necklaces and some of them boasted jewels. He'd never seen so much wealth in one place.

Fish said, "There's probably a lot more. I just picked up what was easy to find and quit when I had as much as I could carry."

Smeds looked at Tully. "And you wanted to cut out because the whole thing was a big bust."

Tully looked at the pile, awed. Then his expression became suspicious and Smeds knew he was wondering if Fish had hidden the best stuff where he could pick it up later. Typical Tully Stahl thinking, and stupid.

If Fish had wanted to hold out he would have just hidden the stuff and not said anything. Nobody would have known the difference. Nobody was interested in that town. Nobody even wanted to think about what happened there.

"What's this?" Fish asked, glancing from Tully to Smeds.

Smeds said, "He was whining about how the whole thing was a big damned bust and he was sick of it and wanted us to go home. But look here. Even if we don't have no luck with the tree we made out like bandits. I could live pretty good for a good long time on a share of this."

Fish looked from Tully to Smeds and back again. He said, "I see." And maybe he did. That old man wasn't anybody's fool. He said, "Timmy, you got a good eye for this kind of thing. Why don't you separate that out into equal lots?"

"Sure." Timmy sat down and ran his hands through the coins, laughing. "Anybody see anything he's just got to have?"

Nobody did.

Timmy *was* good. Not even Tully found any reason to complain about his divvying.

Fish said, "There's bound to be more over there. Not to mention a lot of steel that could be cleaned up and whole-saled if we brought a wagon up and carried it back."

After they squirreled their shares, Tully and Old Man Fish headed back to town. Smeds didn't want to go any-where near the place but figured he had to go along to keep Tully honest. Timmy wouldn't go at all. He was happy building up the woodpile.

Looting the town made for a ten-day full-time job, what with having to clean up all the weapons and some other large items of value and then bundling them protectively and hiding them for later recovery. They came up with enough money and jewelry and small whatnots to make a heavy load for each of them.

Even Tully seemed pleased and content. For the moment.

One night, though, he said, "You know what bugs me? How come nobody else in the whole damned city of Oar ever got the same idea I did? I'd have bet my balls that after this long we'd be up to our asses in guys trying to glom on to that spike."

Old Man Fish grunted. "I've been wondering why no one's come to see what happened to the garrison."

Nobody had any ideas. The questions just sort of lay there like dead fish too ripe to be ignored and too big to shove out of the way.

Fish said, "I reckon it's time we torched her and seen if she's going to do it or not. That woodpile gets any bigger Timmy ain't going to be able to throw them that high."

Smeds realized he was reluctant to take the next step. Tully didn't seem too anxious, either. But Timmy had a grin on ear to ear. He was raring to go.

Tully leaned over and told Smeds, "Little dip did some torch work back in town. Likes to see things burn."

"We got a good day for it here," Fish said. "A nice breeze to whip up the fire. A hot, sunshiny day, which is when we know it's asleep the deepest. All we have to do is look in our pants and see if we got some balls, then go do it."

They looked at each other awhile. Finally, Smeds said, "All right," and got up. He collected the bundle of brush that would be his to throw. Fish and Timmy got theirs. Tully had to go along.

They lit the bundles off down in the bottom of the hole the monster dug, then jumped out and charged the mountain of sticks from the windward side. They heaved their bundles. Tully's, thrown too far away, fell short, but that did not matter.

They ran like hell, Smeds, Timmy, and Fish in straight lines, Tully zigging and zagging. The tree did not wake up before they'd all made the cover of the woods.

The fire had reached inferno proportions by then.

Random bolts of blue lightning flailed around. They did not come for long, though.

Smeds could feel the heat from where he crouched, watching. That was one bitch of a bonfire. But he was not impressed. What he was, mainly, was sad.

The fire burned the rest of the day. At midnight Timmy went to check it out and came back to say there was still a lot of live coals under the ash and he hadn't been able to get near it.

Next morning they all went to look. Smeds was astounded. The tree still stood. Its trunk was charred and its leaves were gone, but it still stood, the silver spike glittering wickedly at eye level. And it did not protest their presence, no matter how close they got.

That was not close enough. There was a lot of heat in the ash still. They hauled water from the river and splashed down a path. Timmy Locan volunteered to take the pry bar and go pull the spike.

"I can't believe it," Tully said as Timmy leaned on the bar and the tree didn't do anything about it. "I can't goddamned believe it! We're actually going to do it!"

Timmy grunted and strained and cussed and nothing happened. "This son of a bitch ain't going to come! Oh!"

It popped loose. Timmy grabbed at it as it sailed past, grabbing it left-handed for a second.

Then he screamed and dropped it. "Oh, shit, that bastard is hot." He came running, crying, and shoved his hand into the last bucket of water. His palm was mostly red and beginning to show patches of blister already.

Fish took a shovel and scooped the spike out of the ashes. "Look out, Timmy. I'm fixing to dump it in there."

"My hand . . ."

"Ain't good to do a bad burn that way. You head back to camp. I got some salve there that'll do you a whole lot better."

Timmy pulled his hand out. Fish dumped the spike. The water hissed and bubbled. Fish said, "You carry the bucket, Smeds."

Just as Tully said, "We better make tracks. I think its starting to wake up."

It was hard to tell against that sky, but it did look like there were tiny flecks of blue out on the ends of the smallest surviving twigs.

"The spike ain't conducting heat into the heartwood anymore," Fish said. "Scat," he told the backs of a lot of pumping legs and flailing elbows.

Smeds looked back just before he plunged into the woods. Just as the tree cut loose with a wild, undirected discharge. The flash nearly blinded him. Ash flew in clouds. The pain and disappointment and . . . sorrow? . . . of the tree touched him like a gentle, sad rain. He found tears streaking his face and guilt in his heart.

Old Man Fish puffed into camp one step ahead of Tully, who was embarrassed because the old-timer had outrun him. Fish said, "We got a lot of daylight left. I suggest we get the hell on the road. Timmy, let me look at that hand."

Smeds looked over Fish's shoulder. Timmy's hand looked awful. Fish didn't like the look of it either. He stared at it, grunted, frowned, studied it, grunted again. "Salve won't be good enough. I'm going to collect up some herbs for a poultice. Thing must have been hotter than I thought."

"Hurts like hell," Timmy said, eyes still watery.

"Poultice will take care of that. Smeds. When you get that spike out of the bucket don't touch it. Dump it on that old blanket. Then wrap it up. I don't think anybody ought to touch it."

"Why the hell not?" Tully asked.

"Because it burned Timmy badder than it should have.

Because it's a bad mojo thing and maybe we shouldn't ought to take any chances."

Smeds did it the way Fish said, after the old man went hunting his herbs. After he dumped the bucket he moved the spike to a dry part of the blanket with a stick. "Hey! Tully! Check this. It's still hot even after it was in that water." Passing his hand above it he could feel the heat from a foot away.

Tully tried it. He looked troubled. "You better wrap it up good and tie it tight and put it right in the middle of your pack."

"Eh?" Tully didn't want to carry it himself? Didn't want it in his control every second? That was disturbing.

"You want to come give me a hand awhile here?" Tully asked. "I can't never get this pack together by myself."

Smeds finished bundling the spike, went over, knowing from his tone Tully had something he wanted to whisper.

As they stuffed and rolled and tied, Tully murmured, "I decided not to do it on the way back. We're still going to need them awhile. We'll do it later, in the city sometime."

Smeds nodded, not saying he wasn't going to do it at all, and was going to try his damnedest to see that Fish and Timmy and he himself got fair shares of the payoff for the spike.

He had a good idea what was going on inside Tully's head. Tully wasn't going to be satisfied with the big hit they'd made already. Tully was thinking Fish and Timmy made good mules. They could haul their shares back. Once they got to town he could take them away.

Smeds had a suspicion Tully wasn't going to be satisfied with a two-way split, either.

XX

Our fire burned down till it wasn't nothing but some patches of red. Once in a while a little flame would shoot up and prance around for a few seconds, then die. I stared up at the stars. Most were ones I'd known all my life, but they had moved to funny parts of the night. The constellations were all askew.

It was a good night for shooting stars. I'd spotted seven already.

"Uncomfortable?" Raven asked. He was watching the sky, too.

He startled me. He hadn't said anything since back around lunchtime. We didn't talk much anymore.

"Scared." I had lost track of time. I had no idea how far we'd come or where we were, except that it was one goddamned long ways from home and down in the south.

"And wondering what the hell you're doing here, no doubt."

"No. I think I got a handle on that. My trouble is I don't like having to sneak everywhere, like a thief. I might get treated like one."

I did not add that I did not like being in places where the only person who could understand me was him. If something happened to him . . . That was what scared me the most.

It was too awful to think about.

I said, "But it's too late to turn back."

"Some say it's never too late."

So he was thinking about his kids again, now he was plenty safe from the risk of actually having to deal with them. Also, maybe, he was having second thoughts about our ride into the unknown.

Opaque as they were to me, and maybe even to him, powerful emotions were driving him. They had Darling's name hung all over them, though he never mentioned her. One monster of a guilt was perched on his shoulders, flapping and squawking and pecking at his eyes and ears. Somehow he was going to silence that beast by catching his pal Croaker and passing the word about what happened in the Barrowland.

It didn't make no sense to me. But people never do, a whole lot.

Maybe the determination was starting to wear thin. It was one thing to take off after a guy expecting to catch him in a few weeks and a few hundred miles and something else to be on the track still after months and months and thousands of miles. People aren't built to take that without any letup. The road can blunt the most iron will.

He let the edges of it show when he said, "Croaker's been gaining on us again. He doesn't have to be as careful as we do. We have to speed it up somehow. Else we're going to chase him all the way to the edge of the world and still never catch him."

Hell. He was talking to himself, not to me. Trying to find some enthusiasm he had misplaced somewhere back up the road. There wasn't no way we were going to kick up the pace any. Not without giving up any thought of watching out for trouble from the people in the countries we were going through.

We were pushing so hard now we were killing ourselves slowly.

I glimpsed something off to the north. "There. Did you see that? That's what I was telling you about the other day. Lightning from a clear sky."

He missed it. "Maybe it's storming up there."

"Just keep an eye peeled."

We watched a series of flashes so dim their source had to be way over the horizon. Usually that kind of lightning lights up or silhouettes the tops of clouds.

"There isn't one cloud," Raven said. "And we haven't seen one for weeks. And I'd bet we won't see any as long as we're crossing this steppe." He watched another flash go. He shivered. "I don't like it, Case. I don't like it at all."

"Yeah? What's up?"

"I don't know. Not exactly. But I got that tingle again, that bad feeling I got in Oar, that set me off on this crusade."

"The thing from the Barrowland?"

He shrugged. "Maybe. But that wouldn't make sense. If it was really who I thought it was, he ought to be busy taking over the empire and making himself safe from a few loose Taken who might still be hanging around."

I'd had some time now to do some thinking about what might have moved in the Barrowland and could have had so much impact on Raven. There was only one answer that fit, though it didn't seem likely. They had burned his body and scattered the ashes. But they hadn't been able to find his head.

"If it's the Limper we really might have trouble. Nothing he ever did made a whole lot of sense. Not to us mortals. He was always crazy as a loon."

He gave me a surprised look, then a soft smile. "No sawdust between your ears, is there, kid? All right. Put those brains to work trying to figure out why even a crazy wizard would be chasing us around the world. On the thousand-to-one that really is him raising a fuss up there."

I laid back and started watching for shooting stars again. I counted six more, not really thinking about the Limper because that wasn't an idea worth taking serious. Limper didn't have no love for Raven, but he sure didn't have a grudge big enough to go chasing him, neither. Crazy or not.

"Between a rock and a hard place." It sort of just slipped out.

"What?"

"Tighten up the buckles on your ego, brother Corvus. It ain't us he's after. If it's him."

"Eh?" His eyes tightened up into a suspicious squint. That made his cold, hawkish face look more predatory than ever. I had to go use that family name.

"He's after the same thing we are. The Black Company."

"That don't make sense either, Case."

"Hell it don't. It's the only way you can get it to make any sense at all. You're just not thinking about the world the way one of the Taken would. You got a pretty screwed-up eye, but you still think people is people. Them Taken don't and never did. To them people are just tools and slaves, live junk to use and throw away. Except for the one that was so powerful she made them *her* slaves. And she's riding with your buddy Croaker, far as we know. Right?"

The idea sank in. He turned it over, looked at the sharp edges, grunting and shaking like a dog shitting peach seeds. After a while, he said, "She's lost her powers but she hasn't lost what she knew. And that was knowledge enough to conquer half a world and tame the Ten Who Were Taken. She'd be one big prize for any wizard who could lay hands on her."

"There you go." I closed my eyes and tried to sleep. It took me a while.

XXI

The old man sat quietly. When he moved at all he did so slowly and carefully. His status was ambiguous. He had chased these people across a continent, damned near killing himself, and for what?

For nothing, that's what. For nothing.

They were lunatics. They ought to be locked up for their own protection.

The woman watched him from about twenty feet to his left. She was a blue-eyed, stringy-haired blonde about five feet six inches tall, in her middle twenties. She had a square jaw, a too broad, lumpy bottom, and a goofy manner that made you wonder if anybody was home behind those watery eyes. And for all that, there was something strongly sensual there.

She was deaf and mute. She could communicate only via sign language.

She was in charge. She was Darling, the White Rose, the one who had put an end to the Lady's dark dominion.

How the hell could that be? It didn't add up.

Off to his right was a man who watched him with the warmth of a snake. He was tall, lean, dusky, hard as a stone with less sense of humor. These days he dressed in black, which had to be a statement of some sort, but who could tell what? He would not talk. He flat refused. Which is why they called him Silent.

He was a wizard himself. The tools of his trade lay scattered around him. As though he expected their unwilling guest to try something.

Silent's eyes were as black as jet, hard as diamonds, and friendly as death.

Damn it! A man made one mistake and four hundred years later they still wouldn't let him live it down.

There were three more of them around somewhere, brothers with the surname Torque who seemed to have no given names. They went by absurdities like Paddlefoot, Donkey Dick, and Brother Bear, except that Donkey Dick became Stubby when Darling was in listening distance, even though she couldn't hear.

All four men worshiped her. And it was obvious to everyone but her that the one called Silent entertained romantic ambitions.

Lunatics. Every single one.

Something behind him yelled, "Seth Chalk! What treachery are you up to now?" and exploded in giggles.

Wearily, for the thousandth time, he replied, "Call me Bomanz. I haven't used Seth Chalk since I was a boy." He did not look around.

It had been a long, long time since he had been Seth Chalk. At least a hundred fifty years. He had no exact count. It was a year since he had escaped the thrall of a sorcery that had held him in stasis most of that time. He knew the intervening years of strife and horror—the years of the rise and growth of the Lady's empire—only by repute, after the fact.

He, Bomanz or Seth Chalk, was a living artifact from before the fact. A fool who had had no business surviving it, who wanted to use these last unexpected gift years to expiate the guilt that was his for his part in the awakening and release of the ancient evil.

These idiots were not ready to believe that, no matter that he'd damned near gotten himself killed keeping that dragon off them during the big final throat cutting in the Barrowland last winter.

Damned fools. He had done all the damage he could do in one lifetime.

The three brothers came from somewhere up forward, joined the watch. So it was not one of them who had shouted. But Bomanz knew that. Two of the three could not speak any language he understood. The third managed Forsberger so brokenly it was not worth his trouble to try.

The fool who could understand a little of Bomanz's antiquated Forsberger could not sign. Of course. So any communication not heard directly by Silent or lip-read by Darling got garbled and lost.

Only the stones communicated like regular people.

He did not like talking to rocks. There was something perverse about holding converse with rocks.

The trouble with being here was that the human beings, though lunatics, were the sanest, most believable part of the furnishings.

For the first time in his life, if he wanted to build cloud castles he had to go look down.

They had press-ganged him at that camp in the Windy Country. He was on the back of one of those fabulous monsters out of the Plain of Fear, a windwhale. The beast was a thousand feet long and nearly two hundred wide. From below it looked like a cross between a man-o'-war jellyfish and the world's biggest shark. From up top where Bomanz was, the broad flat back looked like something from an opium smoker's pipe dream. Like the imaginary forests that might grow in those vast caverns said to lie miles beneath the surface of the earth.

This forest was haunted by enough weird creatures to populate anyone's fancy nightmare. A whole zoo. And all sentient.

The windwhale was going somewhere in a hurry but was not getting there fast. There had been head winds all the way. And every so often the monster had to go down and tear up a couple hundred acres to take the edge off its hunger.

The damned thing stank like seven zoos.

A couple weird characters had singled him out for relentless harassment. One was a little rock monkey, mostly tail, no bigger than a chipmunk. It had a high, squeaky, nagging voice that made him remember his long-dead wife, though he never understood a word it said.

There was a shy centauroid creature put together backward, with the humanlike part in the rear. That part of her was disturbingly attractive. She seemed intrigued by him. He kept catching glimpses of her watching him from among the copses of uncertain organs that bewhiskered the windwhale's back.

Worst, there was a lone talking buzzard who had a smattering of Forsberger and a wiseguy mouth. Bomanz could not get away from the bird, who, if he had been human, would have hung out in taverns masquerading as the world's foremost authority, armed with an uninformed and ready opinion on every conceivable subject. His cheerful bigotry and who-cares ignorance drove the old man's temper to its limit.

Things called mantas, that looked like sable flying versions of the rays of tropical seas, symbiotes of the windwhales, with wingspans of thirty to fifty feet, were the most dramatic and numerous of his nonhuman companions. Though they looked like fish, they seemed to be mammals. They lived their whole lives on the windwhale's back. They were ill-tempered and dangerous and they bitterly resented having to share their territory with lesser life-forms. Only the will of their god contained their spite.

There were dozens more creatures equally remarkable, each more absurd than the last, but they were more shy of humans and stayed out of the way.

Discounting the mantas, the most numerous and pestiferous tribe were the talking stones.

Like most people Bomanz had heard tales of the deadly talking menhirs of the Plain of Fear. The reality seemed as gruesome as the stories. They were as shy as an avalanche and deadly pranksters. They were responsible for the Plain's deadly reputation. Near as Bomanz could tell, what everyone else considered murderous wickedness they considered practical jokery.

What could be more hilarious than a traveler who, following false directions, stumbled into a lava pit or had his mount snatched out from under him by a giant sand lion?

The stones, in the form of menhirs as much as eighteen feet tall, were the stuff of a thousand stories, hardly a one pleasant. But the seeing and hearing and having to deal with was an experience that made the stories pall—though the stones were on their best behavior now.

They were under constraint, too.

The stones had no language difficulties. Happily, many were a laconic sort. But when they did go to talking their speech was sour, acidic, caustic. The lot were verbal vandals. So how the hell come they were the ones their god had made his diplomatic corps?

It was no wonder the Plain of Fear was a wide-open madhouse. The tree god running it was a twenty-four-karat lunatic.

The stones were gray brown, mostly, without visible orifices or organs. Most were as shaggy with mosses and lichens and bugs as any normal boulder that lay around keeping its mouth shut. They intimidated the hell out of Bomanz, who liked to pretend that he was not scared of any damned thing.

There were moments when he came close to blasting them into talking gravel.

Weird damned creatures!

Every hundred miles the windwhale dropped till its belly dragged. Members of every species, including the Torque brothers, would start singing a merry "Heigh-ho!" work song and would converge on whichever menhir had made itself most obnoxious recently. Hup-hup, over the side it would go, to the accompaniment of dire threats and foul curses. Those stones that pretended to senses of humor would yodel fearfully all the way to the ground.

Damnfool crazies.

No matter how the bleeding rocks fell, they always landed upright, catlike.

The show scared the crap out of the rare peasant unlucky enough to witness it.

The stones were the Plains creatures' and tree god's communications lifeline. They spoke to one another mind to mind—though Bomanz was not about to give them credit for true sentience. No one would tell him squat, but he suspected Old Father Tree himself was running this operation—whatever this operation was—from the nether end.

One of those little things he found disconcerting was the fact that no matter how many stones went over the side, the menhir population never diminished. In fact, some of the same old stones turned up back aboard.

Goddamned insanity.

"Hey, Seth Chalk, you sour old fart, you figure out how to screw us over yet? Gawh!"

The talking buzzard had come. Bomanz replied with a gentle, tricky gesture, consisting of wrapping his hand around the bird's neck. "Just you personally, carrion breath."

Eyes watched. Nobody moved. Nobody took it seriously. The Torque brothers whooped it up. "Way to go, old man!" Paddlefoot gobbled in his outlandish lingo. "Tie his goofy neck in a knot."

"Morons!" Bomanz muttered. "I'm surrounded by morons. At the mercy of cretins." Louder. "I'm going to tie your neck in a knot and braid your toes if you don't lay off the Seth Chalk and start calling me Bomanz."

He turned loose.

The buzzard flapped off squawking, "Chalk's on a rampage! Beware! Beware! Chalk's gone berserk."

"Oh, go to hell. Marooned with lunatics."

General laughter and foolery of a sort he had not seen since his student days. But Darling and Silent neither laughed nor stopped watching him. What the hell did he have to do to make them understand that he was on their side?

"Hah!" It hit him out of the blue. An epiphany. They did not distrust him because it was he whose bumbling had wakened the old evils and loosed them to walk the earth for another dark century. He had done his part in the rectification. No. They knew what had moved his researches in the first place. His quest for tools with which to gain power. His fathomless infatuation with the Lady, which had so distracted him he had made the mistakes that had allowed her to break her bonds.

They might believe he had been broken of his hunger for power, but would they ever believe he was free of his thing for that dark woman? How could he convince them when he had yet to convince himself? She had been a deadly candle to many a man's moth and the flame did not lose its attraction by being out of sight or out of reach.

He grunted, prized himself off his butt. His legs were stiff. He had been seated a long time. Darling and Silent watched him amble past a stand of something that looked like pink ferns ten feet tall. Little eyes peeped out warily. The ferns were some sort of organ. The mantas used them for an infant creche.

He went as far as his acrophobia let him. It was the first he had looked overboard in a week.

Last time they had been over water. He had been able to see nothing but haziness and blue all the way to undefined horizons.

The air was clearer today. The view was very nearly monochromatic again, but this time brown. Just a few hints of green flecked it. Way, way ahead there was something that looked like it might be smoke from a big fire.

They had to be two miles high. There was not a cloud in the sky.

"Soon you will have your chance to prove yourself, Seth Chalk."

He glanced back. A menhir stood four feet behind him. It had not been there a moment before. They were that way, coming and going without sound or warning. This one was a little more gray and mica-flecked than most. It had a scar down its face side six inches wide and seven feet long where something had scraped through lichen and weathered surface stone. Bomanz did not understand talking-stone civilization. They had no obvious hierarchy, yet this one generally spoke for them when there was official speaking to be done.

"How so?"

"Do you not feel it, wizard?"

"I feel a lot of things, rock. What I feel most of all is grumpy about the way you all have been doing me. What am I supposed to feel?"

"The mad psychic stink of the thing that you sensed escaping the Barrowland. From Oar. It is no farther away now."

The talking stones spoke in a dead monotone, usually, yet Bomanz sensed the taint of suspicion that lay in the menhir's mind. If he could tell the old evil was stirring from as far as Oar, when it was weak, how was it that he could not sense it now, when it was so much stronger?

How was it that he, too, was alive when he was supposed to be dead?

Did he know about the resurrection of the shadow because it had been one with his own? Had they conspired together and come out of the unhallowed earth of the Barrowland together? Was he a slave of that old darkness?

"It was not that that I sensed," Bomanz said. "I heard the scream of one of the old fetish alarms being tripped when something moved that should not have. That isn't the same thing at all."

The stone stood silent for a moment. "Perhaps not. Nevertheless, we are upon the thing. In hours, or a day or two, as the winds decide, the battle will be joined. Your fate may be determined."

Bomanz snorted. "A rock with a sense for the dramatic. It's absurd. You really expect me to fight that thing?"

"Yes."

"If it's what I think it is . . ."

"It is the thing called the Limper. And the thing known as Toadkiller Dog. Both are handicapped."

Bomanz sneered and snorted. "I'd call being without a body something more than a handicap."

"It is not weak, this thing. That smoke rises from a city still burning three days after its departure. It has become the disciple of death. Killing and destruction are all it knows. The tree has decreed that it be stopped."

"Right. Why? And why us?"

"Why? Because if it continues amok its course will someday bring it to the Plain. Why us? Because there is no one else. All who had any great power were consumed in the struggle in the Barrowland except thee and we. And, most of all, we do it because the god has commanded it.''

Bomanz muttered and grumbled under his breath.

"Prepare yourself, wizard. The hour comes. If you are innocent in our eyes you must be guilty in his.''

Of course. There could be no ground in the middle. Not for him. He did not have the strength to hold it. Never had had, if the truth be known, though he had deluded himself in the years of his quest for knowledge about those who had been enchained by the ancients.

Did he know remorse for the horror brought on by his fumblings? Some. Not as much as he thought he should. He told himself that because of his intercession at the penultimate moment, his self-sacrifice, the outbreak of darkness had been far gentler than it could have been. Without him the night might have lasted forever.

The old man ambled away from the stone, rapt in his own thoughts. He did not notice the stone turning jerkily, keeping its scarred face toward him. The menhirs never moved while being watched by human eyes. How they knew they were being watched no one knew.

Bomanz's meander took him to the aft end of the windwhale. Small rustlings accompanied him. Chaperons. If he noticed he ignored them. They had been with him always.

He settled upon a soft, unprotesting lump of whale flesh about chair height. It made comfortable sitting. But he knew he would not be staying long. The windwhale was especially fetid here.

For the hundredth time he contemplated escape. All he had to do was jump and use a levitator spell to soften his fall. That was well within his competence. But not within the compass of his courage.

His fear of heights was not totally debilitating. Should he fall, he would retain enough self-possession to save himself. But there was no way he could bring himself to take the plunge voluntarily.

Resigned, he looked back the way he had come. Home, such as it was and had been, lay a thousand miles away. Maybe a lot farther. They were passing over lands of which he had never heard, where all who saw it marveled at the great shape in the sky and had no idea what it was.

There was no guarantee he would step into friendly lands if he did go over the side. In fact, the terrain below looked actively hostile.

Hell with it. He had gotten himself into this. He would ride it out.

"Hunh!"

He was an old man but his eyes were plenty sharp.

The high, clean air allowed him to see a long way. And up north, at the edge of discernment when he looked at them a fraction of a point off directly, were two dots at an altitude even higher than that of the windwhale. To be visible at all at that distance they had to be the size of windwhales.

Bomanz snorted.

This monster was the vanguard of a parade.

He chuckled then. There were rustles nearby, the natives disturbed by his amusement. He chuckled again and rose. This time he strolled the length of the windwhale before he alighted again, as far forward as he dared go.

The smoke was much nearer. It rose higher than the windwhale. He saw hints of the fires that fed the column, which had begun to develop a bend in its trunk down lower. Grim. Maybe the rock was right. Something had to be done.

This was the dozenth such city, though the first they had come to still in its death throes. The progress of the insanity was an arrow pointing due south, a craziness that could make sense only to the crazy himself.

The windwhale began rumbling with internal flatulences. The horizon tilted, rose. Mantas piped and squealed behind Bomanz. He got a death grip on his seat.

The monster was headed down.

Why? It was not time to drop a menhir. It was not feeding time.

Mantas hurtled past in pairs and squadrons, spade-headed darts spreading across the sky, headed toward the city and its coronet of circling carrion birds.

"There is a good wind running a mile below us, wizard." Bomanz glanced back. His scar-faced stone friend. "If it holds we will overtake the destroyer shortly after nightfall. You have only that long to prepare."

Bomanz glanced around again. The stone was gone. But he was not alone. Darling and Silent had come to stare at the stricken city. The dark man's face was impassive but Darling's was a study in empathetic agony. That touched the soft-headed, softhearted side of the old man. He faced her, said, "We will put an end to the pain, child." He spoke carefully so she could read his lips.

She looked at Silent. Silent looked at her. Their fingers flew in the speech of the deaf. Bomanz caught part of the exchange. He was not pleased.

They were discussing him and Silent's remarks were not complimentary.

Bomanz cursed and spat. That bastard had it in for him for no damned reason.

The mantas decimated the carrion birds, used the updraft from the fires to soar high, then returned to the windwhale carrying a feast for their young. They settled down to nap.

But there was no real relaxation for anyone. The windwhale had dropped till it was only half a mile high. It passed the city, scudding along at twenty miles an hour. Soon the monster had to climb back into less vigorous air so as not to catch up before nightfall.

The scar-face stone returned when Bomanz was not looking. When he did notice it, he said, "I feel it now, rock. It reeks of corruption. And I still have no idea what I could do to hurt it."

"Worry not. There is a new decree from the god. You are not to reveal yourself except in extreme circumstance.

Our attack will be exploratory, experimental, and admonitory only.''

"What the hell? Why? Go for the kill, I say. Hit him with everything the one time he don't know we're coming. We'll never get a better shot.''

"The god has spoken.''

Bomanz argued. The god won.

The windwhale began shedding altitude at dusk. Soon after nightfall Bomanz spied the campfires of an army ahead. A pair of mantas took to the air to scout. They returned, reported whatever they reported. The windwhale slanted down toward the encampment, cutting a course that would rip through its heart.

Mantas poured off the windwhale's back, scrambled around and over one another in a search for updrafts.

Bomanz felt the old terror moving closer. It was restless but did not seem alert.

The ground came up and up. Bomanz clung to his seat and awaited certain impact, now unconcerned by the insult inplicit in the fact that a dozen menhirs had moved into position around him and Darling, and her thugs were spread out ready for trouble.

The windwhale leveled out. Campfires slid out of sight beneath it. The screaming down there was almost inaudible because of the creak and rumble and intervening bulk of the giant of the sky. Bomanz felt the shock of the old evil, caught completely unprepared. It went into a pure black rage.

Just as it began to respond mantas swooped in from every direction. They cut the heart out of the night with the glare of the lightnings they discharged from the store in their flesh. Bolts stabbed around by the hundred, keeping the old horror so busy guarding himself he had no chance to counterattack.

The windwhale dumped tons of ballast and began a slow ascent, struggling to gain altitude against the weight of plunder.

Bomanz could not see the monster's underside and was glad. Its tentacles would be grasping men and animals and anything else it considered edible. It was an intelligent beast but it did not exempt other intelligences from its food supply if they were its enemies.

Many of the Plain races ate their enemies.

Bomanz found the idea repugnant in practice, yet it had a certain moral allure. How vigorously would men prosecute their wars if they had to eat those who fell before their swords?

Interesting. But how to impose the requirement?

The mantas began returning. Near as the old man could tell, they were very pleased with themselves.

It was over. The windwhale was up and safely away and now preoccupied with its digestion. Bomanz rose. Time to turn in.

As he passed Darling, Silent, and the scarred menhir, he said, ''Next time the bear is going to bite back. You should have stuck him while you had him.''

XXII

The "bear" was stunned, numb, immobile within the desolation of his camp, desperately trying to grasp the sense of his sudden misfortune.

His entire existence was a headlong assault upon adversity. Having something go sour was never a surprise. But a disaster of these proportions, with its implication of vast, previously unconsidered forces in motion, had for the moment obliterated his initiative. He lacked even his usual insane volition driven by the engine of rage.

The beast Toadkiller Dog was less stricken. Its memories of the son of the tree were fresh. It had not deceived itself when it came to that sprig's connection with its sire. It had been but a matter of time till Old Father Tree showed an interest.

Toadkiller Dog had been to the Plain of Fear. He had come face-to-face with the god. His memories of the confrontation were not sweet. He had been lucky to escape.

But that had been a profitable adventure. He had seen the Plain firsthand. Now what he knew might become a useful tool. If the wicker man would listen.

Unlikely.

It was not now the half-rational thing that had been the Limper before. It had become so self-centered, so self-involved, as to be the hub of a solipsistic universe.

The beast prowled the camp, past men and the remains of men. Shock lay upon the survivors like a smothering quilt. Only a few understood what had happened. He heard mutterings about the wrath of the gods. Those men did not know how truly they spoke.

It would be hard to hold them together if that theory gained credence. Problems of conscience were endemic already.

There was faint hiss, a crack, and a blinding flash. The beast's fur stood straight out. Little blue sparks pranced and crackled amidst it, though the bolt had missed.

Soldiers scurried around like hens in a panic.

That sniper had attained a tremendous speed, falling from several miles high. It came and went too quickly for any response. Even in daylight there would have been little chance to get it.

Flash. *Crack!* Screams. A man pranced in a shroud of will-o'-the-wisp fire.

So there it was. Having made its presence known, the windwhale was embarking on a program of terrorism and attrition that would not stop till the wicker man proved he could stop it.

Toadkiller Dog snarled at the wicker man till the glaze left his rheumy eyes and he nodded once, sharply. He began to shake so hard he creaked and squeaked. He was trying to control his rage.

To yield might prove fatal.

One of those bolts, accurately delivered, could destroy his toy body, leaving him next to powerless, his army at the mercy of the monster above. Somewhere out there, planing around the camp, were mantas watching for a chance at the quick kill missed during the surprise attack.

The shaking faded. In a controlled whisper the wicker man said, "Kill those campfires. They light us as targets." Then he began the slow, painful process of surrounding himself with spells against the mantas' bolts.

Toadkiller Dog limped around snapping and growling to make the soldiers hurry.

Dousing the fires did not help. The mantas came in all night. Their accuracy did not decrease. Neither did it improve.

The things seemed more interested in harassment than killing. In keeping everyone awake and frightened of the moment the next blow would fall. It was a weakling's way to fight. Though no tears fell from the sky when a bolt did splatter a soldier.

The minions of the tree god were trying to panic and disperse the Limper's army. That puzzled Toadkiller Dog. They were not that tender of heart.

Men slipped away by twos and threes.

He galloped as fast as he could on three real legs and a wooden one, yelping and nipping and driving them back, and in interim moments trying to get a feel for that monster in the sky. Some of the deserters objected to his bullying. He had to kill a dozen before everybody got their minds right.

Something familiar about a few of the lesser life sparks up there.

The beast sensed the wicker man's summons. He trotted over. Spells now enfolded the wicker man in layers of protection. Pain leaked out.

Toadkiller Dog was amused. The more surely the old shadow guarded himself, the greater was his pain. To make himself absolutely safe the Limper would have to subject himself to an agony that would rob him of all reason, to the point where he might not be able to get back out from behind the layered defense.

The beast wondered if they knew that up there.

The wicker man knew the answer. "The one they call the White Rose is riding the windwhale, shaping their tactics."

Toadkiller Dog woofed in exasperation. The White Rose! Soft of heart but bitterly lethal of maneuver. It all fell into place. She had locked them into no-win positions already. Without doing her conscience an injury. The Limper could suffer protecting himself or ease the pain and get blown off his withy steed. They could watch their army evaporate through desertion or terrorize the men into staying and have them mutiny.

And, from what he recalled of the White Rose, there would be a third and subtler option, which she would push them toward. But she could not comprehend the kind of murderous obsession driving the Limper. She would leave opportunities and openings. She would give second chances when the only workable choice would be to go for the throat.

It was a night when hell was in session. No one rested. The Limper hid so deeply in his defenses he could do nothing to stay the harassment. The pace of the attacks increased as dawn neared, as though the White Rose wanted them to know she could make their day more horrible than had been their night.

The army was half-gone when the sun rose. The tree god had won the first round.

His creatures refused a second round by day. The mantas cleared the sky. The windwhale floated miles up and miles to the south. The Limper collected his ragtag horde and began marching toward his next conquest.

The time of easy killing was over. Now those who stood in the Limper's path were warned of his coming. Always that monster out of the Plain of Fear hung overheard, a sword of doom ready to fall at the slightest lapse in attention.

The White Rose made no mistakes. Whenever the Limper launched an attack the mantas came fast and hard, trying to force him to cower inside his spells of protection. He fought back, brought a few down. Increasingly, he held back in hopes the windwhale would stray too close. He looked for new weapons in the ruins of his conquests.

The White Rose made no mistakes. Not once. But the maniacal determination of the Limper kept his army moving, gaining on his quarry. Till he gained his revenge, even the enmity of the tree god was just an annoyance, the whine of a mosquito.

But after the kill . . . Oh, after the kill!

XXIII

Smeds said, "There's something wrong."

"I'm beginning to get your drift," Tully said. "You think there's something wrong." Smeds had said so five times. "So does Timmy." Timmy had agreed with Smeds three or four times.

"They're right," Fish said, venturing an opinion for the first time. "There should be more industry. Carts on the road. Hunters and trappers." They were out of the Great Forest but had not yet reached cultivated country. In these parts the tide of civilization was on the ebb.

"Look there," Timmy said. He pointed, winced. His hand still hurt him.

A burnt-out cottage lay a little off the road. Smeds recalled pigs and sheep and wisecracks about the smell when they had been headed north. There was no smell now. Fish lengthened his stride, going to investigate. Smeds kept up with him.

It was grisly, though the disaster lay far enough in the past that the site was no longer as gruesome as it had been. The bones bothered Smeds the most. There were thousands, scattered, broken, gnawed, mixed.

Fish examined them in silence, moving around slowly, stirring them with the tip of his staff. After a while he stopped, leaned on his staff, stared down. Smeds moved no closer. He had a feeling he did not want to see what Fish saw.

The old man settled onto his haunches slowly, as though his own bones ached. He caught hold of something, held it up for Smeds.

A child's skull. Its top had been smashed in.

Smeds was no stranger to death, even violent death, and this was old death for someone he'd never known. It should have bothered him no more than a rumor from the past. But his stomach tightened and his heartbeat quickened. He felt a surge of anger and unfixed hatred.

"Even the babies?" he muttered. "They even murdered the babies?"

Fish grunted.

Tully and Timmy arrived. Tully looked bored. The only death that concerned him was the one awaiting him personally. Timmy looked unhappy, though. He said, "They killed the animals, too. That doesn't make sense. What were they after?"

Fish muttered, "They killed for the sake of the blood. For the pleasure of the deed, the joy in the power to destroy. For the pure meanness of it. We know too many like that already."

Smeds asked, "You think it was the same bunch that killed everybody back up there?"

"Seems likely, don't it?"

"Yeah."

Tully grumbled, "We going to hang around here all day? Or are we going to get hiking? Smeds, you decided you like it out here with the bugs and furry little things? Me, I want to get back and start enjoying life."

Smeds thought about wine and girls and the scarcity of both in the Great Forest. "You got a point, Tully. Even if five minutes ain't going to make any difference."

Fish said, "I wouldn't go living too high too sudden, boys. Might set some folks to wondering how you got it and maybe some hard guys to figuring how to get it away from you."

"Shit," Tully grumbled. "Quit your damned preaching. And maybe give me credit for a little sense."

He and Fish went off, Tully grousing and Fish listening unperturbed, with a patience Smeds found astounding. He was ready to strangle Tully himself. Once they hit the city he didn't want to see his cousin for a month. Or longer.

"How's the hand, Timmy?"

"Don't seem like it's getting any better. I don't know about burns. You? My skin's got black spots where it was the worst."

"I don't know. I saw a guy once burned so it looked like charcoal." Smeds hunched up a little, imagining the heat of the spike in his pack burning between his shoulder blades. "We get to town, you go see a doc or a wizard. Don't fool around. Hear?"

"You kidding? The way this hurts? I'd run if I didn't have to carry this damned pack."

The road was festooned with old butcheries and destructions. But the disaster had not been complete. Nearer the city there were people in the fields, and more and more as the miles passed, backs bowed with the weight of tragedies old and new.

Man is born to sorrow and despair. . . . Smeds shuddered his way out of that. *Him* wallowing in philosophical bullshit?

They crested a rise, saw the city. The wall was covered with scaffolding. Despite the late hour, men were rebuilding it. Soldiers in gray supervised. Imperials.

"Gray boys," Tully grumbled. "Here comes trouble."

"I doubt it," Fish said.

"How come?"

"There'd be more of them if they were looking for trouble. They're just making sure the repairs get done right."

Tully harumphed and scowled and muttered to himself but did not argue. He had overlooked the obvious. Imperials were sticklers for getting things done right, obsessive about keeping military works in repair.

The only delay was occasioned by the construction, not by the soldiers. Tully was not pleased. He was sick of Fish looking smarter than him. Smeds was afraid he would start improvising, trying to do something about that. Something stupid, probably.

"Holy shit," Smeds said, soft as a prayer, half a dozen

times, as they walked through the city. Buildings were being demolished, rehabilitated, or built where old structures had been razed. "They really tore the old town a new asshole."

Which left him uncomfortable. There were people he wanted to see. Were they still alive, even?

Wonderstruck, Tully said, "I never seen so many soldiers. Least not since I was a kid." They were everywhere, helping with reconstruction, supervising, policing, billeted in tents pitched where buildings had been razed. Was the whole damned city inundated with troops?

Smeds saw standards, uniforms, and unit emblems he'd never seen before. "Something going on here," he said. "We better be careful." He indicated a hanged man dangling from a roof tree three stories up.

"Martial law," Fish said. "Means the wise guys are upset. You're right, Smeds. We walk real careful till we find out what's going on and why."

They headed for the place Tully stayed first, it being closest. It was not there anymore. Tully was not distressed. "I'll just stay with you till I get set," he told Smeds.

But Smeds had not paid any rent, so they had thrown his junk into the street for scavengers—after cashing in his empties and stealing what they wanted for themselves—then had let the room to people dispossessed by the disaster.

Fish's place had gone the way of Tully's. The old man was not surprised. He said nothing. He did look a little more gaunt and haggard and slumped.

"So maybe we can all stuff in at my old lady's place," Timmy said. He was jittery. Smeds figured it was his hand. "Just for tonight. My old man, he don't like anybody I hang around with."

Timmy's parents owned the place they lived, though they were as poor as anybody else on the North Side. Smeds had heard they got it as a payoff from the gray boys for informing back in the days when there was still a lot of Rebel activity in Oar. Timmy would not say. Maybe it was true.

Who cared anymore? They'd probably been on the right side. The imperials were more honest, and better governors, if you were at a social level where who was in charge made any difference.

Smeds did not give a rat's ass who ran things as long as they left him alone. Most people felt that way.

"Timmy! Timmy Locan!"

They stopped, waited while an older woman overhauled them. As she waddled up, Timmy said, "Mrs. Cisco. How are you?"

"We thought you were dead with the rest of them, Timmy. Forty thousand people they killed that night. . . ."

"I was out of the city, Mrs. Cisco. I just got back."

"You haven't been home yet?"

People jostled them in the narrow street. It was three-quarters dark but there were so many soldiers around nobody needed to run inside to hide from the night. Smeds wondered what the bad boys were doing. Working?

"I said I just got in."

Smeds saw he did not like the woman much.

She went all sad and consoling. Even Smeds, who did not consider himself perceptive, saw she was just busting because she was going to get to be the first to pass along some bad news.

"Your dad and both your brothers . . . I'm sorry. They were trying to help fight the fires. Your mother and sister . . . Well, they were conquerors. They did what conquerors always do. Your sister, they mutilated her so bad she ended up killing herself a couple weeks ago."

Timmy shook like he was about to go into convulsions.

"That's enough, madam," Fish said. "You've buried your blade to the heart."

She sputtered, "Why, the nerve . . ."

Tully said, "Piss off, bitch. Before I kick your ass up around your ears." He used that gentle, even tone Smeds knew meant maximum danger.

So. Cousin Tully had a little canker of humanity hidden away after all. Though he would not admit it on the rack.

"I can't handle this," Timmy said. "I think I better stay dead."

Fish said, "That woman won't let you rest in peace, Timmy."

"I know. I'll do what I got to do. But not now. I know a place called the Skull and Crossbones where we can put up cheap. If it's still there."

It was there. It was a place the invaders would have ignored as too contemptible to burn. It made Smeds think of a hooker still working twenty years past her prime, pathetic and desperate.

An imperial corporal sat in a chair out front, leaning back against a wooden wall that had forgotten the meaning of paint. He held a bucket of beer in his lap. He seemed to be napping. But when they were a few steps from the door he opened his eyes, checked them over, nodded, took a drink.

"Catch his emblem?" Smeds asked Fish inside.

"Yes. Nightstalkers."

The Nightstalker Brigade was *the* crack outfit in the northern army, rigorously trained for night operations and combat under wizard's war conditions.

Smeds said, "I thought they were out east somewhere, trying to finish the Black Company." The proudest honor on the standard of the Nightstalkers was their defeat of the Black Company at Queen's Bridge. Before Queen's Bridge those mercenaries had been so glibly invincible that half the empire had been convinced the gods themselves were on their side.

"They're here now."

"What the hell is going on around here?"

"Guess we better find out. What we don't know could eat us up."

Timmy talked to the owner, whom he knew slightly. The man claimed he was full up with the dispossessed. None of those guests were evident. He hinted he might find space, though, if fate took a hand. Fishing for a bribe, Smeds figured. Which he would follow with a deep gouge.

"How much leverage on fate are we talking?" Timmy asked.

"Obol and a half. Each."

"You goddamned thief!"

"Take it or leave it."

The Nightstalker corporal stepped past Smeds and Timmy and plunked his bucket down in front of the landlord, who had gone as pale as death. "That's twice today, dogmeat. And this time I heard it myself."

The landlord gulped air, grabbed the bucket, and started to fill it.

"Don't try," the corporal said. "Offer me a bribe and you'll stay on the labor gang forever." He eyed Timmy and Smeds. "You guys pick yourself a room. On old Shit for Brains here for a night."

"I was just joshing with the guys, Corporal."

"Sure. I could tell. You had them rolling around on the floor. Bet you'll have the guy in the black mask in stitches. He loves you comedians."

Smeds asked, "What's going on around here, Corporal? We've been out of town."

"I could tell. I guess you can see your basic situation. Some bandits and deserters tore the place up. They wasn't too happy about that, down to the Tower. Since we was in the neighborhood we was one of the outfits got to come in and keep order. The brigadier, she started out life in the slums of Nihil, she figures here's a chance to get even with the kinds of assholes who made life hell when she was a kid. So you got thieves hanging from the roof trees. You got your pimps and priests and pushers, your sharpers and your fences and your whores won't learn no better working on the labor gangs eighteen hours a day so your regular citizens can get on with putting their lives back together.

"You ask me, she's too damned lenient. Gives them too many chances. Shithead here, the famous profiteer, he's done used up two of his shots now. First time he got paraded through the streets with a sign around his neck and got a week on the labor gang. This time he gets thirty

lashes and two weeks. Because he's got all that shit between his ears and ain't going to learn dick about how he
can't get away with it, next time they're going to drag him
over to Mayfield Square and stick a spear up his butt and
let him sit on it till he rots."

The corporal took a long drink from his refilled bucket,
wiped his mouth on his sleeve, grinned. "Brigadier says
let the punishment fit the crime." He took another long
drink, looked at the landlord. "You ready to go do it,
asshole?"

As he was about to follow the landlord into the street,
the corporal paused. "I reckon you boys will be fair to
your host, here, and treat his place right. 'Less you're
looking for careers in construction." He grinned again and
went.

"God damn!" Tully said.

"Yeah," Smeds agreed.

Fish said, "I have a feeling we're not going to be
comfortable in this new Oar."

"Not for long," Smeds said. "But sufficient unto the
day. Right now I need to get drunk, get laid, get a night's
sleep somewheres besides on the ground."

"Not necessarily in that order," Tully said.

Timmy put on a strained smile. "A bath wouldn't hurt
anything, either."

"Let's get doing what we got to do."

XXIV

We come over this hill after what seemed like forever without seeing people and there across a valley was this walled place that covered maybe a hundred acres. The wall wasn't much. It was maybe eight or ten feet high and no thicker than the kind of stone walls cotters put around their sheepfolds.

"Looks like a religious retreat," Raven said. "No banners or soldiers or anything."

He was right. We'd seen places with the same look before, but never so big. "Looks old."

"Yes. It has a feel to it, too. Peaceful. Let's go look."

"Don't look like a place Croaker would pass up, eh?"

"No. He has a bad case of the curiosities. Let's hope he hung around long enough to let us gain some ground."

We went over and found out our guesses were right. Raven got his wish. The place was a monastery called the Temple of Traveler's Repose and was a kind of warehouse for knowledge. It had been sitting there soaking it up for a couple thousand years.

We found out the guys we were chasing had stayed long enough to teach one of the monks a little Jewel Cities dialect. In fact, they'd only left that very morning.

Raven got all excited. He wanted to head right on out and the hell with the sun was going to hit the horizon in another hour. I wanted to hit him over the head and slow him down. That monastery looked like a damned good place to take a day off and get human again.

"Look here, Case," he cajoled, "they'll be making camp by now, right? Traveling with a wagon and a coach the best they could've done is twenty-five miles. Right? We go all night we can grab off twenty of that, easy." He learned that about the wagon and coach from the priest.

"And then we die. You maybe never need a rest, but I need a rest and the horses need a rest and this looks like the perfect place to do it. Hell, look at the name."

He made exasperated noises. After all this time I still didn't understand that catching Croaker was the most important thing in the world. He was so damned tired himself his thinking was as screwy as a possum's.

He wasn't the only one running shy of a full load. That priest came down with both feet solid on Raven's side.

Raven grinned when he said, "He claims the omens are so bad they aren't letting anybody onto the grounds. They're even chasing people out."

I had enough of the lingo, learned from Raven, to have gotten part of that. Also something about "the bad storm coming down from the north." I saw I wasn't going to win this round neither, so I said the hell with it and added a few comments that would have disappointed my old potato-digging mother. I went and shared my misery with the horses. They understood me.

Raven worked a deal for some supplies and we headed out. I wondered how much farther to the edge of the world. We'd already come farther than I'd ever believed possible.

We didn't talk much. Not because I had the sulks. I'd given up on them and went fatalistic a long time ago. I think Raven was brooding about that bit I'd caught that he hadn't mentioned. A bad storm coming down from the north.

In the Jewel Cities lingo "bad" can mean a couple three different things. Including "evil."

There was barely any light left when we came to a strip of woods. "Going to have to walk this part," Raven said. "That priest said the road through is good enough, but it's going to be hard to follow in the dark."

I grunted. I wasn't thinking about the woods. My mind was on the funny-looking hills on the other side. I'd never seen anything like them. They were all steep-sided, smoothly rounded, covered with a tawny dry grass and nothing else. They looked like the humped backs of giant animals snoozing with their legs tucked up underneath them and their heads turned around behind them, out of sight.

They were very dry, those hills. The light to see them hadn't never been good, but I was sure I'd seen a few black burn scars before it got too dark to see anything.

The woods were bone-dry, too. The trees were mostly some kind of scruffy oak with small, brittle leaves that had points almost as sharp as holly leaves. They were a sort of blue-gray color instead of the deep green of oaks in the north.

A feeble excuse for a creek dribbled through the heart of the wood. We watered ourselves and the horses and took time out for a snack. I was too tired to waste energy talking, except to say, "I don't think I got what it takes for another fifteen miles. Uphill."

Half a minute later he surprised me by saying. "Don't know if I got what it takes, either. Only so far you can go on willpower."

"Hip bothering you?"

"Yes."

"Might ought to have it looked at."

"Good job for Croaker, since he done it. Let's see how much we got left."

We managed about six more miles, the last couple up the dry grass hills, before we sort of collapsed by silent agreement. Raven said, "This time we'll give it an hour before we hit it again."

He was stubborn, that bastard.

We hadn't been there five minutes before I spotted evidence of that bad storm from the north. "Raven."

He looked. He didn't have nothing to say. He just sighed and helped me watch the lightning.

There wasn't a cloud between us and the stars.

XXV

Toadkiller Dog, carrying the wicker man, eased over a ridge line, halted. He shivered.

For leagues now they had sensed the presence of that place over there, an aura ever increasing in intensity and its ability to irritate. If they were sons of the shadow this was a fastness of the enemy, a citadel of light. There were few such places left.

They had to be expunged when found.

"Strange magic," the wicker man whispered. "I don't like it." He glanced at the northern sky. The creatures of the tree god were up there somewhere, just beyond sight.

This was not a good place to be, sandwiched between them and that place.

The wicker man said, "We'd better do it fast."

Toadkiller Dog had no desire to do it at all. He would bypass, given a choice.

He had choices, of course, but not many. He might get away with defying the wicker man once. That once had to be saved. In the meantime he responded to the ego of the wicker man, doing the insane, the stupid, sometimes the necessary, biding his time.

The army presently numbered two thousand. The men had collapsed in exhaustion the moment their commanders stopped moving. The wicker man summoned two to help him dismount.

They were rich men, every one. Their packs bulged with the finest treasure taken from cities their masters had devoured and from fallen comrades. Few had been with the army more than two months. Of the two thousand only a hundred had crossed the sea with the Limper. Those who did not desert had no cause to be optimistic about a long life.

The wicker man leaned against Toadkiller Dog. "Scum," he whispered. "All scum."

Close. Most with any spark of courage or decency deserted quickly.

The wicker man eyed the sky. A faint smile stretched the ruin of his mouth. "Do it," he said.

The soldiers groaned and grumbled as they stood to arms, but stand to they did. The wicker man stared at the temple. It abused his confidence, but he could not discern any concrete cause. "Go!" He slapped Toadkiller Dog's shoulder. "Scout it, damn you!"

He then assembled the surviving witchmen from the northern forest. They had not been much use lately, but he had a task for them now.

There wasn't a breath of warning. One moment the night was still except for the chirp of crickets and the uneasy rustle of men on the brink of an assault, the next it was alive with attacking mantas. They came from every direction, not fifty feet high, in twos and threes, and this time their lightning was not their most important weapon.

The first flights ghosted in and dropped fleshy sausage-shaped objects four feet long. Boiling, oily flame splashed everywhere. Toadkiller Dog howled in the heart of an accurately delivered barrage. Soldiers shrieked. Horses screamed and bolted. Baggage wagons caught fire.

The wicker man would have screamed in rage had he been able. But had he had the capability, he would not have had the time.

He had begun preparing a snare. And while he had concentrated on that they had caught him flat-footed.

He was enveloped in flame. He dared not think of anything else.

He suffered badly before he shielded himself with a chrysalis of protective spells. He was sprawled on the

earth then, his wicker body charred and broken. His pain
was terrible and his rage more so.

Bladders continued to fall. Mantas that had dumped
theirs returned with their lightning. The wicker man extended his charm to include a pair of shamans. One struggled to lift the wicker man's battered frame. The other
found the tag ends of the Limper's charm and began to
weave it stronger.

The remnant of the wicker man waved a blackened arm.

A manta tumbled from the night, little lightning bolts
popping and snapping around it.

The wicker man waved again.

Toadkiller Dog charged the temple. Most of the men
followed. A quick, successful assault would mean shelter
from the horror in the sky.

That horror pursued them. The air above the Limper had
become too dangerous.

Fire bladders fell and blossomed orange, finishing the
baggage and supplies. Safe now, the wicker man forgot
the fires. He chained his anger. He returned to his inter-
rupted task

As Toadkiller Dog neared the monastery wall something
reached out and flicked him away the way a man flicks a
bug. Soldiers tumbled around him.

There would be no shelter from the devils in the sky.

Yet a few men did keep going, their progress unim-
peded. Why?

The mantas came down on rippling wings. Toadkiller
Dog hurled himself into the air. His jaws closed on dark
flesh.

The wicker man murmured while the two shamans recovered something from the smoldering remains of a wagon.
He beamed at them, oblivious to the surrounding holocaust.

The thing they brought him was an obsidian serpent,
arrow-straight, ten feet long and six inches thick. The
detail was astonishingly fine. Its ruby eyes blazed as they
reflected the fires. The witch doctors staggered under its
weight. One cursed the heat still trapped in it.

The wicker man smiled his terrible smile. He began singing a dark song in a breathless whisper.

The obsidian serpent began to change.

Life flowed through it. It twitched. Wings unfolded, long wings of darkness that cast shadows where no shadows should have been. Red eyes flared like windows suddenly opened on the hottest forges of hell. Glossy talons, like obsidian knives, slashed at the air. A terrible screech ripped from a mouth filled with sharp, dark teeth. The thing's breath glowed, faded. It began trying to break away, its gaze fixed on the nearest fire.

The wicker man nodded. The shamans released it. The thing flapped shadow wings and plunged into the fire. It wallowed like a hog in mud. The wicker man beamed approval. His lips kept forming words.

That fire faded, consumed.

The thing leaped to another. Then to another.

The wicker man indulged it for several minutes. Then the tenor of his whisper changed. It became demanding, commanding. The thing shrieked a protest. A fiery haze belched from its mouth. Still screaming, it rose into the night, following orders.

The wicker man turned his attention to the Temple of Traveler's Repose. It was time to see by what sorcery the place kept itself inviolate.

The shamans took hold and carried him toward the temple wall.

XXVI

Bomanz's knuckles were white. They ached. He had a death grip on some windwhale organ. The monster had dropped low enough that the flash and fire and chaos down below gave him a clear perspective of just how far he was going to fall if he relaxed his grip for an instant. Silent and Darling were close by, watching. One false move and Silent would give him a kick in the butt and a chance to see if he could fly.

It was testing time. The White Rose had orders to stop the old horror here, where there might be help from its victims. This time she had woven him into her plan.

In fact, he had the feeling he *was* the plan.

She had not explained anything. Maybe she was playing woman of mystery. Or maybe she really did not trust him.

He was in charge—till he did something unacceptable and bit a boot with his butt on his way to doing a swan dive into hell.

Menhirs seldom got any feeling into their speech. But the one that materialized behind his left shoulder managed sorrow as it reported, "He's shielded himself. Neither fire nor lightning can reach him."

The surprise had seemed a wan hope, anyway, but a long shot worth trying. "And his followers?"

"Decimated again. The monster is unconquerable, though. He suffers, but pain just makes him angrier."

"He's not invincible at all. As you will see if I get close to him."

Bomanz's least favorite talking buzzard cackled wildly.

104

"You're big-timer, eh? Ha! That thing is gonna squish you like a bug, Seth Chalk."

Bomanz turned away from the bird. His stomach flopped as he looked down again. The buzzard was determined to get his goat. He was amused by the bird's optimism. He had learned self-control in a hard school. He had been married for thirty years.

"Isn't it time you stones made your move?" He tried a disarming smile, a man with nothing on his mind but the issue at hand.

A little scheme had begun to fester in the back of his head. A way to put that snide vulture in his place.

The stone said, "Soon. What will you contribute to the farce?"

Before he could temporize the buzzard shrieked, "What the hell is that?"

Bomanz whirled. That damned bird wasn't scared of anything, but it was squeaky with fear now.

Vast dark wings spanned the night, masking the moon and stars. Fires animated wise and evil eyes. Another limned huge needle teeth. Those malignant eyes were fixed on those who rode the windwhale.

Silent made frantic warding signs that did no good.

Bomanz did not recognize the thing. It was nothing of the Domination, brought out of the Barrowland. He was an expert on those and believed he knew every rag and feather and bone that had gone into them. Neither was it something of the Lady's empire or she would have made it her own thing during her heyday. So it had to be loot from one of the cities desolated since the Limper had come out of the empire.

Whatever its provenance, it was dangerous. Bomanz began putting himself into that trance from which it was easiest for him to meet a supernatural challenge.

As he opened himself to the energies of another level of reality, fear struck. "Get on to the next phase!" he shouted at the scarred menhir. "Now! Recall the mantas! Get everybody off this damned thing!"

Fire-edged wings beat the night. The red-eyed thing streaked toward the windwhale.

Bomanz used the strongest warding spell he knew.

The monster tortured the night with its shriek of pain. But it came on, its path deflected only slightly. The windwhale shuddered to its impact.

All across the windwhale's back talking menhirs began vanishing, leaving baby thunderclaps.

The talking buzzard cursed like a stevedore and flailed at the air. Young mantas screeched in fear. The Torque brothers rushed Bomanz, shouting questions he did not understand. They were going to throw him off.

Darling stopped them with a gesture.

Below, the windwhale's belly opened and gave birth to a boiling globule of fire. Heat rolled up its flanks. A huge shudder ran its length. Bomanz's knuckles grew whiter. He wanted to move back but his hands had a will of their own and would not turn loose.

Another explosion tore the windwhale's belly. The great sky beast dropped a short distance. Upset became panic. "We're going down!" one of the Torques shouted in his barbaric eastern gabble. "Oh, gods, we're going down!"

Darling caught Bomanz's eye and in peremptory sign language ordered, "Do something!" She was not rattled.

Before he could respond the air filled with icy water spraying from organs on the leviathan's back. Despite the departure of the menhirs the windwhale had begun to lose buoyancy. It was shedding ballast high, hoping that would dampen the fires.

The chill water helped stifle the panic.

Mantas began coming in out of the night, fluttering into the spray. The instant they came to rest their young scrambled onto their backs, followed by other Plains creatures. Once a manta had all the weight it could bear, it flopped to one of the slippery, downsloping launch slides that allowed them to hurtle into space.

Another explosion shook the windwhale. It began a slow buckle in the middle.

Darling approached Bomanz. She looked like she would

put him over the side personally if he did not start doing something more than gawk and shake.

How could she stay so damned calm? They were going to die in a few minutes.

He closed his eyes and concentrated on the author of the disaster. He tried to pump himself up.

He did not know what that thing was but he would not let it intimidate him. He was the Bomanz who had slain a grandfather of dragons. He was the Bomanz who had walked into the flames, daring the wrath of the Lady in all her majesty and strength.

But his feet had rested upon solid ground those times.

Softly, surely, he murmured the calming mantras, following with the unleashing cycles that would allow him to slide free of his flesh.

In a moment he was adrift in the whale's belly, floating through the flames, watching the dark fire-eater. Only because it fed so gluttonously had the windwhale not yet been consumed by a holocaust.

He added his skills to the self-protective efforts of the windwhale and the damping of the fire-eater's feeding. The flames began to dwindle. He tried to move subtly and do his work unnoticed by the predator. That thing had only one thought. Soon the windwhale could manage the fires alone.

The fire-eater tried to breach another gas bladder. Bomanz slapped it away. It tried again, and again, and again, failing, till it flew into a frustrated fit.

While it was out of control Bomanz insinuated tendrils of sorcery. With a jeweler's touch he evicted the commands of the wicker man. He replaced them with one overwhelming imperative: destroy the wicker man. Consume him in darkness, consume him in fire, but rid the earth of his noxious presence.

Bomanz retired to his own proper flesh. Physical sight showed him the stars masked by fire-edged wings that spanned half the sky. Those wings tilted. The body they supported dropped toward the place Old Father Tree wanted defended at all costs.

Bomanz glanced at Silent and Darling. The dusky, humorless wizard smiled slightly, nodded, made a small gesture to indicate that he had witnessed a job well done.

So maybe he was finally off the shit list.

He watched the fire-eater strike.

"Damn!" It was plunging toward the compound. Limper must have broken in.

The windwhale had fallen a long way, too. It was in easy striking distance for the wicker man. The giant of the sky had buckled in the middle, become a sagging sausage. It had no more ballast to shed. Neither could it control its motion through the sky. It was at the mercy of the wind, heading south, still losing altitude.

Silent and Darling joined Bomanz. He demanded, "Why did you stay? Why didn't you get the hell off?"

Silent's fingers danced as he relayed to Darling.

"Knock it off with the waggle fingers. You can talk."

Silent gave him a hard look. He did not say anything.

The windwhale lurched. Bomanz grabbed an organ stem as he hurtled toward the monster's side and a drop still three thousand feet till it was over. A gobbet of flame rolled up, singed him. He cursed and clung for his life. The windwhale continued to reel and shudder. It began making a hollow, booming noise that might have been a cry of pain.

An overlooked spark had tangled with a slow leak from a gas bladder. The game was about over. There was nothing to be done this time.

He was going to die in a few minutes. For some reason he could not get as upset as he thought he should. Mostly he was angry. This was not the way for the great Bomanz to go out, just dragged along, without an audience and no great battle to die in. Without a legend to leave behind.

He cursed continuously, in an unintelligible mutter.

His thoughts, more agile than ever he pretended, scurried around in frantic search for a way to make sure the wicker man went with him.

There was none. He had no weapon but the fire-eater, which was a javelin thrown and now beyond his control.

The windwhale began settling more rapidly. Fire crept up the aft half of the monster. The bend in its middle grew increasingly pronounced. The sucker was going to break up. "Come on. That half is going to go." He began climbing the steepening slope of the fore half. Silent and Darling scrambled after him.

Another explosion. Silent lost his footing. Darling grabbed a treelike organ with one hand, caught him with the other. She hoisted him to his feet.

"That ain't no woman," Bomanz muttered. "Not like I ever saw."

The rear half of the windwhale began falling faster than the front half. Secondary explosions hurled comets of whale flesh into the teeth of the night. Cursing monotonously, Bomanz continued his scramble away from disaster—every second wondering why he bothered.

The fear began to come, feeding on his helplessness. His talents were of no avail. He could do nothing but run from the conquering fire till there was nowhere left to flee.

Yet another explosion ripped and wrenched the windwhale. Bomanz fell. Below, the aft half of the monster tore free and fell away, the whole enveloped in flames. The rest of the windwhale bobbed violently, trying to return to horizontal. It yawed and rolled while it bobbed. The old sorcerer hung on. And cursed.

A whimper caught his ear.

Not five feet away he saw the glowing eyes of an infant manta. When the windwhale fragment began to stabilize he crawled thither. "They forget you, little fellow? Come on out here."

The kit hissed and spat and tried to use its lightning. It could generated no more than a spark. Bomanz dragged it out into the moonlight. "You are a tiny one, aren't you? No wonder they missed you." The kit was no bigger than a half-grown cat. It could not be more than a month old.

Bomanz cradled the infant in the crook of his left arm. It

ceased struggling almost immediately. It seemed content to be held.

The old wizard resumed his journey.

The windwhale had become as stable as it could. Bomanz eased nearer the side. He looked down just in time to see the other half hit ground.

Silent and Darling joined him. As always their faces were emotionless masks, one dusky, one pale. Silent stared down at the earth. Darling seemed more interested in the baby manta. Bomanz said, "Under two thousand feet now. but that's still a long way to fall. And there's still *that* to concern us."

That meant the small fires still burning back where the rear half had broken away. One of those could reach another gas bladder any minute.

"We should get as far forward as we can and hope for the best." He tried to sound more hopeful than he felt.

Silent nodded.

Bomanz looked around. The monastery was burning merrily, fired by the fire-eater. So that had worked, some. But when he listened the right way he could sense a knot of rage and pain seething amidst the flames.

The Limper had survived again.

And *his* scheme had worked some, too.

XXVII

I had a hard time believing it. Raven had given up. His hip must have hurt a lot more than he wanted to admit.

He had not moved since he had gone down, and hadn't said nothing since his body beat down his will. I think he was ashamed.

I really wished the son of a bitch would figure out that he didn't have to be a superman. I wasn't going to make him stop being my buddy because he was human.

I was as wiped out as he was but I could not lay down and die. That show up around the monastery was getting flashier all the time. In fact, some of the fireworks was headed our way. That made me too nervous to crap out, though even my toenails were tired.

Another blast. A rose of fire bloomed in the sky. A big hunk of something started falling, spinning off smaller hunks of fire.

I realized what I was seeing.

"Raven, you better get your ass up and look at this mother."

He grunted but he didn't do it.

"It's a windwhale, asshole. Out of the Plain of Fear. What do you think of that?" I saw a couple get wiped during the big bloodletting up to the Barrowland.

"So it seems."

Mr. Ambition had rolled over. His voice was cool but his face was fishbelly white, like he'd stepped around a corner and bumped noses with Old Man Death.

"So how come it's here?" Then I shut up. I'd imagined up a reason.

111

''Not for me, kid. Who on the Plain would know where to look for me? Who would care?''

''Then . . . ?''

''It's the battle of the Barrowland, still going on. It's the tree god head-to-head with whatever I felt breaking loose up there.''

Light flashed. Fire busted out of one end of the part of the windwhale that was still up. ''That thing isn't going to stay up there much longer. Should we go see if we can do something?''

He didn't say anything for at least a minute. He looked up at the humpbacked hills like he was thinking maybe he had enough left to go catch Croaker after all. He couldn't be more than five, ten miles away, could he? Then he levered himself to his feet, wincing, obviously favoring his bad hip. I didn't ask. I knew he'd claim it was just the chill air and cold ground.

He told me, ''Better get the horses. I'll drag our stuff together.''

Big job you took on yourself there, old buddy, since we basically just dropped in our tracks when we couldn't go anymore.

Since he didn't have much to do he mostly just stood there watching that flying disaster cross the sky. He looked like he was being asked to mount the gallows and put the noose around his own neck.

''I've been thinking, Case,'' Raven said as we came down off the knee of the most northerly of those goofy humped hills, headed northeast, chasing that drifting windwhale fragment.

''Brooding is the word I would have picked, old buddy. And you been at it since the day they finally put the Dominator down. Looks like that explosion a while back was the last one.''

The fragment was drifting on a course that would intercept ours. A few fires flickered on one end. It was turning end for end slowly but had stopped its fall.

''Maybe. But you say something definite like that, the

gods will stick it to you. Let's just hope it clears the woods. Be rough landing in there.''

"What were you thinking?"

"About you and me, Croaker and his gang, the Lady, Silent, Darling. About all the things we had in common but still couldn't get along."

"I didn't see all that much you had in common. Not once you got past having the same enemies."

"Neither did I for a long time. And none of them saw it, either. Else we all might have tried a little harder."

I tried to look like I gave a shit at three in the morning.

"Basically we're all lonely, unhappy people looking for our place, Case. Loners who'd really rather not be but don't know how. When we get to the door that would let us in—or out—we can't figure out how to work the latch string."

I'll be damned. That was about as open-up-and-expose-what's-inside a remark as I ever got out of him. Filled with longing and conviction. Well shave my head and call me Baldy. I been right up here beside him since a couple years ago. You don't see the changes going on in people when you're standing up close.

This wasn't the Raven I'd first met, before his ego and misadventure had gotten his soul trapped among the shadow evils of the Barrowland, before its cleansing. He had returned from the prison of the heart dramatically altered.

Hell, he wasn't even the same man who had spent all his time drunk on his ass in Oar, neither.

I had kind of mixed feelings. I'd admired and liked and gotten along pretty good with the old Raven.

Maybe I would again once he got through his transition.

I did not know what to say to him, though I was sure he wanted a response. His knack for befuddling me never changed. "So did you figure out how to work it?"

"I have an unsettling premonition, Case. I'm almost paralyzed by a dread that I'm about to find out if I've learned anything." He stared at that piece of windwhale.

I checked it, guessed it was about two miles away and five hundred feet up. The breeze was bringing it to us.

"We going to chase it back into the hills if it carries that far?"

"You tell me, Case. This was your idea." He paused to whisper to his horse. The animals were not excited about hiking around at night either. Even if they didn't have to carry anybody.

Flame mushroomed out of the windwhale. Before the roar of the explosion reached us, I said, "We're not going to have to worry about climbing any hills."

The windwhale came down fast, turning end for end. When it was about two hundred feet off the ground some chunks fell off and it stopped coming down so fast. I had a pretty good idea where it would hit. We hurried toward the spot.

Then what was left nosed down, sped up, and hit the ground about a mile away. It bounced back into the air, maybe a hundred feet high. It kept coming, straight at us now.

At the peak of its bounce it exploded again.

It bounced two more times before it stayed down and just slid to a stop.

"Be careful," Raven said. "There might be more explosions." Fires still burned on the windwhale. Somewhere inside it was making a noise like somebody beating on the granddaddy of all bass drums.

I said, "It ain't dead yet. Look there." The end of a tentacle lay just a couple yards from me. It was jumping around like a snake with a toothache.

"Unh. Let's hobble the horses."

Excited all to hell, Raven was. Like he spent his whole life hanging around windwhales so close he could smell their bad breath. And this one had that all over.

I caught something in the firelight. "Hey! There's people up on top of that sucker."

"There had to be. Where?"

"There. Right over that black patch." I pointed. Some guys up there were hauling around on something.

Raven said, "Looks like somebody trying to get somebody else out from under something."

"Let's get up there and give them a hand." I left my horse unhobbled.

Raven grinned at me. "The exuberant folly of youth. Where does it go?"

I started climbing a blubbery, stinky cliff. He went looking for a bush to tie the horses to, that being easier than messing with hobbles. I was halfway to the top before he started after me.

The flesh of the windwhale was sort of spongy and definitely smelly, with the odor of burned flesh added. The flesh trembled with pain and failing life. Such a noble monster. I wanted to cry for it.

"Raven! Hurry up! There's three of them up here and a big fire burning back there."

Right then there was a baby explosion. It knocked me down. Gobs of fire splattered the ground. Some of the dry grass caught.

There would be trouble if that spread.

By the time Raven dragged his carcass up I had the woman across my shoulders and the old man, who was the only one on his feet, was tying her so she wouldn't slide off. Finished, the old boy whipped around and starting trying to drag a frondlike piece of windwhale off somebody else.

Panting, Raven looked at me, looked at the woman, grumbled, "It had to be, didn't it?"

I said, "Hey, this broad is solid as a rock. Or she's got a lead butt. She weighs as much as I do."

"How about you get her down?" He muttered, "I'm getting too old for this crap," and headed for the old man. "You. What the hell are you doing here?" He wasn't surprised to see the guy under the frond, though. Having Silent drop out of the sky was just the kind of trick he expected the fates to pull on him.

He was shaking as he helped the old man lift the frond. The old man started fussing over Silent. A black lump of a something glommed on to his shoulder made a sound like a kitten crying.

"Hoist him up!" the old wizard ordered. "Carry him. We don't have time for me to bring him around."

I started down then. Whatever else they said I missed. Pretty soon they started down after me.

Something whispered overhead. The lump on the wizard's shoulder mewled again. A screech tumbled down from the dark. The windwhale's mantas had come to circle their dying partner.

What happened to mantas when their windwhale died?

"Ouch!" Raven yelled. "Watch where the hell you're stepping!"

At the same time the old man said, "The arrogance of you, man! The bloody insufferable, conceited arrogance. You, without claim or right, demand—demand!—explanations of me. Of *me*! The conceit of you surpasses comprehension. I should be asking you what you're doing here, fluttering around ahead of the Limper. Are you his forerunner? His death scout? Will you get moving? Before we get crisped like bacon?"

I got my feet on the ground, watched them. Raven was thoroughly pissed. Maybe he never figured out that he wasn't a lord anymore and the world wasn't going to jump when he barked. And he never did have sense enough to be scared of the right people. People like old Bomanz, who could probably turn him into a frog if he got aggravated.

Raven didn't get to shoot off his own mouth. Another explosion almost shook him and the old man off the windwhale. A big shudder rolled through the monster. That drumbeat stopped. The beast let out with a deep groan that said everything there was to say about death and despair.

The mantas upstairs made keening sounds. Mourning sounds. I wondered how they would manage now.

The windwhale stopped shaking. The wizard yelled, "Get out of here before the whole thing blows!"

•   •   •

Raven was staggering toward the horses when it happened. The blast beggared everything we had seen before. I ducked away from a blast of hot air. It hurled Raven forward. He fell on his face. Bomanz, though closer to the explosion, rode the blast, staying upright with footwork that reminded me of my old mother dancing. He looked like he was in pain.

When the ring in my ears went I heard the sad song of the mantas, again or still.

The windwhale became its own funeral pyre.

Flying chunks started grass fires all around. The horses were upset. We were not safe yet.

Raven crawled, unable to get back up. I felt like a total Daryl Dipshit standing there doing nothing to help, but my legs just wouldn't move.

The wizard caught up, hoisted Raven. They cussed each other like a couple of drunks. I got my feet going finally and leaned into the heat. "Come on, you guys. Knock it off. Let's throw this dork on a horse and get out of here before we all get turned into pork cracklings."

I already had the woman across one saddle like a sack of rice. We had to do so much running her front side was going to be one miserable bruise.

"Move it!" I yelled. "There's a breeze coming up." I scooted back and got hold of the animals before they decided they were smarter than us and headed for the high country.

While we hoisted Silent, Raven got his first good look at Darling. She was all beat to hell. Blood leaked from her mouth, ears, and nose. Her exposed skin was all bruised or blood-caked. Silent looked about as bad, and so did the wizard, pretty much, but Raven did not care jack shit about them.

"They can be healed," Bomanz said before Raven could start fussing. "*If* we get them away from here before the grass fires get us."

That and me heading out without waiting around for him got Raven moving. He followed me, leading the horse with Darling on it. Bomanz did not wait for either of us.

He headed around one end of the nearest grass fire, which the breeze was pushing toward the sleepy, humpbacked hills.

Raven went to muttering and cursing again. Bomanz was headed north, cradling the manta kit, which squeaked cheerfully at creatures that glided invisibly above our heads. Raven still wanted to catch his old crony, but I guess he decided it would not be smart to challenge the sorcerer right off, when he was in a bad mood, too.

I kept glancing back at the burning windwhale till we got too far into the woods to see it. It seemed to me there had to be some kind of lesson there, some kind of symbolism, but I couldn't unravel it.

XXVIII

Smeds walked into the Skull and Crossbones out of bright morning sunshine. When his eyes adjusted he spotted Timmy Locan in a dark corner at a tiny table for two. At first it looked like Timmy was just sitting there staring down at his bundled hand. When he got closer, though, Smeds saw Timmy's eyes were tight shut. Moisture glittered on his cheeks.

Smeds sat down across from Timmy. "You go to a doc like I said?"

"Yeah."

"Well?"

"He charged me two obols to tell me he didn't know what was wrong and he didn't know what to do about it unless I want him to cut it off. He couldn't even help with the pain."

"You need a wizard, then."

"Point me at the best one in town and turn me loose. I can afford him."

"That ain't a him, Timmy. It's two hers. Gossamer and Spidersilk. Top blades from Charm that just took over."

Timmy wasn't listening. "You hear what I said, Timmy? We got two bitches here straight from the Tower. Came in last night. Bad mojo. They're supposed to find out what happened up to the Barrowland. Tomorrow or the next day they're going to borrow a battalion of Nightstalkers and head up there. It's all over town."

Timmy still did not listen close enough to suit.

"You get it? They're going to get up there and find out

119

that somebody messed with that tree. They're going to be out for blood, then.''

Timmy ground his teeth a moment, said, ''Be good advertising.''

''What?''

''Fish says he don't think there's any way they can trace us as long as we just sit tight and keep our mouths shut. Meantime word gets around to all the wizards. Them that's interested will get here and start looking for the spike. Then we put it up for bids.''

Smeds was less fond of that idea all the time. Too damned dangerous. But the rest of them, even Fish, were convinced that a sale could be made safely. They didn't believe that all wizards were crazy-mean and liked to screw people and hurt them just for the fun of it.

''It's just a business deal,'' Tully kept saying. ''We sell. They pay off and get the spike. Everybody's happy.''

Dumb shit. Everybody would *not* be happy. There were a skillion wizards and only one silver spike. Every damned one of them was not only going to be trying for it for himself, they were going to be out to make sure nobody else got it first. Whoever did get it might want to cover his tracks so nobody came looking to take it away from him.

Tully kept saying bullshit whenever Smeds started worrying. Even when Smeds reminded him that that was the way wizards carried on in every story you ever heard.

''I think I know where's a guy who can work on your hand, Timmy.'' Smeds recalled one of his aunts talking about a wizard down on the South Side who was mostly pretty honest and decent as long as you paid him what you owed him.

The street door opened. Light spilled inside. Smeds glanced around, saw the Nightstalker corporal and a couple of his buddies. The corporal raised a friendly hand. Smeds had to reciprocate or look like a shit. Then he had to stay there talking awhile so it didn't look like he was walking out because a bunch of gray boys had walked in. He used the time to tell Timmy about the wizard his aunt knew.

"So you want to try him?"

"I'm ready to try anything."

"Let's go, then."

The wizard was a smiling, tubby, apple-cheeked little dork with thin white hair that stuck out every which way. He came on like he'd spent his whole life waiting just for them. Smeds understood why his aunt liked the man. She was so sour and ugly that a blind dog would not wait for her except to go away.

Smeds did most of the talking because he did not trust Timmy not to blurt out more than he needed to in his eagerness to get rid of his pain. "Some kind of infection that's turning his hand all black," Smeds said.

"And making it ache," Timmy said. There was a hint of a whine in his voice. Timmy Locan wasn't a whiner.

The wizard said, "Let's open her up and look at it, then." He pulled Timmy's hand down onto his worktable, went after the bandage with a thin, sharp knife. He smiled and chattered as he worked and when he laid the bandage open he said, "It does look a bit nasty, doesn't it?"

It looked a lot nasty to Smeds. He had not seen Timmy's hand unwrapped in a week. The area of blackness had tripled in size. It now covered Timmy's whole palm and had begun to creep round to the back. The blackened flesh had a puffy look.

The wizard leaned down, sniffed. "Funny. Infected flesh usually smells. Close your eyes tight, son." Timmy did and the pudgy man started poking his hand with a needle. "What do you feel when I do this?"

"Just a little pressure. Ouch!" The needle had pricked unblackened flesh.

"Strange. Very strange. I've never seen anything like it, son. Try to relax." The wizard went to a shelf and took down a baroque brass doohickey that was not much more than a one-foot empty circle supported by six eight-inch legs. This he placed astraddle Timmy's hand. He pinched powders and dribbled drops into pockets in the brass gizmo, made with some mumbo jumbo. There was a flash and a puff of noisome smoke. A shimmer like heat off pavement appeared within the confines of the circle.

The wizard stared into that.

Smeds could not see that it made any difference.

But the wizard's smile went away. The color left his cheeks. In a squeaky voice he asked, "What have you boys been into?"

"Huh? What do you mean?" Smeds asked.

"Surprised I didn't see it sooner. The mystic stench is there. But who would have thought it? The boy has had his hand on something polluted with the essence of evil. Something pregnant with the blood of darkness. A powerful amulet, perhaps. Some periapt lost in ancient times and just now resurfacing. Something very extraordinary and hitherto unknown in these parts. Have you boys been grave robbing?"

Timmy stared at his hand. Smeds met the wizard's eye but did not say anything.

"You wouldn't have been breaking any laws digging wherever you ran into whatever caused this. But you could get in deep if you don't report it to the imperial legates."

"Can you do anything for him?"

"They pay good rewards."

"Can you do anything for him?" Smeds demanded.

"No. Whatever caused this was created by someone far greater than I am. Assuming it to have been an amulet, the burn can be cured only by someone greater than the man or woman who created the amulet. And that someone would have to have the amulet itself to study before trying to effect a cure."

Shit, Smeds thought. Where were you going to find somebody big enough to undo the Dominator?

You weren't. "What else can you do? If you can't just fix him up?"

"I can remove the tainted flesh. That's all."

"What's that mean in plain language?"

"I can amputate his hand. Here. At the wrist would do it today. If that's the way you decide to go you'd better do it soon. Once the darkness works its way into the larger bones there won't be any way to tell how far or how fast it's spreading.''

"What about it, Timmy?"

"It's my *hand,* man!"

"You heard what he said."

"I heard. Look, wiz, you got something that will stop the pain long enough for me to think straight?"

The pudgy man said, "I could put a blocking spell on that would help for a while, but it would hurt worse than ever when that wore off. And that's an idea you'd better get into your head. The longer you stall, the worse the pain is going to get. In another ten days you're not going to be able to stop screaming."

Smeds scowled. "Thanks for just not a whole lot. Do the painkiller thing for him and let us go talk it over."

The wizard sprinkled powders, mumbled, made mystic passes. Smeds watched Timmy relax a little, then even manage a feeble smile.

Smeds asked, "That it? Come on, Timmy. Let's hit the road."

The wizard said, "I need to wrap that again. I don't *know* that it would, but it if came in contact with someone else it *might* communicate itself. If the original evil was potent enough."

Smeds's insides knotted and curled as he tried to recall if he had ever touched Timmy's hand. He didn't think he had.

He barely waited to get Timmy outside before he asked, "Old Fish ever touch that when he was taking care of you?"

"No. Nobody did. Except that doc I had look at it. He poked it a couple times with his finger."

"Unh." Smeds did not like it. It was getting complicated. He did not like things complicated. Trying to untangle them usually made things worse.

They had to have a sitdown with Tully and Fish. He knew what Tully would want to do: drag Timmy out in the country somewhere, cut his throat, and bury him.

Tully had the soul of a snake. He had to break loose.

The sooner the better. Right now probably wouldn't hurt. Except then how would he get his cut of whatever the spike went for? Shit.

"Timmy, I want you should go get drunk, have a good time, but do some serious thinking and get your mind made up. Whatever you want to do, I'll back you up, but you got to remember it affects all of us. And keep an eye on Tully. Tully ain't a guy you want to turn your back on when he's nervous."

"I'm not stupid, Smeds. Tully ain't a guy I'd turn my back on when he wasn't nervous. He ever tries anything cute he's got a nasty surprise coming."

Interesting.

Smeds figured he had some deciding to do himself. Like, with the town up to the gutters in gray boys and their bosses about to find out the spike was gone from the Barrowland, was it time to hit the road and get lost someplace they'd never think to look? Was it time to do something with the spike so it would be safer than it was in his pack back at the Skull and Crossbones? He'd already had a cute idea how to handle that. An idea that might turn into a kind of life insurance if he went ahead and did it before he told the others what he had done.

Damn, he hated it when things got complicated.

There was a hell of a row with Tully when they all got together. Tully seemed a little shorter on sense every day.

"You think you're some goddamned kind of immortal?" Smeds demanded. "You think you're untouchable? There's the goddamned grays out there, Tully. They decide to get excited, they'll take you apart one piece at a time. Then they'll give the pieces to Gossamer and Spidersilk to put back together so they can make you tell them what they want to know. And whatever you tell them then, it won't be enough. Or do you think you're some kind of hero that would hold out against the kind of people that learned to ask questions in the Tower?"

"They got to find me before they can ask me anything, Smeds."

"I think we're finally getting somewhere. That's what I've been saying for the last ten minutes."

"The hell. You've been jacking your jaw about running off to some ass-wipe place like Lords. . . ."

"You really think you could stay out of their way here? Once they knew what they were looking for?"

"How they gonna . . . ?"

"How the hell should I know? What I do know is, these ain't no half-moron bozos from the North Side. These are people from *Charm*. They eat guys like us for snacks. The best way to stay out of their way is not to be around where they're at."

"We ain't going nowhere, Smeds." Tully was turning plain stubborn.

"You want to stand around waiting for the hammer to hit you between the eyes that's fine with me. But I ain't getting killed because you got ego problems. Selling that spike off and getting rich would be nice, but not nice enough to die for or go to the rack for. All these heavies turning up here before we even start trying to find a buyer, I'm tempted to let it go to the first bidder just to get out from under."

The argument raged on, bitterly, inconclusively, with Fish and Timmy refereeing. Smeds was as angry with himself as he was with Tully. He had a nasty suspicion he was just blowing a lot of hot air, that he would not be able to walk out on his cousin if it came to a decision. Tully was not much, but he was family.

XXIX

Toadkiller Dog lay in the shade of an acacia tree gnawing on a shinbone that had belonged to one of the wicker man's soldiers.

Only a dozen of those had survived that grisly night when they had taken the monastery. Half of those had died since. When the breeze blew from the north the stench of death was overpowering.

Only two of the witch doctors had gotten through alive. Barely. Till they recovered, he and the wicker man were in little better shape than they had been in the beginning, back in the Barrowland.

Toadkiller Dog kept one eye on the mantas gliding overhead and around the monastery, eternally probing for soft spots in the shell of magic shielding the place. Bolts ripped through any they found. Only one in a hundred did any damage, but that was enough to guarantee eventual destruction.

The wicker man's triumph over the windwhale had given a respite of two hours. Then another windwhale had appeared and had resumed the struggle. There were four of them out there now, at the points of the compass, and they were determined to avenge their fallen brother.

Toadkiller Dog rose, bones creaking and aching, and zigzagged his way between dangerous spots to the low, thin wall that surrounded the remains of the monastery. He limped badly. His wicker leg had gone in the conflagration that had come when the Limper's firedrake had turned back upon him.

He consoled himself with the knowledge that the Limper

was worse off than he was. The Limper had no body at all.

But he was working on that.

How the hell had they managed that turnaround?

Toadkiller Dog rose on his hind legs, rested his paw and chin on top of the wall.

The picture was worse, as he had expected. The talking stones were so numerous they formed a circumvallation. Groves of the walking trees stood wherever the ground was moist, feasting. They had to endure eternal drought on the Plain of Fear.

How long before they moved in and began demolishing the wall with their swift-growing roots?

Squadrons of reverse centaurs galloped among the shadows of gliding mantas, practicing charges and massed javelin tosses.

That weird horde would come someday. And there would be no turning them back while the Limper had no body.

They would have come already had they known how helpless were the besieged. That was the only smart thing the Limper had done, getting himself out of sight and lying low, so those creatures out there did not know where he stood. He was counting on the White Rose to think he was trying to lure her into a trap by pretending to be powerless.

The Limper needed time. He would do anything, would sacrifice anyone, to buy that time.

Toadkiller Dog turned away and limped toward the half-demolished main structure of the monastic complex. A frightened sentry watched him pass.

They knew they were doomed, that they had become rich beyond their hopes but at the cost of selling their souls to death. They would not live to enjoy a copper's worth of their stolen fortunes.

It was too late now, even to find hope in desertion.

One man had tried. They had him out there. Sometimes they made him scream just to remind everybody they were irked enough to take no prisoners.

Toadkiller Dog squeezed through the tight halls and down steep, narrow stairs to the deep cellar the Limper had taken for his lair. Down there he was safe from the monster boulders and whatnot the windwhales dropped when the urge took them.

The Limper had set up in a room that was large and as damp and moldy as might be expected. But the light there was as bright as artificial sources could make it. The sculptors needed that light to do their work properly.

The bodiless head of the Limper sat on a shelf overlooking the work in progress. Two armed guards and one of the witch doctors watched, too. The actual work was being done by three of the dozen priests who had survived the massacre of the monastery's inmates.

They had no idea what their reward would be if they did a good job. They labored under the illusion that they would be allowed to resume the monastery's work when they finished and their guests departed.

In the southwest corner, the highest of the enclosure, there was a small spring. The monastery drew its water from this. Below the spring, kept moist by its runoff, lay a bed of some of the finest potter's clay in the world. The monks had been using it for ages. The Limper had been delighted when he had learned of the deposit.

The sculptors had the new body roughed in to the Limper's satisfaction. It would be the body he'd always wished he'd had, not the stunted, crippled thing he'd had to endure when he'd had a body of his own. With the head on it this would stand six and a half feet tall and the body itself would fit what the Limper imagined was every maiden's dream.

About a third of the detail work was done and it was very good work indeed, with all the tiny wrinkles and creases and pore holes of a real human body, but with none of the blemishes.

Only one of the three monks was doing any sculpting. The other two were keeping the clay moist, basting its surface with oil that would keep that natural dampness in.

Toadkiller Dog glanced at the clay figure only long enough to estimate how much longer their good luck would have to hold. He was not reassured. Surely those things out there would stop procrastinating in a day or two.

He retraced his route to the surface, prowled from wall to wall, eyeing potential routes of escape.

When the hammer fell he was going out of there at a gallop, straight at the talking stone and jump over. They would not expect him to bolt and leave the Limper to his fate.

He would find a more reasonable patron somewhere else. The Limper was not the only one of the old ones who had survived.

XXX

It was not a companionable camp where we were set up east of the monastery, where the smell of bodies wasn't as bad. I mean, I did my best and me and the Torque boys and the talking buzzard and a couple of the talking stones had us some pretty good bullshit sessions around the old campfire. But the rest of them acted like a bunch of little kids.

Raven wasn't going to talk to Darling unless she made the first move. Silent wouldn't have nothing to do with Raven on account of he thought Raven was going to try to steal his girl. A girl he never really had. Darling wasn't talking to Raven because she figured he owed her about twenty giant apologies and he had to pay off before she gave him the time of day. And she was pissed at Silent because he was being presumptuous, and maybe at herself some, too, for maybe having given him grounds for his presumptions.

Just between you and me and the pillow book, I don't think she's no blushing virgin.

But maybe that's just wishful thinking. Been so long since I been in rock-throwing range of a woman that the females of those back-assward centaurs are looking good.

The Torque boys swear by them.

Old wizard Bomanz ain't getting along with nobody. He's full up to his eyeballs with ideas about how this show ought to be run and there ain't nobody will listen to him but the talking buzzard. The buzzard's name is Virgil but the stones call him Sleazeball or Garbagemouth on account of the high intellectual content of most of his conversation.

Already I'm getting blasé about all those weird critters. They kind of rattled me at first, but we been here eight days now. If I ignore what they look like I knew stranger guys in the Guards.

What I can't figure is why we're sitting around. From what I hear there's only a few guys holed up in that monastery. With what we got we ought to be able to take the Limper even in top condition. But Darling is the high lord field marshal here. She says we wait.

She gets her orders from Old Father Tree. Must be he's happy so long as the Limper is buttoned up in a sack where he can't cause nobody no grief.

Raven said, "I misjudged her. She's not just sitting on her hands."

"Eh? What?" I wanted to go to sleep. So suddenly he wanted to talk.

"Darling isn't just sitting here. There's a dozen kinds of these Plain creatures so small you don't notice them or so much like something you're used to seeing you don't pay any attention. She's got those sneaking in and out of there all the time. She knows every breath they take. She's got somebody on every one of them all the time. The mantas and centaurs and rock dropping are all for show. If the order comes down, the real main attack will be carried out by the little creatures. They won't know what hit them in there. She's a genius. I'm proud of that girl."

When it came to sneaky petcy I figured she had some pretty good teachers, hunking around with the Black Company all them years. I told him, "Why don't you go tell her she's a genius, you're proud of her, you still love her, will she forgive you for being such a butt way back when? And let me get some sleep."

He didn't go see Darling. But he did get pissed at me and left me alone.

Not that that did much good for long.

What nobody knew but maybe Silent—since Darling can't hear and she can't lip-read the stones because they got no mouths—was that she already had the go-ahead from the boss tree. She was just waiting for the right hour to give the signal.

Naturally she timed it for when I just got sound asleep.

Things were quiet in the basement where the Limper was hiding out. There was one armed guard, one shaman overseeing, one monk keeping the clay moist, and two more making a leg for Toadkiller Dog.

The earth shook. A windwhale had hit the building with an extra big stone. Everybody moved to protect the claywork.

A dozen Plain creatures exploded out of cracks and shadows. Little missiles flew. Little blades flashed. The fastest creatures climbed all over the soldier and the shaman. They let the monks escape. Once the soldier and witch doctor went down the creatures began defacing the claywork.

It was the same elsewhere. None of the Limper's men survived.

That monster Toadkiller Dog came flying out of the monastery and landed smack in the middle of a gang centaurs. Blades flashed. Javelins flew. So did bodies. Then the monster broke loose.

Mantas swarmed overhead so thick they kept running into each other. The thunder of their lightnings made a drumroll.

The monster got to the barrier of talking menhirs and walking trees. He jumped over that, too. His fur smoldered and his flanks were pincushioned with darts. The walking trees tried to grab hold of him. His strength was too violent for them.

He kept right on coming, straight at us.

Menhirs popped into his way, stalling and tripping him. Mantas tried to cook him. Centaurs galloped with him, pelting him with javelins and dashing in to try to hamstring him. Me and Raven and the Torque boys all put three or four arrows apiece into him. He never seemed to notice. He just kept on coming, howling like all the wolves in the world at once.

"Go for its eyes!" Raven yelled. "Go for its eyes!"

Right, old buddy. Sharpshoot when I'm shaking so bad I figure if I live through this one I'm going to be cleaning the brown out of my drawers for a month.

The monster was only about forty feet away when Silent said hello by smacking it in the face with a bushel of snakes, snakes that hung on and tried to crawl into its ears and mouth and nostrils.

The snakes never slowed it down but they did take its mind off whatever it had planned for us. It just plowed through.

I went flying ass over appetite. As I sailed through the air I saw Darling step in, as cool as if she was in a kitchen slicing bread, and take a cut with a two-handed sword I wouldn't have figured a woman could lift. She was a little high. She hit ribs instead of opening the thing's belly.

I hit ground and spent the next couple minutes doing an astronomical survey of a couple hundred newly hatched constellations.

A savage rain shower soaked me and brought me out of it and to my feet, where I realized that I hadn't been rained on after all. A windwhale had passed over, dumping a little ballast to slow its fall as it came down after Toadkiller Dog.

The monster was still headed west. Right behind it was a shimmery something that looked like an elephant with a nest of tentacles for a head. Bomanz's contribution to the cause.

That was the last minute when anything made sense.

The talking stones went berserk, started popping all around. Walking trees jumped up and down. Centaurs ran in circles. Everything that could talk started yelling at everything else. The windwhales went to booming and started dropping like they meant to commit suicide by smashing into the ground. The scarred-up menhir was jabbering at Silent in a lingo I didn't get and Silent was practically doing a combination flamenco and sword dance trying to tell Darling what the rock was saying.

I stumbled over to Raven and said, "Old buddy, this looks like a good time to duck out of the party. Before the keepers come to drag them all back to the asylum."

He was watching Silent. He said, "Hush." And a minute later, "The tree god has called the whole thing off. Something's happened up north. He wants everybody to drop everything and head for home."

I looked around. Two windwhales were on the ground already. Critters were piling aboard. The only talking stone around anywhere was the one hanging out with Silent. "There goes our whaleback ride to catch your buddy Croaker."

XXXI

The young tree in the Barrowland had been in a coma since the fire, intelligence damped down while its hurts healed. But there came a day when externals finally registered. There was a bustle and fuss in the Barrowland such as had not been seen since the great battle that had taken place there.

Curious, and compelled by the mandate of his father, the tree dragged himself out of his fugue, though he was far from completely healed.

The Barrowland was crawling with soldiers of the shadowed western empire. He sensed the foci of power that had to be their commanders. They were going over every inch of the surrounding ground.

Why?

Then the memories came. Not in a flood, thankfully. In snippets and dribbles. In reasonable temporal order. The thing that came to dig, the horror it uncovered. The death that had come out of the forest and fallen upon the town. The fire . . . The fire . . . The fire . . .

The soldiers went rigid with fear and awe and fled in terror as the lightning crackled among the branches of the tree. Their captains came out and gaped at the fierce blue light washing the Barrowland.

The tree concentrated its entire intellect upon its immediate forebear and finally, after so many weeks, passed the news of its great failure.

XXXII

The twins Gossamer and Spidersilk strode toward the now quiet tree in lock step. Both wore black leather helmets that hid them completely. Their outfits were mirror images of one another, just as their bodies were. Though their powers were an order of magnitude less deadly and ferocious than those of any of the Ten Who Were Taken, they made the world think otherwise by aping the style and dress of their predecessors.

Thus they successfully donned the mantle of what it was their ambition to become. And if they survived long enough they might hone their wickedness till they were, indeed, indistinguishable from old terrors now mostly gone from the earth.

Thus doth evil breed.

The twins halted three yards from the tree, their fear carefully concealed from their soldiers. They stopped. They stared. They circled the tree, going opposite directions. When they met where they had started they knew.

Their black hearts were heavy with fear, but also entertained a spark of wicked hope.

They summoned their lieutenants. In half an hour the troops were headed for Oar.

The hell with the Limper. There was bigger game afoot.

XXXIII

It was late afternoon. Smeds looked up from his work on the wall. He grinned. Two more hours and his sentence to the labor battalion—three days for petty vandalism and malicious mischief—would end. And the damned spike would be tucked away safe in a place no one could find. Only he would know that it lay in a pocket in the mortar under a certain merlon stone twenty-seven east of the new east-side tower overlooking the North Gate.

Smeds was smugly proud of himself for having thought of such a nifty hiding place. Who would think of that? Nobody. And if by some remote chance somebody did, who would go tearing down the whole damned wall to find it? They would pay for the information.

He grinned again.

His imperial overseer scowled but did not crack his whip. That whip had taught Smeds quickly to keep up his share of the work even while he was daydreaming.

His grin died not because the overseer disapproved but because the cloud of dust to the north, that had been approaching for several hours, had come within a mile of the wall and had disgorged two hurried black riders. They had to be Gossamer and Spidersilk.

They knew about the spike.

Man, they had come back fast. He did not like what that implied.

At least maybe now Tully would get a convincing glimpse of what these people were really like when they had their gloves off.

Time came without a bite from the whip, despite his

having wandered off into reveries about a young woman he had met the day before he had let himself get caught painting an obscene slogan on a pre-imperial monument. It had cost him to get a professional letter writer to teach him to inscribe the slogan. He could not read or write his own name.

That girl was going to be waiting for him tonight, a scant fourteen years of ripening heat.

He came down out of the scaffolding thinking of a bath and fresh clothing and there was Old Man Fish waiting for him to get his release, a simple formality involving snipping a wire from around his neck. "What's up?" Smeds asked.

"I figured somebody ought to come make sure they let you go when they were supposed to. Tully couldn't be bothered. Timmy's still laid up."

Timmy had let the wizard take the hand the morning Smeds had started his sentence. "He all right? Did it work?"

"Looks like. No problem with that kind of pain. Let's go."

They walked a way, not talking much. Smeds looked around through narrowed eyes. They were tearing down three times as fast as they were rebuilding. There were clear areas that covered a dozen acres. The gray boys had been more evident since the bunch from the north had come in, but now they were everywhere. Platoons of the Nightstalkers moved around quickly and purposefully. Soldiers from other outfits seemed to be posted on every corner. Twice they were stopped and asked to state their names and business.

Unprecedented.

"What the hell is going on?" Smeds asked.

"I don't know. They were just getting started when I was coming to get you."

"Gossamer and Spidersilk got back from the Barrowland about two hours ago. I watched them from the wall. They were in a hell of a big hurry."

"Unh. So there it is." Fish glanced over, his bushy

white eyebrows two ragged caterpillars arching their backs. "Did you put it into the wall?"

Smeds did not answer.

"Good. I figured that's what it had to be. You couldn't have done better. And I just forgot I even thought you might have been up to something like that."

They walked along listening to the rumors running the streets. One refrain kept coming up. The imperials had sealed the city. Anybody who wanted could get in but they weren't going to let anyone out till they found someone or something they wanted bad. A house-to-house search had begun already and they were being as thorough as imperials always were.

"We got a problem," Smeds said.

"We have more than one."

"I told Tully till I was blue in the face."

"Maybe you should have said let's stay. Contrary as he's been, he might have decided he had to get out."

"I'll remember that. We got to have a sitdown, all four of us. We got to pound some facts into Tully's skull."

"Yes. Or just do what has to be done whether he likes it or not."

"Yeah."

They turned into the street that led past the Skull and Crossbones. The shadows made Smeds jumpy. He expected a Gossamer or Spidersilk to come bounding out of every one. He had forgotten his date entirely. "Nothing to do now but cover our asses and try to ride it out. They don't find anything they'll figure the spike went on down the road."

"Maybe."

"They have to loosen up sometime. You can't keep a city like Oar locked up very long."

"They don't find it easy, Smeds, they'll try looking hard. Maybe offer some rewards. Big ones, considering the trouble they're going to already."

"Yeah."

"I saw the doc Timmy visited. Remember? I'm pretty

sure he caught whatever Timmy had. He had that same look.''

Smeds stopped walking. "Shit."

"Yeah. And then there's the wizard that did his hand. Two arrows pointing straight at us and too late to dodge them by running away. We have some hard choices to make."

Smeds stood staring into the twilight indigo behind spires rising from the heart of the city. Here it was. What he had been afraid this would come to from the beginning, only it wouldn't be Fish and Timmy he'd have to stick a knife in. "I think I can do it if it has to be done. You?"

"Yes. If that's the decision."

"Let's go get a drink and look at the angles."

"You don't want to drink much. If that's the move we're going to make. That wizard will have to be done quick. He isn't stupid. It won't be long before he figures out that what the grays are looking for might be the same thing that burned Timmy's hand. And not much longer for him to realize he's the cutout between us and them. He won't be easy if he's looking for us to come."

"I'm still going to have to have one long one."

Into the Skull and Crossbones. It was the neighborhood social hour but there were tables available. The landlord did not have the sort of personality that brought in the free-spending hordes. To Smeds's relief his cousin was prominent among the missing.

Neither of them spoke till a pitcher had been delivered and Smeds had downed a long draft. He wiped his mouth on his sleeve. "Been thinking. The way I see it, we got a whatchamacallit, quorum, right here. You and me. Timmy can't do anything even if he wanted. And Tully would just argue and fuss and try to take over and make everybody do things his way. Then he'd screw it up and get us all killed."

"True."

"So what are we going to do?"

Old Man Fish smiled softly. "You telling me to decide?

You want me to tell you what to do? So that way it isn't your fault, you were just doing what you were told?''

Smeds hadn't thought of it that way consciously. But there was a truth there that startled him.

"That's all right," Fish said. "You just needed to have that up where you could look at it and see if you were trying to be a weasel. How do you feel about doing it?''

That was an easy one. "I don't want to. Those guys never done nothing but try to help us when we asked. But better their asses than mine. I ain't going to let them take me down because I know I'm going to feel bad about doing what, as far as I can see, is the only thing that'll keep the grays off.''

"So you just talked yourself into it.''

Smeds thought about that. His stomach knotted up. "I guess so.''

"That's one vote for action.''

"You go the other way, we have to get Timmy or Tully to kick in a tiebreaker." Some foolish part of him harkened to a hope that he would be voted down. Another part said it would be nice to be alive to have a guilty conscience.

"I'm with you." Fish managed a weak smile. "No tie. I don't like it either. But I don't see any other way out. You think of one, let me know. I'll be plenty happy to change my mind." Fish poured himself a beer.

Smeds's stomach just kept knotting and sinking.

XXXIV

Toadkiller Dog slipped into the monastery as silent as death. The windwhales were not yet below the horizon, scudding north, inexplicably abandoning their mission when it lacked only a touch of being complete. The monster was puzzled in the extreme but it did not allow that to paralyze him. He had enough distractions in the form of a thousand wounds and pains.

He slipped through the ruins and down into the subbasement, where he surprised a monk in the process of sabotaging the claywork. One snap of his jaws ended that, though it was probably too late to salvage anything.

He went over and stared at the head floating in the keg of oil. He was not a fast thinker, but steady, and he got where he wanted to go given time. The debate of the hour was whether or not there was any value in continuing an alliance with a thing so obviously mad and out of control.

The head stared back, awake and aware and completely helpless. The monster was not a subtle or reflective sort and so did not think it ironic that fate kept rendering helpless what was possibly the most powerful and most dangerous being in the world.

The head stared with great intensity, as though there was some critical message it *had* to get across. But what little unspoken communication had existed between them in the past no longer worked.

Toadkiller Dog whuffed, snapped the head up, and carried it out of the monastery. He concealed it in a place he thought would be safe, then limped away wearily.

It was start-over-from-scratch time and he had no idea,

really, where to find the kinds of recruits he would need to do the tasks he needed done. He knew only where not to look. They had left nothing but desolation behind them in the north.

He did not hurry. He did not feel pressed. He would live till he ran into something powerful enough to kill him.

He thought he had all the time in the world.

XXXV

There were lights in the wizard's place. "He live alone?" Fish asked.

"I don't know," Smeds said. The wizard seemed to be the wealthiest man in his neighborhood. He had real windows.

A shadow moved across a paper shade.

"Doesn't matter anyway. There's no guarantee he won't have friends in, or a client."

Smeds started. He had not thought about the chance of this becoming a massacre. He glanced up the street, the direction the patrol had gone. The gray boys were all over the place. This had to go down quick and quiet. "You able to do your part?"

"Yes. I'm working myself up the same way I did before we attacked at Charm. Big wizard, little wizard, the risks are pretty much the same."

"You were at Charm? I didn't know that."

"I was young and dumb. I don't kick it around. The grays are still fighting that one. They don't want to let anybody who went there die of old age."

"Patrol."

They faded into the shadows between two buildings, got down as low as they dared without sprawling in the garbage and dogshit. At the same moment light spilled from the wizard's doorway. A woman emerged. The clip-clop of the soldiers' boots picked up. They reached the woman as she reached the street.

"Evening, ma'am," one said. "You're out late. Consulting the wizard?"

There was not enough light to see it but Smeds knew she would be looking from one soldier to another, scared, trying to decide if she had good reason to be. She croaked, "Yes."

"May we have your name? We have to keep track of everyone who comes and goes."

"Why?"

"I don't know, ma'am. It's orders. It's the same all over town, wherever there's anybody in his line of business. Me and Luke being naturally lucky, we got this here clown on our beat that don't seem like he's going to get done all night."

"You can go loaf in a tavern or whatever it is you'd rather be doing. I was his last client tonight."

"Yes ma'am. Right after we get your name and how to find you if we need to talk to you again."

The woman sputtered but gave the soldiers what they demanded. The grays usually got what they wanted.

"Thank you, ma'am. We appreciate your cooperation. The streets being what they are at night, Luke will walk you over to make sure you get there safely."

Smeds grinned. That was one slick gray boy.

The silent partner set off with the woman. The other soldier resumed his patrol. Smeds rose. "We're lucky, he'll really stop off for a beer."

"To get any luckier than we've just been the bastard wizard would have to be in there dying of heart failure right now. You ready?"

"Yes."

"Let's get it over with. Quietly."

Smeds dashed across the street. Quietly. Fish was supposed to give him time to get around back. Then Fish, whom the wizard had not met, would knock on the front door. Smeds was supposed to get in—quietly—and come at the wizard from behind.

The tactic made no sense to Smeds but he was not the general here.

He stopped, astonished. A side window stood open to

let in the cool night air. He paused to catch his breath, then peeked.

The room was the one where the wizard had seen Timmy the first time they had come. The wizard was in there, puttering around, putting things away and mumbling to himself.

This was better than any back door.

Fish's knock, when it came, was so discreet Smeds almost missed it. The wizard cocked his head, looked like he was trying to make up his mind whether or not to answer. Finally, muttering, he left the room.

Smeds hoisted himself through the window, went after the man. He did not recall the floor being creaky. He hoped his memory was playing no tricks because he was taking no precautions against floor noise. He drew his knife as he moved.

The nerves went away. It seemed almost as though he was a bystander in his own mind. He noted that he was moving much more fluidly than was usual, ready for anything in the midst of any movement.

The wizard growled, "Keep your pants on," and started fumbling with the latch as Fish knocked for the third time.

Smeds peeked carefully.

The wizard was at the door, ten feet away, back to him, just opening up.

Fish asked, "Professor Dr. Damitz?"

"Yes. What can I do—"

And that was it.

Smeds saw the wizard rise onto his toes and start to raise his hands as he moved out to get the man from behind. Then Fish was pushing into the house, supporting the wizard, kicking the door shut behind him. He saw Smeds, was surprised. He started lowering the wizard to the floor. "How did you get in so fast?"

Smeds looked at the dead man. "Open side window. How come you did it that way?" The handle of a long knife stuck out under the wizard's chin. There was not much blood.

"Blade went straight into the brain. No chance for him to do any witch stuff while he was dying."

Smeds stared at the body. Now he understood the plan. Fish had sent him around back just to get him out of the way.

"You all right? How do you feel? A little shaky?"

"I'm all right. I don't feel much of anything at all."

"Did he keep written accounts or records? Something where he might have put down something about Timmy?"

"I don't know. I never saw him do it while we were here."

"We'd better look. You start . . . You feeling something now?"

"Just feeling sorry for that woman after they find him."

"Yeah. Be rough for her for a while. Look around. Try not to mess things up too much. And don't take too long. We got to get out of here." Fish went into the room where the wizard had done his interviews.

Smeds rejoined him five minutes later, carrying a large glass jar and a couple of books.

"What the hell is that?"

"Timmy's hand. I found it in a room in the back. All kinds of weird stuff back there."

"Shit. I'm glad we took time to look." He'd picked out a few books himself. "Let's get the hell out of here and get rid of this stuff. Out the window. We pull it shut, it'll latch itself behind us. I'll go first, see if it's clear."

Smeds's hands shook as he poured the first mug of beer. But it had not been as hairy as he had thought it would be. Still, there was some reaction. More than Old Man Fish was showing.

The hand and books had been cared for. The most dangerous strand had been clipped. Only one thing left to do.

Their benefactor the Nightstalker corporal came in with his beer bucket, beamed around, went for a refill.

"Shit!" Smeds said. "I clean forgot. I had a date tonight."

Fish gave him a few seconds of a commiserating look, then said, "Drink up. Catch a nap. We've got half the job still to do."

XXXVI

It seemed like I never saw Darling do much to deserve her White Rose reputation. Maybe that was because she was so unglamorous when you saw her, just a scruffy, tangle-haired blond broad in her twenties who would have fit right in with the gang back at the potato ranch. Except that she would have looked a lot more worn out now because she would have been dropping kids for ten years.

Besides her being deaf and dumb, which is always hard for the rest of us to keep separate from stupid, I think it's hard to take her serious because she does what she does so easily, so casually. Take that attack on the monastery. Slicker than greased owl shit. And no one would have gotten hurt at all if that monster Toadkiller Dog hadn't come plopping into the middle of those centaurs when he was making a run for it. And that was their damned fault. They got too eager. If they was hanging back like they was supposed to they would have had time to get out of the way.

She sure had the respect of the tree god and all the pull with him she wanted. I think he'd indulge her in anything.

She don't put on no airs, neither.

It was strange for a while. You had Darling in one spot with Silent always close, trying to stay between her and Bomanz and her and Raven at the same time, only Raven and the wizard would not get anywhere near each other because they did not trust each other any more than Silent trusted either of them.

It was all kind of amusing. Because when you are on the back of a monster a couple of miles up in the air, sharing that back with a couple hundred critters that would have you for breakfast if you don't behave, you sure as shit ain't going to get away with nothing, no matter what you'd like to try.

The Torque boys knew that. I knew it. Darling knew it. But those other three geniuses, Bomanz, Raven, and Silent, was so busy being important plugging up the knothole at the center of the universe that that never occurred to them.

The Torques were a little nervous about me, though. I used to be Guards and they was Black Company. They thought I might be lugging a grudge.

But I was saying the White Rose don't put on no airs. Not even being the White Rose. She don't like being called anything but Darling. She did not mind when I came around trying to talk to her. Only Raven and Silent minded. I told Raven to stuff it when he objected and I guess she gave Silent the same message. He didn't do nothing but stand around looking like he was making up his mind where to start carving when I talked to her.

Mind you, these were grown men. Plenty older than me.

It was Raven's fault I could talk to her at all. He had only himself to blame. It was him insisted I learn the sign language so we could communicate in situations where we couldn't talk out loud.

Not that we talked much at first, Darling and me. Just hi-how-you-doing stuff. I wasn't very good at it. She taught me more sign as we went along.

She didn't come right out and say it, but I got the feeling she was starved for somebody to talk to besides Silent. She couldn't say it with him hovering over her like he did all the time.

When I started out the only thing I was really wanting to find out was what she really thought about Raven. I wanted to keep him from making any more of a fool of himself than he already had. Maybe she figured that. She was sharp. She never gave me a chance to work it in.

So after a couple days we were talking about what it was like being country kids growing up with a war going on all around. It was easy to understand why she had gone the way she had. Everybody knew the story so she didn't need to explain.

I told her I joined up to get away from the farm, and from where I stood back then the Rebels didn't look no cleaner than the imperials. Maybe less, because she hadn't come along to start cleaning them up yet. And the imperials got paid. Good, and on time.

She did not seem offended, so I added my secret philosophy of life: any dork who became a soldier for an idea instead of the money deserved to die for his country. You're going to put it all on the table, six up with some other guy, it damned well better be for stakes you can carry away.

That did offend her. It got scorching for a few minutes, then sort of settled down to a sustained low heat, her trying to convince me that there were abstractions worth fighting and dying for and me clinging to my position that no matter how admirable the cause there was no point getting killed for it because even only twenty years down the road nobody was going to remember you or give a rat's ass if they did.

Two days went by that way. I got a feeling that if there hadn't been so much ego getting in the way Raven and Silent would have ganged up on me for hanging around with their girlfriend.

She was easy to talk to. I let out things I never said before because I thought they had no value, considering the source. Stuff about how people and the world worked, like that.

I never realized my outlook was so cynical till I tried to tie it up and put it across in that unsubtle way you have to use with sign.

I told her I could not believe in her movement because it did not promise anything for the future except freedom from the tyranny of the past. I told her that what little philosophy I'd detected driving the movement totally ignored human nature. That if the Rebels ever did manage to topple the empire, whatever replaced it would be worse.

That was the lesson of history. New regimes, to make sure they survived, were always nastier than the ones before them.

I kept after the theme of what did the Rebels offer in place of the empire? In my limited experience the people of the empire were more secure, prosperous, and industrious than they had been before its coming—except in areas where there was an active Rebel presence. I told her that for the great mass of people freedom was not an issue at all. That it was an alien concept, at least as her Rebels seemed to define it.

I told her that for a peasant—and peasants probably make up three-quarters of the population—freedom meant being able to provide for a family and market any surpluses.

When I left home the potato fields and all the rest of it were held communally. The work was long and hard and boring, but no one ever went hungry and even in the lean years there were surpluses enough to provide for a few little luxuries. In my grandfather's time, though, our fields had been just one more parcel among scores owned by one great landholder. The people who lived there were part of the furniture, like the trees and water and game, legally bound to the land. They had any number of obligations to the lord that had to be fulfilled before they could work the land. And of the product of the land they had to hand over fixed amounts to the landholder. First. If it was a bad year the lord could take everything.

But they had not had to walk in the Lady's dark shadow. So they must have been blissfully happy little farm animals.

I told her that the sons of the landholders were all backbones of the Rebel cause now, determined to liberate their enslaved homelands.

I told her I had no illusions about the Lady having any love or concern for the common people. She obliterated existing ruling classes simply to be rid of potential challenges to her own power. She had plenty of disgusting minions whose assigned domains were terrible places to be.

Finally, I argued that the empire was in no danger of

falling apart, despite the fact that she had disarmed the Lady during the showdown in the Barrowland. The Lady had been obsessed with expanding her borders and the reach of her power. She had created an efficient machine to handle the domestic work of the empire. That machine had not been broken.

We had been in the air four days. Evening was coming on and ahead brown gave way to the hazy blue of the Sea of Torments. We had come a long way in a short time. When I thought about all the shit me and Raven went through to get down there to that monastery, damn! This was the only way to travel.

I left off arguing with Darling. I felt a little guilty. As that day had gone on she had argued back less and less. I think I was throwing a lot of stuff at her that she probably hadn't ever thought about. On a smaller scale I've always known people for whom a goal was everything, who never thought nothing about the consequences of the goal achieved.

Of course, I did what everybody else does. I underestimated the hell out of her.

Next day I didn't run into her till around noon. I guess I was avoiding her. But when I did see her she had bounced back.

About the same time I noticed the dark loom of land on the northern horizon and right afterward realized we were losing altitude. The windwhales were sliding into some kind of formation, a triangle above with us below. Mantas were taking to the air, gliding toward the coast.

I asked her, in sign, "Where are we? What is happening?"

She replied, also in sign, "We are approaching Opal. We are going to find Raven's children. We are going to compel him to confront his past."

That was a measure of how much the tree god valued and respected her. Though he had yanked his minions away from that monastery and had ordered them to scurry north because there was no time to lose, he would let

her interrupt the journey for this because it was important
to her.

I figured Raven didn't know what was coming. He'd
probably need a lot of support when it hit him in. I went
looking for him.

XXXVII

There was nothing out at the fourth hour, Smeds reflected. The soldiers were all off somewhere loafing because the bad boys all had sense enough to be home in bed. The bakers had not yet stumbled out to their doughs and ovens. The only sound in the street was that of the drizzle falling, of the water dripping from the roofs. He and Fish made no noise. Fish seemed not to be breathing.

There would be one problem with this one they had not faced with the other. He had seen them both before. On the other hand, they were making their move at this ungodly hour, reasonably expecting to catch him in his bed.

Breaking in should be easy, from what they recalled of the physician's place. The deed itself would have to be done quietly. There was, they suspected, a live-in house-keeper. They did not want to add her to their weight of conscience.

"There it is," Smeds said.

Like the wizard, the physician was prosperous enough to occupy his own freestanding combination home and place of business. The structure was barely a decade old. A few years before it had been built, that part of town had burned during an outbreak of violence between Rebel sympathizers and mercenaries in the imperial service. The middle class had come in to build homes upon the graves of tenements.

"Front door to the house and door to the office," Fish murmured. "Assume a back door. These places all have a little fenced-in garden behind them. Three windows we can see. I'm surprised vandals haven't destroyed that leaded-glass monstrosity.''

The physician's office was scabbed onto the side of his home, set a little back. It had its own little porch and door, and beside the door a marvelously dramatic floor-to-ceiling leaded-glass window six feet wide.

''Go,'' Fish said.

Smeds dashed across and crouched in the slightly deeper shadow beneath the window on the building's right front. His thoughts about the weather were not polite. He was miserable enough without a soaking drizzle added on for frosting.

Fish came across as Smeds rose to test the window. He was not surprised to find it tightly secured. Fish went to the house door, achieved no better result. Smeds crossed behind him and checked the second front window. Solid. He slid around the corner of the house.

Fish was crouched in front of the office door, which he had pushed open about three inches. Smeds joined him, his knife sliding into his hand. ''It was unlocked?''

''Yes. I don't like it.''

''Maybe it's so clients can get in anytime.''

Fish ran his hand up the inside of the door. ''Maybe, but there's a heavy latch catch. Let's be careful.''

''Careful is my middle name.''

Fish pushed the door open, looked inside. ''Clear.'' He slipped in.

Smeds followed, headed for the door connecting with the house. It was unlocked, too. It opened toward him. He pulled. It swung smoothly, soundlessly. He heard a faint *snick* behind him as Fish closed the latch. He saw nothing suspicious in the room before him. He stepped inside.

Maybe it was a whisper of cloth in motion. Maybe it was a little intake of breath. Maybe it was both. Whatever, Smeds spun down and away.

A line of fire sliced across his shoulder blade.

He landed on his knees facing the office, watching a shape collide with Fish. Fish said, ''Shit!'' At the same moment the shape squealed. Then it threw itself sideways and floundered through the leaded-glass window a step ahead of Smeds.

Fish came to the window. "That was him."

"He was expecting us."

"Too damned smart. Figured too much out. Can't let him get away." Fish jumped through the window.

The physician was going for all he was worth, legs and arms flailing. That fat little hedgehog was no sprinter.

Smeds followed Fish. He passed the older man moments later, and gained steadily on his prey, who had gotten a sixty-yard head start. The physician glanced back once, stumbled. Smeds gained ten yards while he was getting his balance. Fear lent him renewed stamina and speed. He stayed the same distance ahead for half a minute.

The physician knew he was not going to outrun anyone. Smeds knew he knew that. Unless he was running in a blind panic he had developed a strategy, had chosen an ultimate destination. . . .

The physician zigged right, into a narrow alleyway.

Smeds slowed, approached cautiously.

Footfalls pounded away in the darkness.

He went after them. He was just as careful rounding another corner, again without need. Gods, it was dark in there! Third corner.

He stopped dead. There were no sounds of flight. He tried listening for heavy breathing but could not be sure he heard anything because his own intruded too much.

What now?

Nothing to do but go forward.

He dropped down and advanced in a careful duck walk. His muscles protested. He was grateful for the toughening they had gotten in the Great Forest.

There! Was that breathing?

Couldn't tell for sure. The echoes of Fish's approach overrode it.

Scrape! Swish!

What must have been a foot missed his face by a fraction of an inch. He flung himself forward but the physician was already moving again. Smeds's knife ripped along his hip.

Smeds went down hard but caught hold of a heel and managed to hang on. He snaked forward, stabbing at the man's calf, his target invisible in the darkness. The man squealed like an injured rabbit.

Smeds was so startled he let go. Then he realized he was letting his man get away. He got up and charged ahead, smashed into the man.

"Please! I won't tell anyone! I swear!"

Pain slashed along Smeds's ribs on this left side.

He flailed away with his knife, hitting anything he could. The physician tried to scream and fight back and run away all at the same time. Smeds held on with one hand, kept hacking with the other. The physician pulled him out into a street.

Smeds kept hacking.

The physician collapsed.

Fish arrived. "Shit, Smeds. Shit."

"Got him."

"You sure he didn't get you, too?"

Smeds looked at himself. He was covered with blood. Some of it was his own.

Somebody yelled up the street. People had begun coming to stoops and windows.

Fish bent, slashed the physician's throat, said, "We've got to get out of here. There'll be soldiers here in a minute." He looked at the dead man's hand. "Unh. A mess. He touched you with that?"

"I don't think so."

"Come on." Fish offered him a hand. "You make it?"

"I'm all right for now."

Fish headed back into the alley.

Smeds began feeling it as soon as the excitement began to go out of him. He knew he would not be able to get away if a chase developed.

Instead of making for the Skull and Crossbones Fish headed into the West End.

"Where we going?" Smeds asked.

"Reservoir. Get you cleaned up. We take you home looking like that the gray boys are going to be around to ask what happened before you can get your boots off."

XXXVIII

I don't know what I expected to see when we got to Opal. Maybe nothing changed from my last time there. I sure wasn't ready for the mess we found. I gaped incredulously as we glided over the ruins, where a few survivors scurried around like frightened mice. I went and told Darling, "Don't look to me like there's much chance we'll find the people you want."

Odds never bothered Darling.

Raven and Silent now had especially black feelings for me. I'd had the gall to tell Darling who she had to find if she wanted to force Raven to face his past. Neither of them wanted that to happen.

Both of them was so busy thinking about themselves they didn't have time to wonder what Darling really thought or felt about anything.

We crossed most of the city. Up north we spied several large, neatly arranged camps. The tents were too numerous to be all army, but they showed us that the imperials were there, responding to the destruction of the city in a quick, orderly fashion. Below, soldiers and civilians were at work leveling way for the new. Though they stopped to gawk, these people did not run away.

Darling ordered us to watch for the standard of the military commander. She figured that was the place to start since the city was obviously under martial law. I couldn't figure why she thought she'd get any cooperation, though.

I asked, "What do you feel about old Raven these days?" I was real careful to keep my hands hid from him and Silent both.

I figured she wouldn't understand what I meant. I was wrong. She signed, "Once I had a child's love for a man who saved me and nurtured me and risked everything to protect me when, long before I could believe it myself, he recognized the role I would play in the struggle with the darkness. That child was like a very little girl in some ways. She was going to marry Daddy when she grew up, and it never occurred to her that things might not turn out that way till she tried to pursue it, and to press it.

"I was never really a girl, or a woman, or a human being to Raven, Case. Even though he did awful things for me. I was a symbol, an expiation, and when I insisted on becoming a person he did the only thing he could do to keep on serving the symbol and not have to deal with a flesh-and-blood woman."

"That is kind of how I always though it was," I signed.

"Many men admire Raven. He fears nothing concrete. He takes no crap from anyone. People who mess with him get hurt, and the hell with the consequences. But those are the only dimensions he has. They are the only dimensions he permits himself. How can I remain emotionally entangled with a man who will not allow himself emotions, however much he did for me in other ways? I appreciate him, I honor him, I may even revere him. But that is all anymore. He cannot change that with some demonstration, like a boy hanging by his knees from a branch to impress a girl."

I grinned because I had a gut feeling that's exactly what Raven had in mind.

Poor sucker. There just wasn't nothing left for him to win. But he wasn't the kind to accept that even if she told him to his face, point-blank.

I wanted to sneak in one or two about Silent, too, but I didn't get a chance. The military headquarters got spotted and the windwhale dropped down and moved up to it, anchored itself in place by dropping tentacles to grab rocks and trees. Its presence overhead was disconcerting to those in the camp.

I like that word, disconcerting. I got it from Bomanz.

Such a sly way to say they were having shit hemorrhages down there.

There was a big hoorah, all kinds of whoop and holler and carrying on, when a bunch of Plain critters ganged up on the scar-faced stone and threw it over the side, almost into the lap of the command staff down there.

Them old boys were pretty shook. I wondered how much more excited they would get if they knew the White Rose her own self was right over their heads. But they wasn't going to try nothing, no matter what they knew. Who'd want to duke it out with four pissed-off windwhales, which is what they would get if they wasn't polite.

Scarstone popped back up. He talked. Silent translated for Darling. I didn't hear anything. The Torque boys had let me know I was supposed to stay back, so I stayed back. Darling made a bunch of signs that I guess the stone could see somehow. It went away. After a while it came back.

After four rounds of that it didn't go away anymore. But the windwhale stayed where it was, so I guessed a deal had been struck.

I went to try to talk it over with Raven. But he was in about as foul as mood as I ever saw, and anyway he had pegged me for some kind of traitor, so I gave it up and went off to shoot the shit with the Torques and the talking buzzard and a couple other Plain creatures that wasn't too shy.

Darling goes after something she usually gets what she wants. This time she got it just before noon next day.

A hoorah broke out downstairs. Darling sent Scarface to check it out. It came back and reported. She got up and walked over to Raven, who watched her like she was the hangman coming. She signed at him. He got up and followed her, again with the eagerness of a man headed for the gallows.

I knew him well enough to see the signs. He was putting himself into a role. I tagged along wondering what it would be. Most everybody else moved closer, too.

Two young people around twenty came puffing up over the side of the windwhale.

So the impossible was possible, the improbable a sure thing. Unless the army down there figured they could placate Darling with a couple of ringers.

The boy looked like Raven twenty years younger. Same dark hair and coloration, same determined face not yet hardened into grimness.

I was only a step behind when Raven got his first look at them. He cursed softly, muttered, "She looks like her mother."

It was plain they had not been told they were here for a family reunion. They were just puzzled and scared. Mostly scared. And more so as the mob closed in around them. They did not recognize Raven.

They did recognize Darling. And that scared them even more.

Everybody waited for somebody else to say something.

Raven whispered, "Do something, Case." Desperately. "I'm lost."

"Me? Hell, I don't even speak the lingo that good."

"Case, help me out. Try to get this moving. I don't know what to do."

All right. I thought of a couple of suggestions for him, but I was never a guy who kicked crippled dogs. I went to work in my feeble Jewel Cities dialect. "You have no idea why you were brought here, do you?"

They shook their heads.

"Relax. You ain't in no danger. We just want to ask about your ancestors. Especially your parents."

The boy rattled something.

"You'll have to talk slower, please."

The girl said, "He said out parents are dead. We've been on our own since we were children."

Raven winced. I figured the voice must be like that of his wife, too.

Silent translated for Darling, who really gave them the eye. Seeing they was Raven's kids, I didn't figure it was so amazing they pulled through.

"What do you know about your parents?"

The girl took on the answering chores. Maybe she thought her brother was too excitable. "Very little." She told me pretty much what I had been able to find out for myself when we were headed south. She did know that her mother had not been a nice person. "We've managed to live her down. Last year we won a judgment that took some of our father's properties from her family and returned them to us. We expect to win more such judgments."

That was something, anyway. The girl had conjured up no special regard for the woman who had brought her into the world.

The boy said, "I don't remember my mother at all. After our births I think she had as little to do with us as she could. I remember nurses. She probably got what she deserved."

"And your father?"

"I have vague memories of a very distant man who wasn't home much but who did visit when he was. Probably out of obligation and for appearance' sake."

"Do you have any special feeling about him now?"

"Why should we?" the girl asked. "We never really knew him, and he's been dead for fifteen years."

I faced Darling, signed, "Is there any point going on?"

She signed, "Yes. Not for their sake. For his."

I asked Raven, "You got anything to put in?"

No. He didn't. I could see him thinking maybe he was going to slide out of this after all.

It wasn't going to be that easy. Darling had me tell them that their father had not died, that he had been harried into exile by their mother's confederates. She had me hit the high spots of their years together.

They had had time to get over being scared. Now they were getting suspicious. The boy demanded, "What the hell is going on? How come these questions about our old man? He's history. We don't care. If he was to walk up right now and introduce himself I'd say so what. He'd be just another guy."

I signed to Darling, "You going to keep pushing it?" and asked Raven, in Forsberger, "You want to call his bluff?"

Negatives all around. Bunch of wimps. So Raven *was*

going to slide out. I told his kids, "Your father was very important in the life of the White Rose. He was a stand-in parent to her for years and she knew how it pained him to be in exile. She stopped here because she wanted to try to give back something of what she'd had and you couldn't."

Neither Raven nor Darling liked me saying that.

I think the girl figured it out about then. She got real carefully interested in Raven. But she didn't say anything to her brother.

I got Darling to agree this was enough and our guests ought to be turned loose. She wasn't satisfied with the way things turned out. What the hell can you do with women? You can give them exactly what they ask for and they'll cuss you because that ain't what they *really* want.

Just before the girl went over the side she turned and told me, "If my father was alive today he wouldn't have to fear that he would be unwelcome in his daughter's house." Then she went.

All right. There was an open door if ever I seen one.

We took off the second the girl hit ground. Darling wanted to get far away before word she was there got to somebody who could do something about it. We lit out northeast, like we was headed for the Plain of Fear.

XXXIX

Every day more people came into Oar, and nobody left. A pigeon could not get out. Several had died trying.

Some elements of the population were growing restless. There were more fights than usual. More people ended up on the labor gangs. The searches went on and on and on. There was not a building in Oar that had not been tossed at least twice, not a citizen who had not been rousted. There were rumors of big tension in high places. Brigadier Wildbrand did not think she owed Gossamer and Spidersilk anything and resented having her Nightstalkers used as bullies for their personal benefit. They were elite troops, not political gangsters.

The nature of the people entering the city changed with time. Fewer were farmers or traders. More and more were dire characters with no obvious trade.

The news about the silver spike was spreading.

Smeds did not like it. It meant big trouble. How did Gossamer and Spidersilk expect to control all those witches and wizards, some of whom might be much more potent than they suspected? And the bullies they brought with them?

Chaos threatened.

Smeds understood the strategy. The twins meant to up the heat and pressure till the spike popped to the surface. If it came up in hands other than their own they were confident they could take it away.

Could they?

Every witch and wizard in town knew that, too. But they had come hunting anyway.

Only Tully was pleased. He thought the situation perfect for the auction he wanted to run. "We got to get the word out," he told the others, over supper.

"Keep your voice down," Fish said. "Anybody in here could be a spy. And we don't get any word out. You heard of anybody offering to buy anything?"

"No," Tully admitted. "But that's because—"

"Because most of them know they can be outbid. You notice the twins aren't offering anything. They figure they can get what they want by divine right, or something."

"Yeah, but—"

"You have no grasp of the situation, Tully. Let me offer you a challenge. . . ."

"I'm fed up with your shit, Fish."

"Indulge me in an experiment. If I'm wrong I'll shout it from the rooftops. If I'm right, you win anyway."

"Yeah? Let's hear it."

Sucked him up again, Smeds thought. His opinion of his cousin declined by the hour.

"Here's two coppers. Go find a kid somewhere away from here. One who don't know you. Pay him to go to the Toad and Rose and tell the bullies there that the wizard Nathan is looking to hire a couple men to help him sneak out of the city tomorrow morning."

"I don't get it."

Smeds said, "Gods, Tully, couldn't you just *once* do something without arguing about it first?"

Fish said, "The experiment will be more instructive if it simply unfolds, explaining itself as it goes."

"Why should I do that asshole Nathan any favors?"

Smeds stood up. "I'll do it. Otherwise we'll be here till the middle of next week."

"I want Tully to do it. I want him to see that there can be a direct connection between his saying something and what happens in the real world."

"You're putting me down again, ain'tcha?"

"Tully," Smeds said, "shut the fuck up or I'm going to brain you. Pick up the goddamned money, hit the goddamned street, find a kid, and pay him to deliver the goddamned message. Now.''

Tully went. Smeds had gotten pretty intense.

"He's going to get us all killed," Timmy said as soon as he was gone.

"How's your hand coming?" Smeds asked.

"Real good. Don't try to distract me, Smeds."

"Easy, Timmy," Fish said. "I think there's a chance this trick will get through to him."

"Want to bet?"

"No."

Smeds would not have taken the bet either.

The wizard Nathan and his four men had rented rooms just up the street from the Skull and Crossbones. The grays came there shortly before dawn. They found five dead men and two rooms torn to shreds. They sealed the area, searched it again, asked a lot of questions. Fish made sure they all got a good look at the mess. He asked Tully, "You starting to catch on?"

"Who would do something like that, man? Why?"

"Nathan was a wizard. If he was going to sneak, that meant he'd found the spike and wanted to make a run for it."

"But he wasn't going to leave town."

"No. He wasn't, Tully. But you said he was."

Tully started to be Tully and argue, but he bit down on it and through for a moment before he said, "Oh."

"Next time you say something without thinking first or checking to see who's listening, that could be us all carved up."

Smeds said, "You maybe went too far to make your point, Fish."

"Why?"

"This ain't over yet. Those soldiers didn't find anything but a mess. They're going to figure whoever made the mess got the spike."

"Yeah. And maybe everybody else will think so, too. Maybe even the guys who actually did it. The next few days ought to be interesting. And part of the ongoing lesson.''

"What're you blathering now?" Tully demanded.

"That was a big gang in that place, eh? Five pro thugs and a sorcerer. Nobody would try to take them alone. I figure there was at least three guys did it. Probably more. Unless they're a bunch that really trust each other they're going to have trouble. Every one of them is going to know *he* didn't get the spike, but he isn't going to be sure about the others.''

Tully said, "Oh," again, and after a while, "This shit is getting scary. I never thought it would get this hairy.''

"Your problem is you never thought," Timmy muttered, but Tully did not hear him.

Fish said, "It's just starting, Tully. It's going to get hairier. And if we want to come out of it with our skins on we're going to have to be very damned careful. These aren't nice or reasonable people. They aren't going to be interested in dealing till they got no other choice.''

It got hairier fast, as more, and more powerful, thaumaturgic treasure hunters poured into the city. Old feuds having nothing to do with the spike flared. The citizenry, pressed from all sides, responded by rioting on a small scale. The twins presided smugly, doing nothing to retard the escalating violence.

Smeds spent a lot of time being sorry he had let Tully get him into this in the first place. Because of the other treasure they had brought home, the living was good, but not good enough, given that he had to watch his every word every minute and spent half his time looking over his shoulder to make sure disaster was not gaining on him.

XL

We were over the Forest of Cloud, south of Oar, east of Roses, west of Lords, hiding out from imperial eyes, too many of which had seen the windwhales cruising far from their proper range over the Plain of Fear. Darling wanted to let a little of the excitement die down before she moved on.

She would not let the tree god hurry her, though he was in a minor frenzy. I did not understand exactly what was up yet, but neither did some of the others, so we were getting an education from old Bomanz, who was suddenly Darling's number-one boy.

"Since you were all there you'll recall that in the course of the battle in the Barrowland the soul or essence, of the Dominator—the most evil being ever to walk this earth—was imprisoned in a silver spike, which was then driven into the trunk of a sapling sired by the tree god of the Plain of Fear." He really did talk that way when he had an audience.

"At the time it was believed that would effectively contain and constrain the residual evil of the man forever. The sapling was the scion of a god, invulnerable, unapproachable, and so long-lived as to be, in practical terms, immortal. As the sapling grew, its trunk would engulf the spike. In time the old evil would not persist in so much as memory.

"However. We thought wrong.

"A band of adventurers succeeded in stunning the sapling long enough to get in and prize the spike out. If we are to credit the sapling's own testimony—and we must,

169

for the nonce, because it is the only testimony we have—none of those men had the least familiarity with the art, and were remarkable only because they came up with an idea that, logically, should have originated with someone devoted to the occult.''

Damn him, he did talk like that when he had an audience. And he wouldn't stop.

"Gentlemen, the silver spike is loose in the world. It's not the Dominator. He's dead. But the undying black essence that drove him remains. And that could be used by an adept to summon, coerce, and shape powers even I cannot begin to imagine or fathom. That spike could become a conduit to the very heart of darkness, an opener of the way that would confer upon its possessor powers perhaps exceeding even those the Dominator possessed.

"Our mission, our *holy* mission, given the White Rose by Old Father Tree himself, is to recover the silver spike and deliver it for safekeeping, at whatever cost to ourselves, before someone of power seizes upon it and shapes it to his own dark purpose and is, in this turn, shaped—perhaps into a shadow so deep there would be no chance ever for the world to win free.''

That bit about "at whatever cost to ourselves" got a big hand. The talking buzzard pulled his head out from under his wing, cracked an eye, went to town heckling the old wizard. That finally distracted him from his windier fancies.

"Buzzard, if you were fit to eat I'd be picking up kindling right now!" he shouted. Then he got back to business. "The tree god has reason to suspect that the spike is now in Oar. The White Rose, Silent, the Torques, and some of our smaller companions will drop into the city. With the help of the underground they will establish a secure base, then will take up the hunt. Raven, Case, and I, because of our considerable familiarity with the site, will go on to the Barrowland to see what can be learned there.''

That started a bunch of bitching. Raven didn't like being sent off someplace where Darling wasn't. I didn't think these guys had the right to draft me into their adventure. I got pretty hot.

Darling took me aside and calmed me down, then convinced me that even if I remained committed to the empire in my heart, helping her in this would not harm me. Maybe she was right when she said the evil she wanted to abort wouldn't respect allegiances or philosophies. That it would divide the world into two kinds of people, its enemies and its slaves.

That was a little heavy to get down in one or two bites but I said all right, I'm just following Raven around anyway. Might as well keep on keeping on.

So that was that. I gave in. I also started giving some thought to going back to herding potatoes as a career. No potato never talked anybody into making a fool of himself.

XLI

Smeds came out onto the porch of the Skull and Crossbones figuring to shoot the shit with Fish, but found the
only empty chair stood between Fish and the Nightcrawler
corporal. He wanted to turn around but felt like he was
committed.

He plopped down. "Hey, Corp. Don't you never do
nothing but sit here and drink beer?"

"Not if I can help it."

"That's the life. I oughta go sign up."

"Yeah? You wouldn't like it. Where was you at three in
the morning?"

"In bed sleeping one off."

"Lucky you. Ask me where I was at three in the
morning."

"Where were you at three in the morning?"

"With about two hundred others guys out Shant, where
they got all those buildings tore down and nothing new put
up yet. Looking for a monster. Some guy reported there
was a monster out there bigger than the Civil Palace."

"Was there?"

"Not even a little one."

"Was the guy drunk?"

"Would a sober man be out there at that time of night?"

"Got something interesting coming here," Fish interjected,
jutting his chin up the street.

Smeds saw three men and a woman. She was not much
to look at and too old to be interesting anyway. But she
looked tough. She carried weapons like a man.

As a bunch they looked as hard and tough as any Smeds

had seen. But what made them stand out was the zoo they carried with them.

The woman had a live ferret draped around her neck and chipmunks peeking out of her pockets. The tall, dark, and darkly clad man who walked to her right carried an unhooded falcon on his left shoulder. The three men behind them—Smeds thought they might be brothers—carried a bunch of monkeys and one big snake.

Smeds asked, "You going to arrest them? They're lugging enough illegal hardware to start their own war."

"And give you boys a show? Eh? My mama's stupid babies never lived to make corporal." Even so, he stuck his fingers in this mouth and whistled. When those people looked he beckoned.

The tall man looked over with tight eyes for a moment, made a slight gesture at the man with the snake. That one came over. The snake looked them over like it was sizing them up for dinner. It gave Smeds the creeps.

The corporal said, "Just a friendly word of advice, pal. The city is under martial law. Ain't nobody supposed to tote a blade over eight inches long. 'Less he's wearing gray."

The snake man went back and told the tall man, who looked at the corporal hard for a moment, then nodded.

"You see that?" Smeds said. "That goddamned monkey gave us the finger."

The corporal said, "I seen that tall guy somewhere before. Down the length of a sword. Hunh! Well. Bucket's empty. Save my chair while I walk my lizard and get me a refill." He went inside.

"What you think of that bunch?" Smeds asked Fish.

"I've seen the tall one before, too. In the same circumstances as the corporal. A long time ago. No problem remembering where or when, either, since I was only ever in one battle."

That just puzzled Smeds. He asked, "You figure they're here after the dingus, too?" He could ask because by now everyone in town had a good idea what was going on.

"They're here for it, yes. They'll help make the game interesting."

"What're you yapping about, Fish?"

"Don't mind me, boy. Just an old man maundering. Ha! I thought so. Isn't there anymore, is it?"

Down the street the animals people had stopped in front of a place Timmy said used to be a butcher shop but these days was just another dump filled up with squatters. The tall man glanced back as though he had heard Fish. Then the whole bunch moved on, indifferent to stares.

The corporal came back out with his full pail and bladder empty. "I ought to give this shit up. Bothers my stomach." He took a drink. "Where were we?"

Fish said, "I was just going to ask you when they're going to unbutton the gates. Going to start getting hungry in here now the farmers won't bring anything in."

"They don't consult me on policy, Pop. But I'll tell you something. I don't think those two bitches give a rat's ass if everybody in Oar starves. They ain't going to go hungry."

Smeds was tired of listening to the corporal. "Going to get me something to drink." He went inside and had a beer drawn, wondered how long the supply would last. And how much more patience the people of Oar had. A while, for sure. Not that many were hurting yet. But if circumstances did not change a big blowup was inevitable.

Timmy Locan came in, got him a beer, stood beside Smeds awhile without saying anything, then suggested, "Let's go for a walk when we finish these."

"All right. I need the exercise."

When they were well away from the Skull and Crossbones, passing through a construction area where they were unlikely to be overheard, Smeds asked, "Well? What's up?"

"You remember that doc that looked at my hand when we first came back?"

"Yeah." More than a twinge of guilt. He and Fish had not told the others what they had done. Tully was so indifferent he had not noticed that the physician and wizard were no longer among the living. Timmy had noticed, though, and Smeds supposed he had some definite suspicions about two such coincidental and convenient murders. "What about him?"

"It looks like he got whatever it was that I had and passed it around to everybody who came to see him. And they passed it on, too. Not like the plague or probably everybody would have it by now. But there's a couple hundred people got it already. The ones that have had it the longest . . . Well, they're worse off than I was. Yesterday a woman who had it killed herself. This morning a guy whose whole arm had gone black killed four of his kids who had it before he killed himself."

"That's awful. That's really gruesome. But it isn't anything we can do anything about."

"I know that. But the thing is, see, the grays have gotten interested. They're grilling everybody with the black stuff. From the questions they're asking you can tell they think there's a connection with the spike. They're trying real hard to find out about everybody who's had it and done something about it, like me."

"I don't think you need to worry, Timmy. They can't trace it back to you."

"Yeah? Those bitches are *serious,* Smeds. What happens after they find out all the trails lead back to that doc, who turned up among the dead right after the stuff started spreading? They're going to figure he had a fatal accident on account of somebody he treated didn't want to be remembered. And they already know the only way to treat the stuff is to cut off whatever it's eating on. So pretty soon the word goes out to the grays to grab amputees. Especially guys with missing hands."

"Maybe you got a point. Maybe we better see what Fish thinks."

Fish agreed with Timmy. There was no reason to think Gossamer and Spidersilk would not go so far are to order the arrest of all amputees. They were determined.

Fish did some heavy thinking. "I reckon it's time to blow some smoke."

"What do you mean?" Smeds asked.

"This situation—the whole city sealed up like a bottle—can't go on forever. There'll be a blowup. When that comes we break loose with everybody else. Till then we buy time by getting them off on a wild-goose chase, or by taking advantage of the potential for chaos they've created."

Smeds was bewildered. He grew more so when Fish said, "Get rid of whatever you've got that's silver. Get gold or copper or jewels or whatever, but get rid of your silver. Smeds, you pass the word to Tully and don't let him give you any shit."

"What's going on?"

"Just do it."

So they did. Even Tully, who had become reasonably serious and responsive since Fish's demonstration of the deadly power of the loose word.

XLII

We arrived in the Barrowland by sliding down ropes with our possessions strapped on our backs. A few Plain creatures joined us. More would after we set up a safe camp. The boss menhir wanted a couple of his flint-hearted buddies there to keep an ear on us. The better to maintain quick communication, he said. Right.

The better to make sure things got done the tree god's way.

"Back where we got started," Raven said as soon as we had our feet on the ground. He'd been getting more fit to live with since Opal. He was almost back to being the old boy I'd known when I first met him.

"Back in the cold and wet," I grumped. It had been the tag end of winter when we'd left. It was sneaking up on winter again now. The leaves had fallen. We could get snow anytime. "Let's don't fool around, eh? Let's do what we got to and get out."

Raven chuckled. "How you going to keep them on the farm after they've seen the big city?"

"A little less ruckus, please," Bomanz said. "We don't yet know there aren't any imperials around."

He was halfway right. We hadn't yet seen that with our own eyes, but the Plain creatures had scouted and reported nothing bigger than a rabbit within five miles. I could trust them on that.

Bomanz had to do some wizard stuff before he was satisfied. Then he let us set up housekeeping and start a fire.

We dragged out with morning twilight and ate some god-awful cold yuck. Then we split up.

I got the town and military compound because I knew them best. Raven took the woods. Bomanz got the Barrowland itself. Near as I could tell he wasn't going to do anything but stand in the middle and take a nap.

The Plain creatures were supposed to do anything they wanted and clue us if they found anything.

I needed to do only a rough once-over to see what had happened in town. There wasn't nothing but bones left. Poking around wasn't as bad as it could have been. I did everything I could think of to find out something useful, then I went back to camp. Bomanz was just about where I'd left him, eyes still closed, but taking little tippy-toe baby steps.

At least he was moving.

Raven came back. "You done already?"

"Yep."

"Find anything?"

"A whole lot of bones. Enough to build an army of skeletons."

"Got you down, eh?"

"I knew all them guys."

"Yeah." He didn't say anything else, just waited. He can be an all-right guy when he isn't busy feeling sorry for himself.

"I figure the Limper and Toadkiller Dog did the killing. But there was somebody else there after them. Somebody went through like a mother picking a baby's nits. There ain't nothing left there that's even remotely valuable."

Raven though about that. "Nothing at all?"

"Picked as clean as the bones."

"That might be an angle to follow up in Oar. Though they would have taken only what they could carry, and that would be the kind of thing that isn't going to make a splash. Unless they did something gaudy. Which if they had they would be in the hands of the imperials already."

Bomanz joined us. He puttered around making tea while Raven told us he'd found two campsites probably used by the guys we were after, but nothing that would help us.

"If there ever was anything here the imperials got to it first."

"And if they had," Bomanz said, "they would have the spike by now."

We'd gotten reports from Oar through the stones. The news was not encouraging. It looked like a couple of imperial bigwigs were out to grab the spike and go into the empire business for themselves.

"You learn anything?" Raven asked.

Bomanz said, "Not much. There were four of them. Probably. They got away with what they did because most of the time the sapling was preoccupied with Toadkiller Dog and did not perceive them as a threat. It thought they were throwing sticks at it as a gesture of defiance."

"Sticks?" I asked.

"They threw sticks at the tree until it was almost buried. Then they set the pile on fire."

Raven muttered, "You don't have to be brilliant to be a god."

I said, "We got them now."

"What?" That Bomanz never did figure out you could be joking.

"All we got to do is look for four guys with splinters in their fingers."

Bomanz scowled. Raven chuckled. He asked, "Do we know anything about these men at all?"

Bomanz grumbled, "We don't even know they were men."

"Great."

Raven said, "Since we can't get anywhere with who, why not work on when? Can we pin down any dates? Even approximately? Then work back from them to whose movements fit?"

That sounded pretty feeble to me and I said so. "Even if Oar hadn't been attacked and half the people killed and the other half kept crazy ever since . . ."

"Forget I brought it up. Well, wizard, is it worth us hanging around here? Or should we go down to Oar and try to smoke them out?"

"Tentatively—pending reports from our allies from the Plain—I'd say we're wasting our time here."

The weirder side of the outfit didn't come up with anything either. At sundown we clambered back aboard our smelly airborne steed planning on having breakfast in Oar.

I was looking forward to my first decent meal in months.

XLIII

Smeds was amazed. That bastard Fish sure could stir some shit.

There was a rumor got started that this silversmith down on Sedar Row—where all the silversmiths and goldsmiths and such were located—had had a guy bring in a giant silver nail and pay him a hundred obols to turn it into a chalice and keep his mouth shut about it. Only this smith had got to celebrating his good fortune last night and had had too much to drink and had bragged to some of his cronies after swearing them to secrecy.

Today a man's life was worthless if he had anything to do with the metalworking or jewelry trades. Those who were out after the spike were getting desperate. They were stumbling over each other and causing a lot of damage in the process. Mostly to one another.

The grays were late getting into the game but when they did they did not fool around, they came with a vengeance, sweeping through the city confiscating every piece of silver they found on the assumption the spike could have been turned into anything by now. They tried giving claim chits but people were having none of that. They had been robbed by the military before.

There was resistance. There was localized rioting. People and soldiers were hurt and killed. But there were too many soldiers and even now most people were not angry enough to rebel.

"Pretty sneaky, Fish," Smeds told the old man, walking down a street where he felt safe talking. "Mean sneaky."

"It worked. That don't mean I'm proud of it."

"It worked all right. But for how long?"

"I figure three, four days. Maybe five if I feed the rumor a couple of new angles. Plus however long it takes Gossamer and Spidersilk to decided the spike isn't in any of the silver the soldiers are collecting up. So we'll be all right for maybe a week. Unless one of the free-lancers stumbles onto us somehow. But in the long run we're still had. They'll get us one way or another. Unless this backward siege breaks. Let even ten people get out of this city and get away and you've opened the whole world up to the search. Because if there's a successful breakout the man who has the spike is sure to be one of the first people gone."

"He is?"

"Wouldn't you figure that if you were in the place of the twins?"

"I guess."

"Every day they send more men to guard the walls. I don't know, but I think they're maybe working against a deadline. If they are, we might use that against them."

"A deadline? How's that?"

"Those two aren't anywhere near top dogs in the empire. Sooner or later their bosses have got to get suspicious about what they're up to. Or one of them might decide to come up here and grab off the spike for himself."

"We should have left the sucker where it was and settled."

"We should have. But we didn't. We have to live and maybe die with that. And make no mistake, Smeds. We're in a fight for our lives. You, me, Timmy, Tully, we're all dead if they ever get close to us."

"If you're trying to scare the shit out of me, Fish, you're doing a damned good job."

"I'm trying to scare you because I'm petrified myself and you're the only one I think is steady enough to help me. Tully doesn't have any backbone at all and Timmy has been living in kind of a daze ever since he lost his hand."

"I got a feeling I'm not going to like whatever you're going to say. What're you thinking?"

"One of us needs to steal some white paint. Not buy it but steal it, because a seller might remember who he sold it to."

"I can handle that. I know where to get it. If the grays aren't sitting on it. What're we going to do with it?"

"Try to change the focus of this whole mess. Try to politicize it."

There he went getting mysterious again. Smeds did not understand but decided he did not have to as long as Fish knew what he was doing.

That evening was the first time Tully asked to borrow money. It was a trivial amount and he paid it back next morning, so Smeds thought nothing of it.

That night was the first night Smeds fell asleep thinking about Old Man Fish and how he seemed to have no conscience at all once you got to know him. It was like Fish had decided he was going to get through this mess and get his share from the spike even if he had to sacrifice everybody in Oar. That didn't seem like the Fish he'd always known. But the Fish he'd always known hadn't ever had anything at stake.

He could not be sure where he stood himself. He was neither a thinker nor a doer. He had spend his life drifting, doing what he had to do to get by and not much more.

He did know that he did not want to die young or even to answer questions on the imperial rack. He knew he did not want to be poor again. He had done that and having money was better. Having a lot of money, like from selling the spike, would be even better.

He could arrive at no alternative to Fish's methods of achieving salvation, so he would go on going along. But with an abiding disquietude.

XLIV

Toadkiller Dog observed the quickening through tight eyes. He was an ancient thing and had dealt with sorcerers all his days. They were a treacherous breed. And the smell of betrayal hung thick in that monastic cellar.

He had located the necessary help more quickly than he had expected, in a country called Sweeps, a hundred miles west, where a bloody feud between families of wizards had raged unchecked for three generations. He had examined the respective families and he decided the Nacred had skills best suited to his needs. He had made contact and had struck a bargain: his help overcoming their enemies in return for theirs reconstructing his "companion."

He had told them nothing about the Limper.

The Shaded clan had ceased to exist, root and branch, sorcerers, wives, and nits that might have grown to become lice.

The twelve leading Nacred were there in the cellar, crowded around the trough of oil where the head, wedded to its new clay body, awaited a final quickening. They muttered to one another in a language he did not understand. They knew betrayal at this point would be painful and expensive.

They had seen him in action during the scouring of the Shaded. And he had been a cripple then.

He had made sure he got his own new limb first.

He growled, just a soft note of caution, an admonition to get on with it.

They did the thing that had to be done. One of the fool monks who had stayed around to restore the monastery served as the sacrifice.

Color flowed over the surface of the gray clay. It twitched and shivered almost as if it were becoming genuine flesh.

The body sat up suddenly, oil streaming off it. The Nacred sorcerers jumped back, startled. The Limper ran hands that had been clay over a body that had been clay. His smile became an ecstatic grin. "Mirror!" he said. His voice was a thunder. He looked at himself, ran fingers lovingly over a face that far exceeded the original at its best.

A bellow of rage nearly brought the ceiling down.

Toadkiller Dog caught one glimpse of what the Limper saw in the mirror.

The gorgeous new fading to reality. Truth. His face as it existed without the cosmetic overlay.

The Limper flung out of the trough, grabbed it up, hurled its contents around the cellar. The Nacreds retreated, shouted back, hastily prepared their defenses. They did not understand what was happening.

Toadkiller Dog understood. He knew the Limper's rages. This one was almost wholly contrived.

He had been looking in the wrong place when he had been watching the Nacreds for treachery. The Limper was the source of the foul smell.

He attacked. And in midleap recognized his error.

The Limper used the trough to deflect his charge, dashed to the doorway he had been blocking with his bulk. The Limper laughed, pranced up the stairs ahead of Nacred spells. Toadkiller Dog flung after him, but too late.

The stairwell collapsed.

Toadkiller Dog started digging.

"It won't be that easy, my fine pup. You thought you would use me, eh? Eh? Me! I let you think you could till you did what I needed done. Now enjoy your tomb. It's better than you deserve but I have no time to prepare you a more suitable fate." Mad laughter. Tons of earth poured in on what had collapsed already.

Toadkiller Dog dug furiously but stopped after a moment, snarled at the panic in the darkness behind him. In the ensuing silence he listened very carefully.

North! The Limper was headed north! He was crazier than ever but he had turned away from his mad quest for revenge.

There was just one answer to that puzzle. He had set vengeance aside in hopes of gathering more power.

Toadkiller Dog growled once, softly, almost amused. The shields were off the claws now.

XLV

If you dipped a wad of cotton in paint, then sponged semicircles around a common center you could create a passable imitation of a rose, Smeds discovered.

After the excitement of the search for Fish's phantom silversmith had died and he had failed to sell the rumor that one of the twins had taken possession already and was hiding it from her sister, the old man had decided to loose his final bolt. To take advantage of the potential for chaos. To add a new level of distraction to the mess plaguing Oar.

Which was why Smeds was out after midnight with a bucket of paint for the third night running. Fish had sent him to mark selected points with the sign of the White Rose to give the impression that there was an angry underground about to respond to imperial excesses.

Fish was after a slower but grander effect this time. He wanted the whole city to hear and begin to hope and believe. He wanted the grays to start worrying. The rest, he said, should take care of itself.

Smeds finished his three roses and headed home. Elsewhere Fish was painting roses of his own. Smeds had done two the night before and three the night before that, all in places where a partisan strike would be appreciated sincerely by the mass of citizens. Slow and easy, Fish said. Let it build.

Fish had had a stroke of luck last night. He had stumbled onto a couple of grays who had gotten themselves killed somehow and had painted white roses on their foreheads, claiming them for the movement he wanted to create out of the collective anger.

Smeds did not like this game. Too dangerous. They had people enough after them from directions enough already. He had worries enough with the spike hunters.

But that was not on his mind as he stole toward the Skull and Crossbones. He was mulling the puzzle presented by Tully. Earlier in the evening Tully had borrowed money from him for the fourth time in eight days, this time a fair sum and before he had repaid the last loan.

Smeds never approached the Skull and Crossbones in a hurry. That Nightstalker corporal would catch him sure, first time he did.

One peek and he knew he wasn't going in the front way. The corporal and his cronies occupied the porch. So it was the long way around and slide in the back.

And that was no good either. He found trouble on the way. And it almost found him.

Two men were lounging inside the mouth of the skinny, scruffy alley that passed behind the Skull and Crossbones. He would have walked into them if one had not coughed and and the other had not told him to shut up.

What was this? Smeds felt no inclination to ask. He settled into a shadow to wait them out.

A half hour passed. Came the hour. Nothing happened except one man coughed and the other told him to shut up. They were bored. Smeds began to nod.

A third man arrived running. "He's coming," he said, then darted over to hide not eight feet from Smeds. Smeds was wide-awake now.

Sure enough, someone was coming, and from the sound of his steps he was a little bit drunk. He was talking to himself, too.

Smeds suffered one startled moment of recognition, then Timmy was into the ambush and the men jumped him so fast he never got a chance to yell.

Smeds almost jumped in. He half rose, half drew his knife. Then he realized that the most he could hope to do was get himself killed by the other two after he got the first one he reached.

What the hell was he going to do?

He was going to follow them. See where they took Timmy, then get Fish and . . . And listen to Fish tell him he didn't have ball one.

For sure too late to do anything here, now. He had to follow them.

He had no idea who they were but a strong suspicion as to what: bully boys for a free-lance spike hunter who had decided to interview citizens who were short a hand.

Following was less trouble than he had expected. Timmy fought them all the way. That kept them from devoting much attention to their surroundings. And they did not go that far, just a quarter mile into an area of fire-gutted buildings condemned but not yet demolished, so bad the squatters had not moved in.

They took Timmy inside one of those. Smeds stood in a shadow and looked at it and wondered what he was going to do and kept hearing Fish say they were fighting for their lives now.

He'd never been much of a fighter. He'd always walked away when he could. When he could not he'd always gotten whipped. He hadn't had the desire or meanness, or whatever, even when he'd had no choice.

Which got him to remembering all the bullies who had taunted and slapped and shoved him around and puzzling the eternal *why* did they do it when he'd never done a thing to them. The old anger bubbled up, along with the nerve-tingling vengeance fantasies, the miasma of bitter hatred.

One of the men came back out of the building, urinated into the street, backed off, and just leaned against the wall. He didn't act like he was doing anything but just hanging out. He wasn't alert enough to be a sentinel.

Smeds staggered forward without the slightest damned idea what he was doing. Besides shaking so bad his toe-nails rattled.

He stumbled, went down on one knee onto a broken brick, could not silence a whining curse, and in the shock of pain suffered an inspiration.

He came up limping, stumbling, muttering to himself.

He headed straight for the man, sort of singing, "Once there was a farmer's daughter, couldn't behave like a maiden ought-er."

The thug was alert now. But he did not move.

Smeds did a pratfall, giggled, got onto his hands and knees, pretended a bout with attempted upchucking, then got his feet under him and headed out. Straight into the wall about ten feet from the man watching him. He backed off muttering, looked at the wall like he couldn't understand where it had come from. Then he put one hand against it for support and started stumbling toward the thug. At a distance of four feet he pretended to take first notice of the man, who was watching more with amused contempt than with suspicion.

Smeds made a little "Gleep!" he hoped sounded startled and frightened and silently thanked whatever gods there might be that he hadn't been recognized. Now if the guy just stayed in character and tried to roll him in the guise of helping . . .

Smeds stumbled and went down onto hands and knees.

"Looks like you had one too many, old buddy." The thug stepped over.

Smeds made gagging sounds. Inside, he was listening to Old Man Fish. "Like taking a woman, Smeds. Slide it in. Don't stab."

The man started giving him a hand up. He did not see the blade in Smeds's palm. Smeds leaned against him and began sliding in between his ribs, into his heart.

One part of Smeds stood outside, guiding his hand. The rest was in a passion of terror and horror, oblivious to the world. Only one coherent thought splashed across that chaos. It was a lie that killing got easier each time you did it.

When he came out of the fog, consciously, he was a hundred feet away, dragging a still-twitching body.

"What the hell am I . . . ?"

Getting it out of sight, of course. Because this was just the start.

He heard a muted scream and realized that another such had opened the first rent in the fog that had possessed him.

Smeds went into the building with the caution and intense concentration of a stalking cat. He compartmented his emotion, did not let them torment him when Timmy screamed. He used the cries to move a few quick steps each time.

What the *hell* was he doing?

The screams came from a basement. Smeds started down the steps, so committed he moved as though under a compulsion. Six steps down he hunkered, then almost stood on his head to get a look around.

The base of the stair ended a few feet from a doorway without a door in it. Light and the screams came through that. Smeds eased down a couple more steps, then carefully lowered himself over the side, got underneath the stair, looked around.

It was hard to see much, but it looked like the fires had been gentle here. This part of the basement was untouched. There wasn't a whiff of old smoke.

He could make our most of what was being said in that other room. Someone was asking Timmy impatient questions. Another two men were bickering about the character Smeds had killed. One was worried that the man had run out, the other didn't give a damn.

Under the stair was not the place to be if someone decided to go looking. The light from the room would give him away. Smeds moved out carefully, got behind a pile of junk to the left of the doorway.

And there he squatted, unable to think of anything to do.

Timmy passed out or something. He wasn't yelling anymore. One man was grumbling about that while the other two went on about the man in the street. The grumbler snapped, "He *has* been gone too long. Give me some peace. Go find him. Both of you."

Two men stomped out and headed upstairs, still arguing. They were the other two who had snatched Timmy.

Smeds rose, stretched, drifted over till he could see into the room.

Timmy was tied into a chair, slumped forward, unconscious. A man bent over him, back to Smeds. Too good to be true. He slapped Timmy. "Come on! Come out of it. Don't die on me now. We're too close to the truth."

Slide it in, slide it in, Smeds told himself, gliding toward the man.

The man sensed danger, started to turn, eyes and mouth opening. . . .

Too late.

Smeds's knife pierced his heart. He made a grisly noise that wasn't quite a scream, tried to get hold of Smeds, folded up.

Maybe it was easier after all. . . . The detachment went. His heart hammered. His hands shook. His breath came in gasps. He stumbled over to Timmy, cut the ropes binding him. . . . Gods! They'd burned out one of his eyes! They'd . . .

Timmy fell over on his face.

Smeds got down and tried to bring him out of it. "Hey! Timmy! Come on. It's me. Smeds. Come on. We got to get out of here before those other guys come back."

Then it hit him. "Shit!" Timmy had croaked. "Son of a bitch! I come in here and risk my ass for nothing. . . ." Except maybe for whatever Timmy told them before he checked out.

Then he felt like a total shit, getting pissed at Timmy for dying and inconveniencing him. Then he got confused, not knowing what to do about the fact that he was in here and still had to get out and there were bodies here something probably ought to be done about.

"Hey, Abel!" somebody shouted from outside. "You better come check this out. Somebody offed Tanker."

Smeds dropped Timmy's hand, frantically jerked his knife out of the dead man—wizard?—and got himself over beside the doorframe as the someone yelled, "You hear me, Abel?" Feet *thump-thump-thumped* down the stairs.

"We're maybe in deep shit here. Somebody stuck a knife in Tanker. . . . What the shit is going on here?"

The man had stopped just outside the doorway.

Smeds came around thrusting at what he guessed should be chest height. . . . and discovered that the big voice belonged to the smallest of the thugs. He turned the thrust into an uppercut, drove his blade up and in under the man's chin, not sliding it, driving it with all the force of panic into the man's brain.

He had not looked the other two in the eye at their moment of realization. Gods! That was scary. He jumped back, stumbled over Abel and Timmy, fell on his back as his victim toppled forward.

Before Smeds was all the way back on his feet someone else called some question downstairs. He dove over to reclaim his knife. The man continued to move, one leg slowly pumping. For a moment he thought of a dog trying to scratch. Crazy.

The damned knife was wedged in bone. It wouldn't come loose. He scrambled around looking for another weapon, any weapon, while the voice from the head of the stairs asked several questions more. All Smeds could come up with was the dead man's own knife, which he pulled from its sheath with a sort of superstitious dread.

He got against the wall beside the doorway again and waited. And waited. And waited.

In time the shakes went away. The nerves calmed some. He realized that his latest victim could be seen from the stairs.

He waited some more.

He had to make a move. The longer he dicked around, the more time there would be for something to go wrong.

His muscles did not want to unlock. He was completely terrified of the consequences of making any move.

But he did, finally, drag himself around far enough to peek through the doorway.

Morning light spilled down from upstairs. It showed him nothing to fear. He made his feet move. He found no trouble on the ground floor. From the doorway he could see nothing but desolation, city badlands where not a soul stirred. He wanted to run, all the way to the Skull and Crossbones.

He bore down, did what had to be done, dragging the body out of the street, to the cellar, where it was less likely to be discovered soon. Then he headed for home. But he did not run, though his legs insisted they had to stretch out and go.

XLVI

We dropped into Oar in the middle of the night but we didn't find Darling and them till noon next day, and then only because we had Bomanz along to sniff them out. They weren't where they were supposed to be. Meantime, I ran into two guys that I knew from when me and Raven were staying in Oar, and they wanted to talk talk talk.

Nobody in town had much else to do.

"Things don't look good," Raven said as we drifted through the streets, following Bomanz's sorcerous nose. "All these people packed in here, no chance to get out, food stocks probably getting low, plague maybe getting ready to break out. The place is ripe. Would have been long gone if this was high summer and the heat was eating up everybody's tolerance. You know anything about these twins?"

He wasn't talking to me. When it comes to sorcerers and sorcery I don't know nothing about nothing except I want to stay out of the way.

"Never heard of them," Bomanz said. "That doesn't mean anything. The Lady had a whole crop coming up."

"How do you think you'd stack up against them?"

"I don't plan to find out."

I spotted a white rose painted on a door. "Look there." They looked. Other people were looking, too, and trying not to be noticed doing it.

"That damned screw-up Silent," Raven growled. "He's talked her into doing something stupid."

"Who you trying to bullshit?" I asked. "When did anybody ever talk Darling into doing something she didn't want to do?"

He grumbled some, then grumbled some more.

Bomanz's nose picked out their hideout then, and after some shibboleth stuff we got into the cellar where Darling was holding court with a gang of leftovers from Oar's Rebel heyday. They didn't look like much to me.

Raven grunted. He wasn't impressed either. He reported the high points of our visit to the Barrowland. That didn't take a minute, even using sign. Then Darling let us in on the situation in Oar, which took a lot longer than a minute.

Raven wanted to know what she was doing, painting white roses around town. She said she wasn't. In fact, she said nobody that had anything to do with the movement admitted doing it. Since none of those roses had been seen before she arrived she thought somebody recognized her in the street and was trying to get something stirred up.

She didn't have a shred of evidence. Didn't seem likely to me. Anybody that recognized her, that wasn't personally committed to the cause, should ought to go for the bounty on her, the way I figured. She would fetch a good price, and Silent not a bad sum, and even the Torque brothers were good for a chunk that could keep you in beans for a long time.

Raven figured it the way I did. But he wasn't going to argue with Darling, so he asked if there had been any progress finding the silver spike.

"None," she signed. "We have been very busy stampeding around old ground already covered by other hunters, finding nothing while we ate their dust. In the meantime our small allies have been busy spying on those other hunters that our brothers of the movement have identified for us."

Bomanz wanted names. He got them. A long string, with a half dozen noted as having enlisted with the deceased.

"You know any of those people?" Raven asked.

"No. But I've been out of touch. The curious angle is, there hasn't been any attention from the Tower. This thing is pulling in every hedge wizard and tea-leaf reader with a smidge of ambition. These twins are pretty plainly up to exactly what you'd expect from their kind faced with an opportunity like this. News like this gets around faster than the clap. It's got to have reached the Tower. Why isn't some real heavyweight up here to sit on those two?''

I suggested, ''Because they don't have windwhales to carry them around and all their flying carpets got skragged back when.''

''They have other resources.''

There wasn't no point worrying about it since we weren't going to come up with an answer.

Raven wanted to know how the other guys were trying to find the spike. He figured maybe the problem was that the hunters were attacking it from the wrong direction.

Darling signed, ''Spidersilk and Gossamer have made repeated direct searches. They also provoke and watch the other hunters, who have been concentrating on finding the men who stole the spike and brought it to Oar.''

I asked, ''How do we know the damned thing is even here?''

Bomanz said, ''You can sense it. Like a bad smell.''

''But you can't tell where it is?''

''Only very vaguely. Right now I'd guess it's somewhere north of us. But I can't narrow that directionality to below about a hundred thirty degrees of arc.'' He raised his arms to show what he meant. ''It's the nature of the thing to maximize the evil around it. If it could be sniffed out easily there would be little chance for the play of chaos. It isn't sentient but it responds to and feeds back the dark emotions and ambitions around it. One way to find the men who brought it out of the Barrowland might be to look for people who were out of town during the proper time period and who have shown changed patterns of behavior. Generally, aggravated tendencies toward indulging weaknesses they've had all along.''

Darling got that from Silent. She signed back, ''That method has been tried. Without success. The Limper's raid killed so many and left people so mixed around that the necessary information cannot be gathered.''

''There's got to be a way,'' Raven carped.

One of the local guys said, ''Gossamer and Spidersilk already thought of it. Get so many bad guys in that the thieves have to panic and do something to give themselves away. Sooner or later.''

"Dumb," Raven said. He sneered. "All they'd have to do is snip a few loose ends, if there were any, and sit tight.''

"That's what they're doing. We think." The guy went off about some really gruesome disease called the black hand that had been traced to a physician that got himself knifed an eyeblink after the twins closed the city. There was still some debate, but a lot thought the black hand maybe got started when somebody accidentally touched the spike barehand, then passed it on when he went to the physician for help. The physician passed it around to his clients and they passed it around some more, till the soldiers rounded them up so they couldn't.

Darling signed, "The twins cleave to this theory. The physician's murder was witnessed. Two men were involved. They have not been identified or even well described.''

The local man went on about theories and about how none of the people with the black hand had had anything to do with grabbing the spike. The twins made sure of that right away. So there was some guy running around who maybe had been fixed up by the doc and that was an angle a lot of hunters were working.

"Maybe," I said. "But what if maybe his buddies was smart enough to put him six feet under?''

Seemed like nobody had thought about that. Nice people tend to think everybody is nice.

"What about them roses?" I asked. "If it ain't your people painting them, who is? And why?''

"A diversion, obviously," Raven said. "If we could catch whoever is doing it we might get a break.''

The local talker said, "Go teach your grandma to suck eggs, fella. We've got everybody we have on the street, calming people down and asking questions. Tonight everybody is going to be watching likely places to put more up. We see somebody, he'll be over here answering questions before he can blink.''

I sat myself down out of the way, fixing to take a nap. "Want to bet they don't walk into it?''

XLVII

Does clay tire? Does the earth? No. The clay man loped northward, hour after hour and mile after mile, day and night, pausing seldom and then only to freshen the coat of grease, spell-supported, that retained moisture and kept the clay supple.

The miles passed away. The hulks of raped cities fell behind. Suns rose and set. He crossed the southern frontier of the northern empire. It was early in the day.

He had not gone far when he realized he was being paced by imperial cavalry. He slowed. They slowed. He stopped. They drifted into cover and waited.

They had been waiting for him. His return had been expected.

How? By whom? For how long? What lay ahead, specially prepared for him?

He resumed his run, but more slowly, his senses keyed.

The cavalry worked in relays, no party riding more than five miles before being relieved. If he turned toward them they retreated. When he held to the road they closed in slowly, as though carefully daring his might. He suspected they wanted him to pursue them. He refused. He followed the road. In time he increased his pace.

A subtle mind opposed him.

After a while the indrift of the riders sharpened, like a charge starting to take shape. . . .

His attention ensnared thus, he nearly missed the slight discoloration, the minuscule sag, in the road ahead. But catch it he did. Pit trap. He hurled himself forward in a prodigious leap.

Missiles filled the air. Several slammed into him, batting him around, and he knew he had been taken. Arrows from saddle bows were whistling around him before he regained his equilibrium. The cavalry to his left had grown a little too daring. He faced them, about to welcome them with death.

A five-hundred-pound stone ripped across his right shoulder so close it brushed away the protective grease. He jumped, whirled. If that had caught him square . . . He sensed no presence on which to spend his wrath. He whirled again. The cavalry were galloping away, already beyond retribution.

He removed the shafts from his body, surveyed the area. There was no pit. Just the appearance of one with a trigger board much better hidden under the dust where his foot must fall if he was going to jump over. Even the stone had been hurled by an engine triggered remotely and fortune had placed him a step out of the line of fire.

That was the first trap. The next was a bridge over a small, sluggish river. Barrels of naphtha had been rigged beneath it, fixed to break open and catch fire when he stepped upon the bridge decking.

This time the diversionary troops waited atop a ridge beyond the river. Light engines hurled missiles at him as he used his power to jam the mechanism meant to breach the barrels and start the fire.

A five-pound rock hit him in the chest, flung him backward. He sprang up angrily and sprinted toward his tormentors.

Held only by a feeble peg, the center section of the bridge collapsed under his weight. The falling timbers smashed the naphtha barrels. A swarm of fire missiles was in the air before he hit water.

They had made a fool of him twice.

They would not live to try a third time.

He came boiling out of the water, up the bank below the burning bridge, into the face of renewed missile fire, bellowing. . . .

He tripped something. A vast net flew up, toward, and

over him. Its cables were as strong as steel but of a sticky, flexible substance like spider silk. The more he struggled, the more tangled he became. And something kept drawing the net tighter and dragging him back toward the water. He would have great difficulty with the verbal parts of his sorcery beneath the river.

The knowledge of the possibility that he might be vanquished by lesser beings stabbed through him like a blade of ice. He was up against something he could not overcome by brute force.

The blow of fear—the existence of which he could not confess even to himself—stilled his rage, made him take time to think, to act appropriately.

He tried a couple of sorceries. The second effected a break in the net just before he was pulled beneath the surface.

He came out of the river carefully, with concentration, and so avoided a trap armed with a blade that could have sliced him in two. Safe for the moment, he took stock. Minor, all the damage done him. But a dozen such encounters could accumulate into something crippling.

Was that the strategy? Wear him down? Likely, though each phase of each trap had been vicious enough.

He proceeded much more carefully, his emotions, his madness, under tight rein. Vengeance could await achievement of the more important triumph in the north. Once he had taken that keystone of power he could requite the world a thousand times for its cruelties and indignities.

There were more traps. Some were deadly and cunning. He did not escape unscathed, alert as he was. His enemies did not rely upon sorcery. They preferred mechanisms and psychological ploys, which for him were more difficult to handle.

Not once did he see anyone other than the cavalrymen who dogged him. He found the gates of the great port city Beryl standing open and its streets empty. Nothing stirred but leaves and bits of trash, tossed by winds from the sea. The hearthstones were cold and even the rats had gone away. Not a pigeon or sparrow swooped through the air.

The murmur of the wind seemed like the cold whisper of the grave. In that desolation even he could feel alone and lonely in spirit.

There were no ships in the harbor, no boats on the waterfront. Not so much as a punt. The haze-distorted shape of a single black quinquirireme hovered beyond the harbor light, well out to sea. There was a statement here. He would not be allowed to cross the sea. He was sure that whichever way he chose to walk along the coast he would find the shores naked of boats.

He considered swimming. But that black ship would be waiting for that. He was so massive that all his energy would have to go to staying afloat. He would be vulnerable.

Moreover, salt water would leak through his protective spells and gnaw at the grease, and then at the clay. . . .

So there was little choice. He must do what they wanted him to do and go around. He pictured the map, chose what seemed to be the shorter way. He began running to the east.

The horsemen paced him the rest of that day. When dawn came they were gone. After a few hours he became confident enough to increase his pace. Curse them. He would do what they wanted and slaughter them anyway.

The miles passed away as they had before he had entered the empire.

As he ran he pondered the hidden purpose behind his having been turned onto this extended course. He could not prize loose the sense of it.

XLVIII

Smeds found Old Man Fish as soon as he had gotten himself some rest. Fish listened intently and watched him through narrowed eyes as he told his tale. "Didn't think you'd have what it takes, Smeds."

"Me neither. I was scared shitless the whole time."

"But you thought, and you did what you had to do. That's good. Think you'd know the man who got away if you saw him again?"

"I don't know. It was dark and I never got a real good look at him."

"We'll worry about him later. Thing we got to do now is get rid of those bodies. Where's Tully?"

"Who knows? Probably sleeping. Why not just leave them where they are? It ain't like they're out where somebody's going to trip over them."

"Because somebody besides you and me knows where they are and he might tell somebody else who might go take a look and maybe recognize Timmy Locan as a guy who used to hang around with you and me and Tully. Get it?"

"Got it." Also, maybe Fish wanted a look just to make sure Timmy had gone out the way Smeds said he had. Smeds was related to Tully Stahl and Fish already had a habit of not taking on faith anything *that* Stahl said.

"So get Tully and let's move."

Smeds went inside the Skull and Crossbones, nodding to the Nightstalkers corporal as he passed. The owner, who didn't have much use for them, scowled at him across the common room. Smeds had to pass close by him. The man asked, "You boys going to pay for your room? You're two days late."

"Tully was supposed to take care of it. It's his turn."

"Surprise, friend. Tully didn't. And he's running a pretty steep beer tab, too. Another day or two, I'll mention it to your buddy the corporal." He grinned wickedly. Nothing he'd like better than to send them to the labor companies.

Smeds held his eye till he flinched, then tossed him a coin. "There's for the rent. I'll tell Tully to cover his tab."

Tully was not asleep. He'd maybe heard some of that. He was pretending. Smeds said, "Come on. We've got work to do." When Tully didn't move, he added, "I'm going to count to five, then I'm going to kick your ribs in."

Tully sat up. "Shit, Smeds. You get more like that asshole Fish every day. What's so damned important you got to get me out of bed?"

"In the street." Meaning he couldn't say there, where somebody might hear. "On our way out you might pay the landlord what you owe him. He's getting edgy. Talking about mentioning you to that corporal."

Tully shuddered. "Shit. That asshole. How about you cover it for me for now, Smeds? I'll get it back to you soon as I can sneak off and tap my stash."

Smeds eyed him. "All right. We'll be waiting outside. Don't fool around." He went out, tossed a heavy coin at the landlord as he passed, said, "Don't give him no more credit," and joined Fish outside. "Back when we hit town I figured my share of the cash take should keep me pretty good for four or five years. How about you?"

"Easy. I'm an old man. My needs are simple. What's up?"

"Tully. You think even a dipshit like him could have blown his whole share already?"

"Tell me about it."

"Tully's been hitting me up for loans. The first couple times he paid me back, but not the last three times. I just now found out he didn't bother to pay the rent and he's running a big beer tab.''

"Yeah?'' Fish looked downright nasty for a second. "I have something to do. When he comes out you and him head out to the place. I'll catch up before you get there.'' He stalked off.

Tully stomped out a minute later. "All right. I'm here. What's so goddamned important? Where's Fish and Timmy?''

"Fish had something to do.'' Smeds thought he knew what. "He'll catch up. Timmy's dead. We're going to bury him.''

Tully looked at him blankly, not watching where he walked. "You're shitting me.''

"No, I'm not.'' Smeds told it in driblets, when no one could overhear. There were a lot of people in the street, moving restlessly, aimlessly. There was tension in the air. Smeds figured the grays wouldn't be able to keep the lid on much longer. A little more patience, a little more care, and they would have weathered the siege.

Wherever they went, wherever there were no grays, people whispered about the white roses, fed the rumor that the White Rose herself had come to Oar and was just awaiting the right portents to start the insurrection.

The grays had spies everywhere, Smeds knew. Spidersilk and Gossamer would have heard of the whispers within an hour of their first muttering. They would have to act, absurd as the rumors might be. Else someone would see something as a sign and would raise the torch of rebellion.

There was another whisper, more sinister, running beneath the foolish hope of an adventure by the White Rose. This one was harder to catch because the rumor mongers were much more cautious in retailing it.

The twins, this fable insisted, had begun to feel pressed for time. They were getting set for mass executions in which they would slaughter the men of Oar till someone bought his life by surrendering the silver spike.

There was no mystery at all now about what was happening to Oar. Everyone knew about the silver spike. The knowledge seemed to signal the opening measure of a long, dark opera of dread.

Tully fussed and worried about the impending massacre till they neared the fire-gutted section where the bodies lay. Then he shifted the focus of his whine. "I ain't going in there, Smeds. They're dead, let them lay."

"The hell you're not. This whole mess came jumping out of your pointy head. You're going to hang in and help the rest of us do whatever it takes to get through it alive. Or I'll break your head personally."

Tully sneered. "Shit."

"Maybe not. But you goddamned well better believe I'll give it my best shot. Move."

Tully moved, startled by his intensity.

Fish caught up a minute later. He exchanged glances with Smeds, said, "There isn't anybody behind us. Slow down while I scout ahead." He went. Two minutes later he signaled all clear and Smeds slipped into the killing place.

The smell of death was in the air already, though not yet strong. Fish growled outside. Tully responded with a snarl but clumped inside. Smeds eased down the cellar stairs and was surprised to find the death room still illuminated by the stubs of some of the candles that had been burning before.

Nothing had changed except that the corpses had stiffened and relaxed again and a roaring swarm of flies had gathered, working their eyes, nostrils, mouths, and wounds.

Tully said, "Oh, shit!" and dumped whatever was in his stomach.

"I've seen worse," Fish said from the doorway. "And there's just a bare chance this scene here could get worse. Sit down in the chair, Tully."

"What?"

"Sit down. Before we get to work we have to have a talk about who got into the money Timmy kept in his bedroll."

Tully started, went pale, tried bluster. "What the shit you trying to pull, Fish?"

Smeds said, "Sit your ass down, Tully. Then tell us how come you got to be stealing from Timmy and mooching from me when you just made the biggest hit of your life."

"What the hell are you . . . ?"

Fish popped him in the brisket, pushed him into the chair. "This here is serious business, Tully. Real serious. Maybe you don't realize. Maybe you haven't been paying attention to what's going on. Look around. Come on. That's the boy. See this? This was our pal Timmy Locan. Just a sweet happy kid you conned into thinking he could get rich. These other guys did this to him. And they were gentle as virgins compared to some of the people who are after us. Look at them, Tully. Then tell us how you've been dicking up, being too damned stupid to be scared, too damned dumb to sit tight and wait the storm out."

Malevolent rage filled Tully's eyes. He looked like he was thinking about getting stubborn where stubborn was pointless.

Smeds said, "You're a screw-up, cousin. You had one damned good idea in your whole damned life and as soon as we get to work on it you got to go and try to mess it up for all of us. Come on. What did you do? Are we all in a hole?"

A flicker of cunning, quickly hidden. "I just made a couple bad bets is all."

"A *couple*? And you lost so much you had to go stealing from Timmy?"

Tully put on his stubborn face. Fish slapped it for him. "Gambling. You dipshit. Probably with somebody who knew you from before and knew you didn't have a pot to piss in. Tell us about it."

The words came tumbling out and they did not disappoint Smeds's suspicions in the least. Tully told an idiot's tale of bad bets made and redoubled bets laid then doubled again and lost again till, suddenly, here was Tully Stahl not only broke but behind a stack of markers that added up to a bundle and the boys holding them were not the sort to laugh it off if he reneged. So he'd had no choice. Anyway, he would have paid Timmy back out of his share as soon as they'd sold the spike, so . . .

Fish cut him off before he started justifying his idiot behavior. Smeds knew it was coming. And knew if Tully went at it he would turn the whole thing around so it was all their fault. He asked, "How much you still owe, Tully?"

That hint of cunning again. Tully knew they were going to bail him out.

"The truth," Fish snapped. "We're going to cover you, yeah. But one of us is going to be there to see you pay off. And then you're not getting a copper more. And you're going to pay back every bit, with interest."

"You can't treat me like this."

"You don't want to get treated like an asshole don't act like an asshole."

Smeds said, "You act like a spoiled brat. . . ."

Fish continued, "You'll get treated a lot worse if you screw up again. Come on. Let's get to work."

Tully shrank from the menace in Fish's voice. He turned to Smeds in appeal. Smeds told him, "I'm not getting killed because you can't understand why you have to act responsible. Grab Timmy's legs and help me carry him upstairs. And think about the condition he's in next time you get a wild hair and go to thinking about doing something. Like anything."

Tully looked down at Timmy. "I can't."

"Yes you can. Just think about what if somebody else was to find him and figure out who he was and who he hung around with. Grab hold."

They moved the bodies upstairs, then waited for nightfall. Fish knew a place not far away that would be perfect, some low ground that turned marshy when it rained and bred diseases. The imperial engineers were using it for a landfill. One day the bodies would lie fifty feet below new streets.

They took Timmy out first, of course. He represented the greatest peril. The man who had been questioning

Timmy went next, then the thugs, with the little one going last. Tully and Smeds did the carrying while Fish floated around watching for the grays or an accidental witness.

It went beautifully. Till the last one.

"Somebody coming," Fish breathed. "Move it. I'll distract them if they spot us."

XLIX

Toadkiller Dog was amused by his companions in misfortune, so eager to spend themselves in the digging yet so loath to do what had to be done to ensure their strength. After four days of increasing hunger he killed the weakest. He fed, and left the remains to the others. It did not take them long to overcome their reservations and revulsion. And that quickened their determination. None wanted to be next on the menu.

But the digging took another eight days.

Only the monster himself came up out of the earth. But that would have been the case had the digging taken only an hour.

He escaped the darkness of underground into the darkness of night. The trail was not hard to find, It had not rained since the hour of the Limper's perfidy. Ha! Headed north again!

He began to trot. As he loosened up he stretched himself more and more, till he fell into a lupine lope that left a dozen leagues behind him every hour. He did not break stride till he had crossed the bounds of the empire and had come to the place where the Limper had encountered a major obstacle. He stopped. He prowled and sniffed till he understood what had happened.

The Limper had not been welcomed back with tears of joy.

He caught something on the breeze, cast about, spied a distant black rider armed with a flaming spear. The rider flung that blazing dart northward.

Puzzled, Toadkiller Dog resumed his journey.

He came to another place where the Limper had had difficulties. Again he saw a black rider with a fiery spear who hurled his dart to the north.

One more repetition and the monster understood that he was being encouraged to overtake the Limper, that he would be guided to the inevitable confrontation, and that the Limper was being stalled all along his northward journey.

What could he do when he caught up? He was no match for that son of the shadow.

A black rider sat outside the gate of Beryl. He threw a blazing spear to the east. Toadkiller Dog turned. He found the trail quickly.

So. The old doom had been forced to take the long road, around the sea. He loped on, gaining two miles for each three he ran. He swam the River Bigotes and the Hyclades and streaked across the seventy silvery miles of lifeless, mirror-flat salt desert called the Rani Poor. He raced between the countless burial mounds of Barbara to reach the forgotten highways of Laba Larada. He circled the haunted ruins of Khun, passed the pyramids of Katch, which still stood sentinel over the Canyons of the Undead. Warily, he circled the remnants of the temple city of Marsha the Devastator, where the air still shimmered with the cries of sacrifices whose hearts had been torn out on the altars of an aloof and disdainful goddess.

The trail grew warmer by the hour.

He came into the province of Karsus, past outposts of the empire where auxiliaries recruited from the Orain tribes guarded the frontier against the depredations of their own kind more ferociously and faithfully than did the imperial legions. A black rider armed with a spear of fire watched him race across the Plain of Dano-Patha, where a hundred armies had contested the right of passage north or south or east and where some legends said the Last Battle of Time would be fought between Light and Darkness.

The Mountains of Sinjian lay beyond, and in their savage defiles he found evidence that the Limper was again being tormented and delayed, again with vicious traps narrowly escaped.

The spoor was heavy and hot and had the taint of newly opened graves.

He came out onto a prominence overlooking the Straits of Angine, where the fresh waters flowed down from the Kiril Lakes to meld with the salty waters of the Sea of Torments. His vantage was not far from that narrowest part of the strait that seafarers called Hell's Gate and overland travelers had dubbed Heaven's Bridge.

Hell was in session down there.

The Limper was on the south shore and wanted to cross over. But on the north shore someone demurred.

Toadkiller Dog settled on his belly, rested his chin on his forepaws, and watched. This was not the place to reveal himself. Maybe at the Tower, if the Limper turned west and sought a vengeance there.

As though they sensed his arrival, those who held the north shore closed up shop and hauled out. The Limper hurled glamorous violences after them. The distance was too great to do them any harm.

The Limper went across immediately. He encountered traps immediately. Toadkiller Dog decided he would hazard a more difficult crossing. After dark.

There was no need to hurry now. He had the quarry in sight. He could bide his time.

He might range ahead and lie in wait. Or he might stalk the enemies of his enemy in order to discover the nature of their game.

L

We got a break. Raven came rolling in where I was reading a book I borrowed from the guy who owned the place where we was staying. "We got a break. Come on, Case."

I put the book aside, got up. "What's happening?"

"I'll tell you on the way." He stuck his head in the next room, yelled and invoked Darling till one of the Torques joined us. We hit the street. He started talking. "One of those little characters from the Plain hit paydirt. He overheard a man telling his cronies about an incident that almost has to involve the men who stole the spike."

I told him, "Slow down. You're getting the soldiers interested." And he was. He was that eager to get at this first assignment from Darling. "What did the guy say?"

"He and two others were hired to snatch a man and then help question him. Which they did. But someone came along and broke it up. This fellow was the only one who got away. We're going to round him up and let him walk us through his adventure."

Right.

It might be the best lead we'd get but it didn't look that great to me. "This guy is shooting his mouth off about what happened to him we're going to have to get in line to talk to him."

"We heard first. Almost direct. We're ahead of the pack. But that's why I'm in a hurry."

I noticed he was hardly limping. "Your hip finally starting to do right?"

"All this sitting around. Nothing else to do but get healthy."

"Speaking of which. I went out for a beer this afternoon. I heard talk there's cholera down near South Gate."

We walked in silence a while. Then the Torque—I still didn't know any of their real front names—said, "That'll tear it, won't it? Get a cholera outbreak going and the pot will boil over, sure."

Raven grunted.

Maybe this wasn't just our best break but our only one. Maybe we had to make it count.

We went into a place with the dumb name Barnacles. Raven looked around. "There's our man. Right where he's supposed to be." His voice had got hard as jasper. He had changed while we walked, turned into a critter like the Raven that had ridden with the Black Company.

Our man was alone. He was drunk. Fortune was smiling today. Raven told us, "You guys have a beer and keep an eye out. I'll talk to him."

We did, and he did. I don't know what he said but I never got a chance to get even with Torque by having him buy the second round. Raven got up. So did our man. In a minute we were all in the street. It was almost dark out now. Our new friend was not full of small talk. He did not seem pleased to be with us.

Raven told us, "Smiley here figured getting fifty obols for showing us around was a lot better than the alternative."

Smiley took us to an alley. "This is where we grabbed the guy."

Raven had asked questions while we walked. "And you didn't know anything about the guy? Like where he was coming from or where he was headed?"

"I told you. This Abel set it up and gave it to Shorts. Shorts just hired me and Tanker to back him up when he grabbed this guy with only one hand that was supposed to come through here. Maybe Shorts knew what was going on. I didn't."

"Convenient."

"Yeah. The more I think about it the more I figure the only reason they had me and Tanker hang around after we got the guy down to the cellar was they planned on us never leaving if they got what they wanted."

"You're probably right. That's the way those kind work."

"And you guys don't?"

"Not when we get cooperation. Show us that cellar."

I was glum. Our big strike looked like it was turning into a pocket of fool's gold. The guys who could give us answers had checked out.

Raven thought we might get something out of a look at the bodies. I was willing to bet all we would get was gagged. "Shit, this is desolate," I said as we was getting close. "How much farther?"

"About a block . . ."

"Hold it!" Raven said. "Quiet!"

I listened. I didn't hear nothing. But my eyes were good at night. By looking slightly to the side of them I could make out some guys. Three of them carrying a fourth. They were headed somewhere in a big hurry.

I told Raven. He asked, "You know this area?"

"Only vaguely."

"Try to get ahead of them. They won't be able to move too fast if they're carrying a body. We'll run them down from behind."

Smiley said, "I'll do a fade now."

Raven replied, "You'll come with us and tell us if you recognize any faces."

Smiley started cursing.

I took off. I figured it was a waste of time but I'd give it a shot. Five minutes and I'd be lost and they'd be long gone.

I went about three hundred yards and found myself on open ground. It looked like the area where we had landed, seen from a different direction. I couldn't see anyone in the open. Figuring they'd been to my left when I started and I'd paralleled them, I moved to my left, along the face of the ruins still standing.

Nothing. Nothing. Nothing. Just like I expected. Where were the others? I worried. I thought about yelling but decided not to. I didn't want to look silly.

I thought I was paying attention but I guess I wasn't.

Somebody stepped out of nowhere and kicked me in the noogies. A perfect shot. The pain exploded through me. I bent over and puked and didn't care about anything else in the world.

He hit me in the back of the head. I went down, rooted up a little pavement with my chin. Somebody got onto me and forced me to lay out flat, facedown. He was not gentle. I wiggled a couple fingers by way of fighting back. He was not impressed.

He twisted one arm up behind me till I thought it was going to break, then whispered in my ear, "I don't want you tromping around in my life, boy. You hear?"

I did not answer.

He twisted my arm a little more. I let out a yell, proving I was getting my wind back faster than I thought.

"You hear me, boy?"

"Yeah."

"Next time I even see you or one of your buddies they're going to be picking up pieces all over Oar. You understand?"

"Yeah."

"You tell that slit she don't mind her own business she's going to be up to her twat in grays. You listening?"

"Yeah."

"Good." He hit me on the head again. I don't know why—maybe because my skull is as thick as my old man used to tell me it was—he didn't put me all the way out. I lay there powerless but aware as he drew a knife across my left cheek. Then he got up and went away and my only companions were pain, nausea, and humiliation.

After a while I got my feet under me and stumbled off to find Raven. I hadn't been whipped up on so bad since I was a kid. The slash burned like hell but wasn't as bad as I'd feared.

I actually found them pretty easy, considering. Only

took me about fifteen minutes. There was a little light now from a big fire burning down south. Later I found out they were getting rid of the bodies of the first hundred people to die from the cholera. The twins must have anticipated epidemics. They'd had the engineers save all the scrap lumber from the demolished buildings.

I stumbled over Raven is how I found him.

He was out cold. He had a slash just like mine.

The Torque was about ten feet away and just starting to twitch and make noises. He had been cut, too.

So had Smiley. Twice. The second cut was about four inches below the first, ran from ear to ear, and was the last wound he'd ever suffer.

They'd done a number on us, all right.

Raven hadn't gotten him a swift kick but a good whack on the head. He was still rocky as we reported. His hands shook badly as he tried to sign to Darling: ''One man, I think. Took us by surprise.'' He was embarrassed.

I don't think I ever saw him embarrassed like that before. But he never got took like that before, either.

I was embarrassed when my turn came because I had to report every word the man had said. I was afraid I was going to have to explain a couple of them.

She surprised me for the hundredth time by not being as ignorant as I expected.

Silent touched his cheek, signed, ''Queen's Bridge.''

Darling nodded.

I had to ask.

Silent signed, ''When we fought the Nightstalkers at Queen's Bridge they took eighteen prisoners. They marked them all on the left cheek and turned them loose.''

''What the hell? Could the soldiers themselves have the spike? Is that why they haven't had any luck finding it? Is the brigadier playing some game of her own?'' I did it in sign. You get into the habit when you're around Darling long.

She looked at me weird for a few seconds, then signed, ''We have to get out of here now. Soldiers—not Nightstalkers—are going to come any minute.''

I saw it then.

Somebody was a mad genius, a wizard at thinking on his feet. In the minutes he'd had us at his mercy he'd put together a plan that could hurl Oar into a whirlpool of chaos and violence.

He had spared us only to spark a greater bloodletting.

The twins' soldiers would grab us, with the marks on us, and eliminate the White Rose menace. Word would get out. A significant portion of the population would start raising hell. Meantime, the twins would take our testimony on the rack and find cause to suspect the Nightstalkers and their commander. There was no love lost there now and there was no way the Nightstalkers were going to let their brigadier be arrested or even relieved of her command.

The Nightstalkers were outnumbered by the other gray regiments but they were the better, tougher soldiers and they would win in any confrontation, unless the twins themselves intervened directly.

Bloody-minded genius. Who could keep his or her mind on the silver spike with all that shit going on?

While I was thinking, Darling was flinging orders left and right. She sent all the little Plain creatures out to scout around and see who was in the neighborhood and to watch for soldiers. She sent the Torque brothers off to warn our Rebel friends. Bomanz and Silent she sent to the area where we got bushwhacked to see if they, with their talents, could pick up anything.

She looked from me to Raven and back again, deciding who should be their guide.

She picked Raven.

Before they could all work up a good scowl for me—I think Silent was pleased that he would not be leaving her alone with Raven—one of the Plain creatures zipped in to report the area clear except for an antiquated wino passed out on the wooden sidewalk half a block away.

Darling signed, "Let us go now."

We all went.

The wave of raids and arrests started less than an hour later.

LI

Smeds looked at Tully across the little table. His cousin was drinking with a grim determination but he was still stone-cold sober. Those bodies. Gruesome. Those men chasing them through the night. Those fires in the south, where they were burning the bodies of cholera victims. Now there were bands of soldiers tramping through the streets, about some nocturnal business that had set the rumors flying. It was not a time to inspire confidence in one's security.

The soldiers—some of them—were troubled, too. Moments before, several Nightstalkers had come in to consult the resident corporal. Now the whole bunch was headed out. They looked like they expected bad trouble.

"It's starting to come apart," Smeds said. He felt breathless.

Shivering, Tully nodded. "If I knew what we was going to go through I would've said screw the spike."

"The big hit, man. I guess when you think about it it wasn't never that easy for nobody that ever made it."

"Yeah. What I did, I never thought it through. Or I would've figured the world would go crazy. I would've figured there'd be just a whole mob of them who'd kill anybody and do anything to get ahold of it. What the hell is wrong with this beer? It's got a kick like a mouse."

"Better enjoy it." Fish appeared out of nowhere. He had a haggard, harried look. He joined them. "It might be the last beer in town." He slumped, wrung out. "I've done what I can. All we can do is wait. And hope."

Smeds asked, "What's going on out there? With the soldiers."

"They're rounding up Rebels. They're going to execute a big bunch in the morning. That ought to set off the explosion that will break the city wide open."

"What if it don't?" Tully asked.

"Then we're screwed. Sooner or later they'll get us. Process of elimination." Fish stole a sip of Smeds's beer. "Cheer up. They're between us and the cholera. Maybe it'll get them before they get us."

"Shit!"

"We ought to get some sleep."

"You kidding?"

"We ought to try. We ought, at least, to get out of sight. Out of sight, out of mind, as they say."

Smeds fell asleep in about two minutes.

He was not sure what wakened him. The sun was up. So were Tully and Fish. Up and out of there. Something made him start shivering. He went to the common room. It was empty.

It hit him as he crossed to the door.

The silence.

The morning was as still as the grave. But for his footsteps he would have feared he was deaf. The door groaned as he opened it.

Everyone stood in the street, looking toward the center of Oar, waiting for something.

The wait was short.

Smeds felt it in the earth before it reached his ears, a monster vibration pursued by an avalanche of rage, a roar almost like a blow.

Fish told him, "They started the executions. I was afraid they would chicken out."

The roar grew louder, rolled closer, as an entire city, in a moment, decided that it had had enough of tyranny and oppression.

The wave came into the street outside the Skull and Crossbones. The people reeled with it.

Then mothers began herding children inside. Men began moving toward city center, in a rage for death, few of them armed because the repeated searches by the grays had turned up most of the privately held weapons. They had confiscated everything but the personal knife.

Smeds decided he must be getting old and cynical. He hadn't the slightest urge to get involved.

Neither did Fish. Tully twitched for a moment, then stood fast.

Many of the men in the street did the same. The rage was like the cholera. Not everyone had it yet. But both would claim many more before they subsided.

Fish got Smeds and Tully inside the Skull and Crossbones and sat them down. "We don't move. We let the rumors come to us. If they turn favorable enough we'll head for the wall whenever it looks like we've got a chance to get out. Smeds, go put yourself a pack together. Stuff you'll need to travel."

Tully whispered, "What about the spike?"

"It can take care of itself."

"Where the hell is it, anyway?"

"Smeds, go pack. I don't know, Tully. I don't want to know. All I care is, Smeds found a place so good nobody else has found it."

Smeds felt Tully's angry stare as he moved away.

The first flurry of rumors spoke more eloquently of human savagery than it did of human nobility.

Despite knowing the mob was in an ugly mood, the regiment handling the executions had been caught off balance by the violence of the outburst following the first execution. They were swamped by the responding fury. Eight hundred died before panicky reinforcements, in no good order, arrived. Several thousand civilians and several hundred more soldiers died before it broke up. The fleeing citizens took a fair supply of arms with them.

Small-to-medium-sized riots bubbled up all over Oar, anywhere the grays appeared weak.

A mob tried to storm the Civil Palace. They were driven

off but they left several fires burning, the worst of which raged out of control for hours.

A huge mob attacked the regiment that had moved in to beef up protection of the South Gate. Many captured weapons surfaced there. The mob overwhelmed the regiment but failed to flush the gate guards and failed to take the top of the wall. Archers posted there soon dispersed them.

Fish did not let Tully or Smeds go out once.

Come nightfall the situation grew both more chaotic and more sinister. The hard-pressed soldiers began to lose discipline, to indulge in indiscriminate slaughter. Youths got out and set fires, vandalized, looted. Individuals pursued private feuds. And the world's densest population of wizards decided to become involved. Decided to gang up and eliminate their toughest competitor.

They rallied a mob and went after Gossamer and Spidersilk. This time the attackers broke through. They exterminated the bodyguard force. One of the twins was injured, maybe killed. The entire center of the city seemed to be afire. And total madness spread with the news. It got so it seemed everyone in the city was trying to murder someone else.

The crowd of wizards turned on one another.

Chaos had not trespassed much in the neighborhood of the Skull and Crossbones earlier. But now it came creeping in with a crash and a clash and a scream.

Smeds said, "We got to get out of here."

Fish surprised him by agreeing. "You're right. Before it gets impossible. Let's grab our stuff."

Tully was too worn out to do anything but go along.

The other hangers-on watched them dully as they slipped out. Half an hour later, without serious misadventure, they had established themselves in the dark murk of a partly collapsed basement barely a hundred yards from the place where Timmy Locan had died.

The madness had no hunger for that part of Oar already gnawed to the bone by the Limper's passage.

LII

Bomanz was bad worried. "There's no limit to the insanity out there. If they keep on they'll continue till there's only one man left standing."

Raven cracked, "Let's make sure that's us."

We had hidden ourselves in the bell tower of an old temple less than a bow shot from the Civil Palace. If I wanted I could peek out and watch the place burn. We didn't let anybody know where we were going to hide out. So far, thanks to the old wizard, nobody had tripped over us.

"You think it's the spike's fault?" I asked.

"Its influence. And the more evil done around it, the thicker the miasma of madness will get."

So why weren't we busting our knuckles on somebody?

Darling was upset about what was happening. Far as I could tell, she was the only one. The rest of us was just scared of it, just wanted to stay out of the way till it burned itself out.

She would have done something if she could.

I asked, "So what we going to do? Sit?" I was thinking how the craziness must have ruined the quarantine on the cholera area.

"You got a better idea?" Raven asked.

"No."

Them that had gone out looking the other night hadn't found nothing. Only good thing turned out to be I got to spend a couple hours talking to Darling without Silent and Raven giving me the evil eye.

"But I feel like the buzzard who got so tired of waiting

223

for something to die he went to thinking about killing something.''

Bomanz said, ''We need to decide what to do if there's a breakout. You can bet if there is the people who know about the spike will be the first ones gone.''

''Everyone will know if it starts moving, won't they?''

''They wouldn't move it. Why should they? It's safe. Or somebody would have found it. They'll just be worried about staying alive till they can sell it.''

''What makes you think they want to sell?'' I asked.

''If they could use it they would have.''

Made sense. That's the way bandits would work. ''So why haven't they tried to hawk it?''

''Because all these assholes here think they can take it away from them and outrun each other.''

I decided to take a nap. Talk was getting us nowhere. We weren't doing nothing but yak and wait on the Plain critters to drop by with reports. When the spirit moved them. They don't think like us. Some got no sense of time at all.

Which is maybe why Donkey Torque sounded so damned surprised after he took a look outside. ''You guys better take a gander here.''

We crowded around him.

We had us a whole new angle on all our troubles. Everybody did.

A new gang had come to town.

A black coach had just rolled into the square in front of the Civil Palace. Four black horses pulled it. Six black riders on six black horses surrounded it. An infantry battalion followed. Surprise. Those boys were all duded up in black.

''Where the hell did they come from?'' I muttered.

Raven said, ''You got your wish, wizard.''

''Eh?''

''The Tower has taken an interest.''

I felt a hand on my shoulder. Darling. I scrunched over so she could get up beside me and see. She left her hand where it was. You can guess how many friends that made me.

Someone got out of the coach. No black for this clown. "A popinjay," Bomanz said.

And me, "I always wondered what that meant."

The peacock looked around at the bodies, at the remains of the palace, said something to one of his outriders. The horseman rode up the steps and into the unburned part of the building. A minute later people started tumbling out. The other riders herded them together facing the clown.

Gossamer and Spidersilk came out. A rider chivied them toward his boss. "Called on the carpet," Bomanz said. "Be interesting to hear that."

There wasn't no doubt who was senior to who down there. The twins did everything but get down on their bellies. A back and forth went on for maybe ten minutes. Then the twins started sending their people scurrying off.

"What now?" Raven muttered.

Next thing the peacock did was set up housekeeping in the only undamaged building in the neighborhood. The temple. Downstairs.

We was stuck.

People started coming to see the new nabob. Brigadier Wildbrand was one of the first. The Nightstalkers had not been involved in any of the fighting so far.

The chaos died away for a few hours while the madmen of Oar digested the news about the new boy in town. Then it blazed up, white-hot.

But it died out, spent, before sundown.

We got the word well after dark, knew why it had gotten quiet.

The Limper was headed for Oar, bent on grabbing the silver spike.·

Oar was not going to let him have it. According to Exile, the new man from the Tower.

"Shit," I muttered. "That Limper has more lives than a cat."

"I knew we should have made sure of him," Raven growled. He glared at Darling. Her fault. She had been so sure she had seen no need to argue with the tree god.

Exile had orders to hold Oar and destroy the Limper. Our spies said he meant to do that if it cost every life in the city.

Shit. The Tower *would* have to send some guy who took his job serious.

LIII

Smeds woke first. Before he had his wits in hand he knew there was something wrong.

Tully was gone.

Maybe he had to go take a leak.

Smeds scrambled out into the unexpected brightness of morning. No sign of Tully. But the nearby street, unused in recent times, was choked with traffic. Every vehicle carried corpses.

Smeds gaped. Then he ducked back down into the ruined cellar and found Fish, shook him till he growled, "What the hell is the matter?"

"Tully's gone. And you got to see what's outside to believe it."

"That idiot." Fish was wide-awake now. "All right. Get your shit. We got to move just so he don't know where to find us."

"Hunh?"

"I've run out of trust for Cousin Tully, Smeds. I want to know where he is, not the other way around. A man who can lose a fortune the way he did? That's stupid to the point of being suicidal. A man who gets over a fit of common sense as fast as he did and goes sneaking off with this city the way it is? I'm pretty close to the end of my patience. Every stunt he pulls puts us all at risk. If he's screwed up . . . I don't know."

"Go look outside."

Fish went. "Damn!" He came back. "We have to find out what's happening."

227

"That's obvious. They're using that landfill to dump bodies from the riots."

"You missed the point. Who thought that up and got all those people to work on it? When we crawled in here they were trying to rip each other's throats out."

They soon discovered that the chaos had not so much died as gone into momentary remission. And not universally. There were hot spots, most surrounding wizards reluctant to embrace a new order that had come in overnight.

The twins from Charm were out and somebody called Exile was in. And Oar was supposed to be girding for another visit from the Limper.

"Things are getting crazy," Smeds said as they approached the Skull and Crossbones.

"There's an understatement if ever I heard one."

Their landlord seemed disappointed that they hadn't been killed in the riots. No. He hadn't seen Tully since he'd wanted breakfast and had stormed out because he couldn't get credit. Wasn't anything to fix, anyway.

"You got nothing?" Smeds asked.

"I got a dried-out third of a loaf I'm gonna soak in water and have for supper. You want to dig around in the cellar you might find a couple of rats. I'll roast them up for you."

Smeds believed him. "Tully didn't happen to say where he was headed, did he?"

"No. He turned right when he left out."

"Thanks," Fish said. He started toward the street.

The landlord asked, "You heard about the re-ward?"

"What reward?" Smeds asked.

"For that silver spike thing all the commotion's supposed to be about. The new guy says he'll give a hundred thousand obols, no questions asked, no tricks, no risks. Just take it in and get the money."

"Damn-O!" Fish said. "A guy could live pretty good, couldn't he? Wish to hell I had it."

Smeds grumbled, "You was to ask me, there ain't no such thing. All them witches and wizards would have found it if there was. Come on, Fish. I got to find that shithead cousin of mine.''

Outside, Fish asked, ''You think he'd try something?''

''Yeah, if he heard. He'd figure we deserve to get screwed on account of we been treating him so bad. Only he don't know where it's at. So he'll have to make up his mind if he can sell me to the torturers.''

''I think he can. Without remorse. There isn't really anyone in this world who really matters except Tully Stahl. He probably started out just figuring to use us, then get rid of us one by one. Only things didn't go as simple as he thought they would.''

''You're maybe right,'' Smeds admitted. ''Guess we got to assume he's going to sell us out, don't we?''

''We'd be fools to give him the benefit of the doubt. You know his habits and hangouts. Look for him. I'll find out where Exile holes up and wait for him to show up there.''

''What if he's already . . .?''

''Then we're screwed. Aren't we?''

''Yeah. Hey. What about *we* sell this guy the spike? A hundred thousand ain't bad. I can't even count that high.''

''It's good. But if the situation is what they say—the Limper coming back—they'll go way higher. Let's let it ride a couple days.''

Smeds did not argue but thought they ought to get what they could while they could get it. ''I'll catch up if I can't find him.''

Fish grunted and walked off.

Smeds began his rounds. He crossed Tully's trail several times. The spike was all the talk everywhere he went. Tully had to know about the reward. He wasn't running to Exile. That was a good sign. Except . . .

Except that a dozen independents had let out that they would go higher than Exile. A witch named Teebank had offered a hundred fifty thousand.

Smeds believed none of them except Exile. He had seen them when the hunt had been a race between thieves. They wouldn't change. They would talk mountains of obols but the payoff, when it came, would be death.

But Tully had that knack for deceiving himself. He might decide they were legitimately offering. Or he might fool himself into thinking he could outwit them. He had an inflated opinion of his own guile.

Smeds soon concluded that the pattern of Tully's movements indicated he was looking for someone.

Likely one of those fabulous purses.

He had no regard left for his cousin.

The evidence suggested Tully was gaining no ground on his quarry. Smeds was, though. He wondered if Tully was getting nervous, knowing they would be after him as soon as they knew he was gone.

Probably.

Smeds caught up but the situation was not suited to the confrontation he had been rehearsing for hours.

He was moving along a street unnaturally quiet even for after the riots, getting nervous about that, when Tully came flying out a doorway a hundred feet ahead and across the way. He hadn't yet gotten stable on his hands and knees when soldiers in black surrounded him. They bound his hands behind him, put a choke cord on him, and led him off toward the center of town.

There were six of those soldiers. Smeds stared numbly, seeing the end of his days. What the hell could he do? Get Fish? But what could Fish do? No two men were going to ambush six soldiers in broad daylight.

He tripped along behind. With each step he became more certain what had to be done, became more sick at heart. No matter that Tully had been ready to write him off.

He ducked into an alley and ran, the energy starting to burn in his veins. He went faster than necessary, trying to leech the growing fear in frenzied physical activity.

His pack hammered against his back. Like half the men in Oar he was carrying his home on his back. He had to get rid of it somehow. Somewhere safe. Most of his take from the Barrowland was in it.

He came on a pile of rubble in deep shadow. No one was around. He buried the pack hastily, hurried on to the point where he wanted to intercept Tully and the soldiers.

They were not in sight. His heart sank. Had they decided to go some longer way?

No. There they were. He'd just gotten way ahead.

He crossed the street to a dark alley mouth. He would run back the way he had come, to his pack, through some useful shadows, on a route barren of witnesses.

The wait stretched interminably. He had time to get scared again. To talk himself into freezing up, almost.

Then they were there, a pair of soldiers out front, a pair behind, one leading Tully by the choke cord and one behind to poke him if he slowed down. Smeds's knife slipped into his hand. It was the knife he'd taken off that man in that cellar.

He flung himself forward, running hard. They barely had time to turn and see him coming. Tully's eyes got huge as he saw the knife come to his throat.

Smeds hit the choke cord and smashed through and in a moment was back in shadows clutching a knife that dripped family blood. Soldiers shouted. Feet pounded after him.

There was very little physical or emotional reaction. His mind turned to the pursuit. Two men, he decided. Very determined bastards, too. He wasn't gaining on them.

He did not want to deal with them but it looked like they might give him no choice.

He knew the place. It was only a few yards from where he had hidden his pack, where the alley was darkest. He would use the trick the physician had tried. If they went on by he would sneak away behind them.

He was amazed at himself. Smeds Stahl, scared, could still think.

He slipped into a crack in a brick wall that, probably, was a legacy of the Limper's visit. It had been improved upon by someone who had used it to get into the building, a thief or squatters. He could slide through and get away, but something that was not concern for his pack stayed him.

He picked up a broken board and waited.

They did not continue their headlong rush once his footsteps stopped. They exchanged breathless words in an unfamiliar language. Smeds grew tense. If they stuck together . . .

He still had the out through the building.

One soldier put on a burst that took him a hundred feet past Smeds. He called to the other. They began moving toward one another.

The one who had not run was much closer.

He did not notice the gap in the wall till Smeds popped out behind his knife. He made one strange noise, surprise that turned to pain.

Smeds tried to pull the knife free as the man fell and the other soldier yelled. It would not come. Goddamn it! Again!

Feet pounded toward him.

He grabbed his board and swung it just as the other soldier arrived. The impact slammed the man against the wall. Smeds hit him again. And again and again, feeling bones crunch, till the broken thing stopped whimpering.

He stood there panting, unaware that he was grinning, till he heard more men coming. He darted toward where his pack lay, realized he did not have time to dig it out, darted back, and tried the knife again. It would not come. Still. Then he was out of time before he could appropriate a weapon from one of the dead men. He slithered through the crack into the darkness inside the building.

Moments later there was an outraged roar from the alleyway.

Smeds kept his head down as he stepped into the street. There was little foot traffic. No one paid him any mind. He set off at a brisk pace, but not one so fast it would attract attention.

What now?

He didn't dare go find Fish. Some damned soldier might recognize him.

But Fish would hear about Tully. Fish would understand. Best thing would be to go back to the Skull and Crossbones and wait. Fish was sure to check there.

As his heartbeat slowed toward normal he became aware of the hollow in his stomach. He had not eaten since yesterday. The Skull and Crossbones was dry. Where could he find something? With stores getting low, nobody might be willing to sell. . . .

It was a meal. Of sorts. A bowl of bad soup and a chunk of stale bread, and the fat old geek who ran the filthy place hadn't tried to rob him.

He was nearly done when a kid blew in, yelled, "Run mister! Press gang!" and sailed out the back.

"What the hell?"

"Press gang," the greasy fat man said. "Round here the grays been grabbing all the young men they can find—"

Two grays stamped in. One grinned and said, "Here's a likely-looking patriot."

Smeds sneered and went back to work on his meal. He did not feel troubled.

A wooden truncheon tapped him on the shoulder. "Come along, then."

"You better hope there's no splinters in that thing. You touch me again I'm going to shove it up your ass."

"Oh, a tough one, Cord. We like them tough, don't we? What's your name, boy?"

Smeds sighed, hearing the voices of all the bullies who'd ever baited him. He turned, looked the soldier in the eye, said, "Death."

Maybe the man saw seven murders in his eyes. He backed off a step. Smeds decided the one who kept his mouth shut was probably more dangerous.

He felt no fear at all. In fact, he felt invulnerable, invincible.

He rose slowly, flipped his bread into the talker's face, kicked him in the groan. A bully had done that to him once. He shoved his chair at the other man's legs and while he was dealing with that shoved his soup into the man's face. Then he grabbed the truncheon away from the first and went to work.

He might have killed them both if half a dozen more soldiers had not showed up to help.

They didn't beat Smeds much more than they had to to get him under control. They seemed to think the whole thing was a good joke on the man with the big mouth.

They dragged Smeds outside and added him to a group of cowed youngsters about thirty strong. Several of the youngsters got told off to carry the men Smeds had injured.

So Smeds Stahl became one of the gray boys. Sort of.

LIV

The little critters was in and out so much I was sure the people downstairs was going to find us out any minute. Bomanz and Silent was having trouble enough keeping curiosity types away without attracting the attention of the new big boy.

Raven was loving every minute of it. "What the hell are you grinning about?" I demanded.

"Those guys with the spike. They got balls down to their ankles."

"Hunh!" He *would* appreciate their brass.

"Come on, Case. Look. One of them decides to cut a deal for himself and winds up getting grabbed by Exile's boys for his trouble. So what do his buddies do? Big rescue attempt, against the odds? Hell, no. Before they get the guy halfway here one man just casually trots through the escort and practically lops the guy's head off. He does it so quick they can't get two descriptions that agree no matter how many witnesses they ask. And when the soldiers get riled and go after the killer, he offs two of them and leaves the rest standing around with their thumbs in their ears."

"Just your kind of fun-loving boy, eh?"

"They have style, Case. I appreciate style. It's a sort of bringing of artistry to even the most mundane—or gruesome—things that have to be done. Bet you something. If the man who made that hit had had five more minutes he would have been wearing a Nightstalker uniform, just to mess with people's minds. It's not the deed. It's how it was done."

Here was a shade of the Raven of old. Maybe the shell was ready to break. "You think these guys are just having a good time, sticking their tongues out at the world, yelling 'Catch us if you can'?"

"No. You don't understand. They're probably hiding out somewhere not fit for a pig. They're probably hungry, filthy, scared, sure they're not going to get out of it alive. But they're not letting it break them. They're going right on clawing at the faces of the wolves and vampires trying to feed on them. You see?"

I agreed mostly because I didn't and if I admitted that we'd end up spending the whole day getting me lessons in never surrender, even if the ground you're holding springs from stupid or wrong.

Agreeing worked. He moved over and got into a discussion with Silent and Darling. All business, I assume, since no sparks flew.

I got into a conversation with Bomanz, who was trying to work his way through some moral catch trap where the spike was concerned. He had some questions that nobody had answers for. I wasn't sure there *were* any answers. That spike was like a drop of black dye plunked into a pool of already murky water, spreading. It had poisoned Oar already. We had resisted it because we knew about it and could think it away consciously. But what would happen if our bunch got lucky and glommed on to it?

Scary.

And what the hell were we going to *do* with the damned thing if we did get it? I never heard none of those clowns talk about that. It was all keep the other guys from grabbing it and doing dirty.

It sure as hell hadn't been safe where they left it before.

I didn't have no ideas. Not that looked like they would work. There wasn't no place in the world you could put it that somebody else couldn't get it back from except maybe if you dropped it in the deepest part of the ocean. And that probably wouldn't do the job neither.

Some damned fish would probably gulp it down before it sank ten feet, then the fish would beach itself or get hooked by some goddamned fisherman with a hidden talent for sorcery and a secret lust for conquest.

That's the nature of evil talismans.

My best notions were to get a bunch of sorcerers together who could elevate it to the outer realm and stick in on a passing comet or to have a bunch break a little hole through to another plane, pop the spike through, and plug the hole.

Both ways was just cheaters that put the problem off on somebody else. The people of the future when the comet came back or the people of the other plane.

I had been picking up bits of the sign exchanges between Raven, Darling, and Silent, without paying much attention, just like you can't help catching snatches of a nearby conversation when it don't really interest you. Raven was getting antsy. He was finger grumbling about all this sitting around waiting for something to happen instead of getting out and making it happen.

He was on his way back all right. That was the old Raven. You got a problem you kill somebody or at least beat the shit out of them.

I was almost tempted to yell, "Hey!" when I caught him voluteering me and him to go look around the landscape where the morning's excitement had taken place. I choked it. Why let the boys downstairs know we were here when Darling could tell him to go soak his head?

Treacherous witch.

She thought it was a great idea. We should drag Bomanz along, just in case a wizard might turn up handy.

Silent grinned all the way around his face. The prick saw himself talking his talk and making his pitch every second we were gone.

I decided I was going for the head recruiter's job if I was going to get stuck as a Rebel for life. The movement could use a few more women. And a few soldiers who weren't screwballs, too.

With a little illusion help from Bomanz we just went downstairs and strutted out the front door, walking like we belonged there. Like Raven said, if we didn't belong we wouldn't've been in there in the first place. Would we?

Balls and style. That's my buddy Raven.

They had carted the body off with all the others but we had no trouble finding the place. There was blood all over and a crowd of kids still hanging around telling each other all about it.

Raven only gave the stains a glance. Bomanz had no use for that scene either. He wasn't looking for dead men.

We strolled down the alley the killer had used to make his escape. I was surprised they didn't have soldiers watching, though I couldn't imagine who they'd think they'd be laying for, either. It just seemed like something some officer would think was a dandy thing to do. If what officers use their heads for is to think.

The place where the two soldiers got killed was a little harder to find because of all the dark. That alley was a creepy place. It felt like it never got light in there. Like a place where people didn't belong at all. A place already claimed by other things, impatient with our intrusion.

Weird thoughts. I shivered.

Maybe the shades of the murdered soldiers were hanging around.

Then Bomanz conjured up a ball of light and hung it out overhead. "That's better," he said. "It got spooky for a minute, there."

He was good for something after all.

"Yeah," Raven said. They started poking around. There wasn't a whole lot to see. I went over to a rubble pile to sit and wait them out. A fat rat sauntered past without so much as a nod to intimidation by a superior species. I chucked a hunk of broken brick at him.

He stopped and eyeballed me over his shoulder, red eyes glowing. Arrogant little sucker. I grabbed another hunk of brick and this time put some arm behind it.

He charged me.

Rabid! I thought, and tried to scramble up the pile while grabbing a broken board to beat him off. The pile collapsed. I went sliding down, kicking and cussing. The rat zagged out, to be seen no more. He took him a good brag to hand his buddies.

Raven got a big chuckle out of the whole thing. "Hail, O Mighty Hunter, Terror of Ratkind."

"Stuff it." I rolled me over and saw about a square foot of raggedy-ass canvas peeking out of the rubble pile. I had me a stroke of cunning. I stood up, dusted me off, and sat back down. They went back to their sniffing around. I dug the thing out, decided it was somebody's backpack, then decided it might be why our villain had made a stand here when all he really needed to do was duck through that hole and leave the soldiers sucking dust.

"What have you got there?" Raven yelled when he noticed. Bomanz didn't say nothing but his beady little eyes lit right up.

They caught on quick. Raven wanted to open the pack right there. Bomanz told him, "This isn't the place. Anybody could come along."

Raven thought about sneaking into the building the killer had used to make his getaway. Great idea, only somebody had boarded up the hole from inside. "Guess we might as well take it back to the temple," he said.

The soldiers were waiting for us at the end of the alley. There were a dozen of them and they were ready for trouble. We would've walked right into them if we hadn't had a tame wizard along to sniff them out.

We backed off to talk. Bomanz supposed all the exits from the maze of alleys would be covered by now. Pretty soon they would come in after us. He could get us out right now but that would take so much flash and show it would get Exile all twisted out of shape.

"Over the rooftops, then," Raven said. Like it was obvious and easy.

"Great idea. But I'm an old man. Sneaking up on five hundred. A wizard, not a monkey."

"Give him the pack, Case. He can cover his own butt and get it home to Mama. We'll play tag with the soldiers."

"Say what? Oh. Yeah. Sure. You're the guy with style.

You play tag with them." But I took the pack off. Bomanz wiggled into it. It was too big for him.

Softly, he told me, "Don't take silly chances. She'll want you to come back."

Chills up the spine, and some more thoughts about what kind of a crazy man was I, being here in the first place. Potato farming never looked so good.

I don't know if Raven heard. He didn't give no sign. We went off and found a way up to the roofs, which was a crazy country of steep pitches, flats, chimneys, slate, copper, tile, thatch, and shingle. Like no two builders ever used the same materials. We stumbled and clunked around and did our damnedest to fall off and break a head or a leg, but something always got in the way.

I might have been better off if I'd busted my bean.

For a while it didn't look like hunking around on the roofs was going to do no good. Whenever we took a peek to see if it was safe, there was some soldiers hanging out. But just when I asked Raven, "How do you like pigeon? 'Cause it looks like we're going to spend the rest of our lives up here," some kind of hoorah broke out back about where we left the old wizard and every soldier in sight headed that way.

I said, "That silly sack probably did something subtle like turn somebody into a toad."

"Must you always be negative, Case?" Raven was having him a good time.

"Me? Negative? The gods forfend! I've never had a negative thought in my life. Where did you get a notion like that?"

"It's clear. Drop on down there."

On down there was a two-story fall to a rough cobblestone landing. "You're shitting me."

"No."

"Then you go first so I can land on you."

"You *are* in a contrary mood, aren't you? Go on."

"No, thank you. I'll just go find me a place where I can climb down."

Maybe I crowded it a little. He gave me a nasty look

and said, "All right. You do what you have to do. But I'm not going to hang around waiting for you to catch up." He rolled over the edge of the roof, hung down, kicked out, let go.

I know he done it just to give me some shit. And he got what he asked for, showing off. He sprained an ankle. When he slowed down cussing and fussing enough, I told him, "You hang on right there. I'll be there in a minute."

I wasn't, of course.

I cut across a couple roofs and found a way to climb down into the street parallel to the one where I left Raven. I hitched up my pants and headed around the corner into the nearest cross street—and ran smack into a whole gang of gray boys.

Their sergeant laughed. "God *damn*! Here's one so eager he came running."

I guess I didn't react too well. I just stood there gawking for about five seconds too long. When my feet finally decided it was time to get moving it was too late. There was five of them around me. They had nightsticks and mean grins. They meant business. The sergeant told me, "Fall in with the rest of the recruits, soldier."

I eyeballed about ten numb-looking guys in a bunch, most of them looking the worse for wear. "What is this bullshit?"

He chuckled. "You just enlisted. Second Battalion, Second Regiment, Oar Home Defense Forces."

"Like hell."

"You want to argue about it?"

I looked at his buddies. They were ready. And I wasn't going to get no help from the other "recruits." "Not right now. We'll talk it over later, one-on-one." I gave him my best imitation of Raven's I'm-going-to-make-a-necklace-out-of-your-toes look. He got the idea.

He wanted to try some bluster but he just said, "Fall in. And don't give us no shit. We ain't no more excited about this than you are."

So that was how I got me back into the army.

LV

Raven waited awhile, then, troubled, hobbled around looking for Case. He didn't find a trace. Case might have stepped off the edge of the earth.

He could spend hours in a futile search that would keep him at risk himself or he could go home and have Silent and Bomanz hunt the easy way.

The pain in his ankle had awakened the old pain in his hip, so that he was stove up in both legs and moved with the spryness of an eighty-year-old arthritic. It was no time for heroics.

He had no trouble entering the temple, reaching the tower, and getting upstairs. Except from his own body. Someone up top had been watching. Silent covered his progress with a curtain of gentle, selective blindness.

Bomanz got after him before he got through the door. "Where's Case? What happened?"

"I don't know. He disappeared. How about you do something for this ankle while I tell it?" He settled with his back against a wall, leg outthrust. He told what there was to tell.

Bomanz poked, prodded, and twisted. Raven winced. The wizard said, "Not much I can do but kill the pain. Silent? You know more about healing than I do."

Silent paused in his translation for Darling, moved in on the ankle without enthusiasm. Bomanz puttered around, muttering, "Got to come up with something of his he had long enough to make his own." Grumble, grumble, paw through Case's few possessions, come up with his journal. "This ought to do it." He shuffled into a corner and went to mumbling and twitching.

Silent did not do much more for Raven's ankle than Bomanz had. The pain was gone but it still did not want to work right when Raven put his weight on it. He wasn't going to win any footraces for a few days.

Everyone waited tensely for Bomanz. No one expressed the common fear, that Case had been caught by Exile's soldiers.

Bomanz finally looked up. "I need the city map."

Silent got it from Darling. Bomanz fussed over it a minute before saying, "He's somewhere in this area."

Raven said, "That's that open area where the windwhale dropped us."

"Yes."

"What the hell is he doing out there?"

"How should I know? Somebody maybe better go out there and find out. Aw, hell! Me and my big mouth." Darling had pointed at him, clicked her tongue, and winked. He was elected.

Raven closed his eyes, relaxed for a few minutes, letting the tension and aches fade. Then he asked, "What was in the pack?"

One of the Torques said, "More money than I ever heard of one guy lugging around. It's in the corner, you want to look it over."

"Don't know if I have that much ambition." But he levered himself up. "Nothing there that was useful?"

"I tell you, I can't remember me a time when found money wasn't useful to me."

That did not sound promising. Raven went through the pack, was disappointed. He looked at Darling. She signed, "Anything?"

He shook his head, but signed, "It does prove that the assassin, and therefore the murdered man, were linked with the theft of the spike. This stuff came from the Barrowland. Some of these kinds of coins haven't been in circulation anywhere else for centuries. But Bomanz told you that already."

She nodded.

"And he could not use anything here to get an idea where the man is, the way he did with Case?"

She shook her head. She got up and started pacing, pausing occasionally to look outside. After a while, she caught Silent's attention, signed, "Slip down and eavesdrop on Exile. Carefully. I do not want him getting too far ahead of us."

Bomanz did not return till after midnight. "Where have you been?" Raven grumped. "You had us worried we were going to lose you, too."

"It's not that easy to get around out there. They have patrols everywhere, trying to keep another blowup from happening. The fighting is sporadic tonight. Exile had Gossamer and Spidersilk doing donkey work, rounding up wizards and whatnot who came here to grab the spike. That's where all the excitement is tonight. Excitement for the future is going to be provided by the cholera. It's showing up everywhere now."

Everyone glared at him. "What about Case?" Raven snapped. "Get to the point, old man."

Bomanz smiled. But there was no humor there. "He's gone back into the army."

"What?"

Darling flashed some signs at Raven. Raven said, "She's right. Quit dicking around and tell it."

"They've put up a camp in that open area. With a fence around it. And they're grabbing every man between fifteen and thirty-five they can lay hands on. They're shoving them in there and calling them the Oar Home Defense Forces Brigade. They may give them a little training so they can use them to do most of the dying if there's an attack, but I think the main reason they're there is Exile wants the most dangerous part of the population locked up where it can't cause any more trouble for the grays."

Darling signed, "How do we get him out?"

"I don't know if we can. He may have to get himself out." He stopped them before they jumped all over him. "I tried. I went to the gate and gave the guards a long sob story about how they had my only grandson and means of support. While they were still being polite they told me there wasn't nobody going to get out of there, and anyway they didn't remember taking in anybody by the name Philodendron Case. I think they would have."

Raven said, "He's technically a deserter even if he's the only man from the Guards still around. He wouldn't have given them his real name."

"I realized that while I was talking. So I gave it up before they got too angry. They were pretty reasonable considering they'd had people after them all day."

Everyone looked to Darling. She signed, "We will leave him there for now. He is safer there than we are here. We have the means if there is a desperate need to communicate with him. We have other matters to concern us. I suggest we give them some attention. Time is running out on us. And everyone else."

LVI

Old Man Fish had grown first troubled, then frightened when Smeds didn't show. Smeds had cared for the problem posed by Tully Stahl alive, but how about the problem of Tully Stahl dead? The grays had the body. If they identified it how long would it be before they discovered who Tully had run with?

Not long enough. Smeds had bought some time but the sands in the glass kept on running and the bodies kept falling.

That was the trouble with this thing. They kept beating the inevitable back, but always the margin was a little narrower afterward. And the cost of holding it at bay escalated and the price of failure became more dreadful while the payoff never looked any better.

He felt no remorse over Tully Stahl. Tully had begged for it. The wonder was that he had lasted so long. But Timmy Locan bothered him a lot. Of the four of them Timmy had been the least deserving of an unpleasant end.

He was about to give up on Smeds and go back to hiding in the ruins when he heard how the grays were conscripting all the citizens of military age they could grab.

Intuition told him what had happened. Smeds was in the army now.

Which was, probably, the safest place he could be. If he'd had sense enough to give them a false name.

The boy had sense.

Old Fish headed for the ruins, to tuck himself away from the eyes of the hunters, and on the way had him an inspiration. Why not hide in plain sight himself? They would argue a little because of his age, but they would take him. And it would be a damned good hedge against the coming privations of the siege. Soldiers, even militiamen, would get fed better than guys hiding in collapsed cellars. And the witch people running Oar should protect their soldiers from the cholera more diligently than they would the general population.

He headed for the camp the grays had set up on the razed ground.

It went about as he expected. They let him in after a little argument and a quick check for signs he was carrying cholera. He gave his name as Forto Reibas, which was a joke on himself and the grays alike. It was the name he had been given at birth but no one had used it for two generations.

LVII

For all the black riders had harassed the Limper into a frothing rage repeatedly with their tricks and traps and stalls, they had used sorcery very little. He did not understand their game. It troubled him, though he did not admit that even to himself. He was confident his own brute strength would carry him, was confident there was no one else in this world any longer who could match him strength for strength.

They knew that. That was what troubled him. They stood no chance against him, yet they harassed and guided him in a way that suggested they had every confidence in the efficacy of what they were doing. Which meant a big and terrible pitfall somewhere ahead.

They had used so little sorcery that he had stopped watching for it. His own style was smashing hammer blows. Subtlety was the last thing he expected from anyone else.

It was not till he came upon the same disfigured tree for the fourth time that he woke to the realization that he had seen it before, that, in fact, his tireless run had been guided into a circle about fifty miles around and he had been chasing himself for hundreds of miles.

Another damned stall!

He controlled his rage and found his way off the endless track. Then he paused to take stock of himself and his surroundings.

He was a little north of the Tower. He felt it down there, somehow mocking, daring, almost calling him to come try its defenses again. An affront, it was.

It seemed likely there was nothing his enemies would like more than to have him waste time beating his head against that adamantine fortress. So he put temptation aside. He would deal with the Tower after he had taken possession of the silver spike and had shaped it into the talisman that would give him mastery of the world.

He headed north, toward Oar.

His step was sprightly. He chuckled as he ran. Soon, now. Soon. The world would pay its debts.

LVIII

Toadkiller Dog loped nearer the Tower, uncertain why he tempted fate so. He sensed the Limper running in circles north of him and was amused. These new lords of the empire were not as terrible as the old, but they were smart. Maybe smarter than any of the old ones except the Lady herself and her sister. He was satisfied that the power had passed into competent hands.

Something he had heard some wise man say. About the three stages of empire, the three generations. First came the conquerers, unstoppable in war. Then came the administrators, who bound it all together into one apparently unshakable, immortal edifice. Then came the wasters, who knew no responsibility and squandered the capital of their inheritance upon whims and vices. And fell to other conquerers.

This empire was making the transition from the age of the conquerer to that of the administrator. Only one of the old ones was left, the Limper. The heirs of empire were out to crowd him off history's stage. Conquerers were too rowdy and unpredictable to keep around if you wanted a well-ordered empire.

He would do well to consider his own place in this nonchaotic future.

He trotted to what he considered a safe distance from the Tower gate, sat, waited.

Someone came out almost immediately. A someone whose vision of the future had room for a timeless old terror like Toadkiller Dog.

They formed an alliance.

LIX

Smeds groaned as he pushed his blanket aside and rolled over. He had bruises on his bruises and aches in every muscle and joint. Sleeping on the ground did not help.

This was the third time he had wakened in this tent he shared with forty men. He was not looking forward to another day in the militia.

"You all right, Ken?" a tentmate asked. He was using the name Kenton Anitya.

"Stiff and sore. Guess I'll get a chance to work out the kinks before the day is over."

"Why keep fighting them? You can't win."

Someone looked outside. "Hey! It snowed. Got about an inch out there."

Jeers and sarcastic remarks about their good fortune.

Smeds said, "Since I was a kid people been kicking me around. I ain't gonna take it no more. I'm gonna kick back and keep on kicking till they decide it's easier to leave me alone." He'd had four fights with the grays running their training platoon already.

Another neighbor said, "You're getting to them. But your tactics aren't so great. Got to use your head a little, too."

That was Cy Green. Already he was pretty much the leader inside the tent. Everybody figured Green wasn't his real name. He didn't wear it very good. Everybody figured he'd been in the army before. He handled the military crap like he was born to it and he always let you know how you could make it easier on yourself—if you wanted to know. The guys liked him and mostly took his advice.

Smeds was reserving judgment. The guy was too much at home for him. He might be a spy. Or maybe a deserter who got swept up by the gray recruiters. Smeds had a notion that at least here in Oar, a deserter with a long military background probably had served with the Guards at the Barrowland.

"I'm open to suggestions, Cy. But I ain't going to back down."

"Look at what's going on, Ken. Originally they worked on you because they wanted to show us what could happen if we weren't good boys. You provoked so easy they kept coming back."

"Over and over. And probably again today. And I won't back down then, either."

"Calm down. You're right. It's gone past what's reasonable. But every time you see red you go for Corporal Royal."

"Only because I can't get to the sergeant."

"But the sergeant and corporal are halfway decent guys just trying to do a job that they don't think there's any point or hope to. Your real problem is Caddy. Caddy waits till they're a hair short of having you under control, then he jumps in and kicks the shit out of you."

Several of the men agreed. One said, "Caddy's got his bluff in on the rest of them."

Green said, "And he's covered as long as he don't kill you."

Smeds didn't really want to talk about it. But they were probably right about Caddy. "So?"

"Go after Caddy if you have to go for somebody. He's the root of the meanness. He's the one going to hurt you. Make him pay. And try to put a leash on that temper. You got to blow up, do it when you're right, not just 'cause you don't like how things are going. Don't none of us want to be here. We keep our heads, maybe we'll all get out of this."

Smeds wanted to throw a fit right then but he held back, mainly because he'd be doing it in the face of common sense, which would cost him the respect he had won.

He was real worried about Smeds Stahl. Smeds Stahl was getting inclined to let himself get carried away. He *did* need to keep a better grip. Or he'd end up doing himself in the way Tully did.

He wondered if it was the influence of the spike.

His determination to do right got a big boost at morning roll.

Fortune was all smiles. The tent next on the left started earlier and he overheard the corporal over there bellow, "Locan, Timmy," so he was ready for the trick when Corporal Royal tried it. He just kind of glanced around dumbly like everybody else, and did not respond at all when Royal tried, "Stahl, Smeds."

They were getting closer. They knew the names now.

He got another shock an hour later. They were stomping around in the mud, doing close order drill. His platoon passed another headed the other way and there in the outside file was Old Man Fish.

Fish winked and skipped to get in step.

LX

Exile watching had become a permanent assignment for Silent. And now it looked like it was paying off. He was excited when he slipped in.

He signed, "They have come up with the names of three men who were regular companions of the murdered man. Timmy Locan. Smeds Stahl. Old Man Fish."

"Fish?" Raven asked aloud.

Silent signed, "Yes. The description was vague but he could be the man who whipped you three."

"*Old Man* Fish?"

Silent smiled wickedly, but signed, "They have been traced to a place known as the Skull and Crossbones, which is abandoned now, except for squatters. But the Nightstalkers had a corporal billeted there till the night the riots started. They are looking for him. They think he can identify the men. Exile feels very close. He is mobilizing all his resources. Also, the Limper is expected tomorrow."

Darling was excited. She looked like she had stumbled onto an unexpected answer. She clapped her hands, demanding attention. "You will prevent them from bringing that soldier to Exile. I want him. Deliver him to Lamber Gartsen's stable."

She had worked hard, using her Plain allies, to take stock of what little remained of the Rebel cause. Gartsen was it.

"Likewise, identify and collect the owner of the Skull and Crossbones. And anyone else who made an extended stay during the appropriate period. Be careful. They have made no great effort to catch us but they know we are here. They will be alert for their opportunities. Outfit yourselves as Exile's guards. Let us go.''

They tried to argue. Arguing with Darling was like arguing with the wind. Faced with no other choice, they went with her, to guard her.

They departed the temple one by one, unnoticed in the press. Darling gathered them two blocks away, took reports from Plain creatures she had sent ahead, signed, ''Exile's guards are billeted in the Treasury Annex. There are twelve there now, off duty. Silent, you and Bomanz will neutralize them.''

No if you can or give it a try. Just do it.

The men were rattled. They were not prepared for a head-to-head with a city very much in imperial hands.

They did not argue this time, though.

Silent knew a spell for putting people to sleep but it was verbally based. Pruned up in disgust, he gave it to Bomanz. The wizards went away. Darling gave them a five-minute start.

Silent awaited them at the annex door. He signed, ''They are asleep.''

Darling countered, ''I want them under so deep they will not awaken for days. Then hidden where they are not likely to be found.''

Silent scowled but nodded.

Shortly afterward, as they donned a guise acceptable on the streets of Oar, Bomanz said, ''Let's keep it neat here. The longer it takes them to figure it out, the longer we've got to take advantage of their costumes.''

Raven grunted. Silent nodded. One of the Torques asked, ''What are these brooch things with the garnet faces? Allegiance badges?''

Silent examined one, set it down quickly, made signs at Bomanz. The old wizard looked at the brooch. ''Allegiance badges, yes, but also a way for Exile to track his people. We'd better do something with them. Like have that idiot buzzard fly them out into the country.''

Darling signed impatiently.

"All right, all right," Bomanz grumbled. "I'm hurrying as fast as I can."

Another half hour passed before they left the Annex. Darling, Raven, and Bomanz rode, guised as black riders. The rest went as foot soldiers. Wherever they went people got out of their way.

Once they cleared the city's center Darling and the injured Torque split off for the Gartsen stable. There was a talking stone there. Darling wanted to get in touch with Old Father Tree. The rest went off to see what they could do about keeping the imperials from getting their hands on anyone who could identify the men who had stolen the silver spike.

LXI

After I figured out I was probably safer in the militia than hanging around Darling I settled down and made myself to home. It was kind of comfortable back in the old rut. Didn't have to do no thinking or worrying.

But I guess I spent too much time running loose. It got old fast. First time I felt like going out for a beer and couldn't I knew I was getting out and staying there.

That idea got a boost when the sergeant had us our first weapons practice. We stood around in the mud while the breeze gnawed on us. Half the guys weren't dressed for it. But that wasn't what got me. That was what the sergeant told us.

"Listen up, you men. We just got word trouble gets here tomorrow. All the learning you're going to get you're going to get today. You want a half-ass chance of getting through alive, pay attention. The only weapon we got to give you is the spear. So that's all we're going to work with." He indicated soldiers who had their arms wrapped around bundles of spears. The spearheads were inside wooden covers so nobody would get stabbed or cut. "These two new guys are experts. They was loaned to us by the Nightstalkers. They're going to run us through the drills. You don't do what they tell you, you get your butt kicked same as if you don't do what I tell you." He gestured at one of the Nightstalkers.

They all learn their piece at the same place, I think.

The Nightstalker stripped the cover off the head of a spear. "This is a spear." He was going to blind us with illuminating information. But I'd played with these toys

257

lots. Those others guys hadn't. Maybe some of them needed to be told. You got to crawl before you walk and walk before you run. Except my littlest brother Radish. The way I remember, he hit the ground running.

"This edge is sharp enough to shave with. This point will go through armor if you put some muscle behind it. The spear is a very versatile weapon. You can stab with it, jab with it, cut with it, slash with it. You can use it to hold your tent up or use it for a fishing pole. But one thing you can't *never* do with it is throw it. It ain't a javelin. You throw it and you don't have shit anymore. You're meat for the first guy that wants you."

So. Rule One.

And so forth. While we froze our butts off.

Came to the part where they start sparring, going through the basic moves. The Nightstalkers called for seven guys to pair off with our regular instructors. I was proud. The recruits had listened to me. Nobody volunteered.

The Nightstalkers grabbed seven guys and started them through the moves. The sergeant took four pairs and his buddy took three.

Just like I figured, when they got moving faster the soldier named Caddy made him a chance to "accidentally" hurt the guy he was sparring with.

The Nightstalker broke it up. "Seven more. Come on."

This one hothead named Ken something was all set to go after Caddy and get his head busted good. I told a couple guys, "Hang on to him. Cool him down. And don't let him pair off with Caddy."

I went up and took the spear from the guy Caddy had decked. His nose was bloody.

Clumsy as Caddy had looked, I figured I could stumble around and get in a "lucky" whack that would slow him down for the rest of the guys that would have to face him. I was rusty but I used to be pretty good with the standard infantry spear. Always was about my best weapon.

The body will betray. I went into a stance without thinking. Caddy looked puzzled. I figured he was mean because everything puzzled him.

The Nightstalker came and moved my hands and feet and butt around into what he considered a more acceptable stance. When he had everybody set he started us through the moves. It got hard to stay looking inept as they came faster. The muscles and bones remembered and wanted to do things right.

Caddy decided to break my nose. When he went for it I stumbled out of the way and accidentally whacked him in the shin. He barked. Somebody in ranks said, "Yeah!" Somebody else laughed.

That did it for Caddy. He came after me.

I stumbled around and tried to make like a scared kid trying to defend himself. Had we been playing for keeps I could have killed him over and over.

Then he gave me an opening a blind man couldn't miss. I tore up his left ear, tripped him, sent him sliding through the mud. I backed off trying to look scared and unable to believe what I'd done.

"That's enough!" our sergeant snapped. "Give me the spear and get back in ranks, Green. Caddy! Go get cleaned up. Get that ear fixed."

I surrendered the spear and moved. The guys were all working hard not to grin.

"Green!" It was the Nightstalker sergeant. "Come here."

I went back. I stood at attention. He looked me in the eye, hard. Then he touched the cut on my cheek. He backed off, took a spear from one of the grays, removed the headguard, threw it aside. "Give him a spear."

It got real quiet. Everybody wondered what the hell, except my sergeant. I thought I knew. Queen's Bridge. But it didn't make no sense. It was over a long time ago. My sergeant tried to argue. The Nightstalker just growled, "Give him a spear."

I gave him my best imitation Raven look and tried not to shake too much as I took the guard off the spear somebody handed me. I didn't throw the guard away. That bastard was serious. I wasn't going to play around and I wasn't going to give up a trick.

He did some fancy moves to loosen up.

My mouth felt awfully dry.

When he turned on me I shifted to a left-handed stance, which guys always have trouble with for a couple of minutes. I kept the guard in my right hand.

He tested me with a thrust toward my eyes. I brushed it away, gently, just manipulating the spear with my left hand. I shot my right forward, cracked his knuckles with the guard. Cold as it was, that had to hurt like hell. In the second the pain distracted him I brought my spear around, still one-handed, in a wild roundhouse edge cut at his throat. He threw himself backward to avoid it. I grabbed my spear with my right hand and went into a clumsily balanced right-handed stance, the butt of my spear forward. I flung myself and the butt of the spear straight ahead and got him under the ribs, taking the wind out of him.

After that it was just a couple of easy moves to disarm him and put him on his back in the mud with the tip of my spear at his throat. The whole thing didn't take ten, twelve seconds.

"You're wrong," I told him. "I wasn't there. But if you was right you should've remembered that the Nightstalkers are only second best, one-on-one."

I lifted the spear, stepped back, put the guard on, handed the weapon to Corporal Royal, headed for my place in ranks. I prayed a lot as I did. Nobody would look me in the eye. The guys were all scared shitless.

The Nightstalker took his time getting up. He was as pale as I've ever seen a guy get without doing a lot of bleeding, which he knew he could have done. He waved off any help. He recovered spear and guard and made a point of cleaning the weapon while forty-seven guys waited for something to happen.

He looked around, said, "You learn something every day. If you're smart. Let's have the next six men up here."

Everybody sighed. Me included. The shit storm was on hold for a while.

I noticed that hothead Ken looking at my cheek like he never noticed the mark there before. Maybe the cold made it show up more.

LXII

With a little sorcery and a little luck Bomanz learned that the men Exile had sent for the valuable corporal had just gone to Nightstalker headquarters and told them to produce him.

"Nothing like getting somebody else to do your work for you," Raven said.

"Sounds like a fine idea to me," Bomanz said. "Why don't we find a place and wait for them to bring him to us?"

As easily done as said. There was just one decent, straightforward route running from the Nightstalkers' headquarters to the heart of Oar.

"Finally coming," Bomanz said. "Silent. Lay down that haze now. Don't make it so thick they smell trouble."

Silent walked a ways away, just kind of stood there. People passing looked at him and stayed as far away as they could. Soon there was a stronger than normal smell of woodsmoke. The air grew hazy.

"This is them," Bomanz said of a tight little group approaching.

As the group came abreast the haze suddenly thickened. Bomanz struck at the escort of four men, flattened them, called his favorite buzzard in to dispose of their allegiance badges.

The four had been escorting a man and a woman. Silent looked at the female and started signing so fast only Raven could follow him. "Brigadier Wildbrand," he said. "We have to take her, too. You don't refuse a gift from the gods."

• • •

Despite their apparel they got into the Gartsen stable without attracting attention. Wizards were handy sometimes. Raven asked the man who met them, Gartsen, "Where is she?"

"Loft."

Raven stepped around a small menhir, climbed, made signs one-handed.

Neither the corporal nor Wildbrand had said a word yet. They had no real idea what their situation was. Till Darling came to look them over. Wildbrand recognized her. The Brigadier said, "Oh, shit. It's true."

Bomanz said, "Tell Darling we're ready to go get the rest of them."

Silent's hands were fluttering. He ignored the old wizard. He asked Darling, "Did you talk to the tree?"

She answered his signs, "Yes. He is troubled. He suggests we remove Case from that camp. Something happened there, involving Case, that he has heard of from his creatures. We will shackle these two and leave them with Gartsen."

Silent started arguing. She donned the clothing of one of Exile's guards. Sometimes she used her handicap for all it was worth. As when she did not want to argue.

Silent and Raven were livid. Neither one believed the tree had mentioned Case at all.

LXIII

Smeds kicked his copper's worth into the discussion. "I ain't hungry and I ain't sick and that's worth something even if I got to be sore and tired all the time." It had been a hard day.

Somebody said, "Yeah. Bet it's hell out there now."

Another said, "What I'm wondering, suppose we whip the Limper? Then back to the same old horseshit till they find their silver whatsit?"

The group grew quiet. That was the first anyone had mentioned the future. Nobody wanted to think about that.

Smeds glanced at Green. Crowded as the tent was, there was a clear space around Green. Nobody understood what had happened this afternoon but they did know there was going to be some shit come down about it. Nobody wanted to be too close to Green when it hit.

Somebody said, "The Limper comes and the shit gets to flying, they're going to be too damned busy to watch me. I see the chance, I'm gone. Even if I have to stick Caddy or somebody."

The sergeant ripped open the entry flap. "Fall out and fall in!"

What now? Smeds wondered. More drills? Hadn't they done enough for one day? Hell! He was too tired to get pissed off.

At least they hadn't been singled out. Every tent was spilling men. As soon as they formed up, the sergeant marched them over to stand with their backs to the stockade. Grays ran around with lamps and torches.

Smeds caught a glimpse of Fish in the back rank of the

platoon two to his left. The old man had done something to darken his hair.

The sergeant called them to attention.

Three dark riders came from the direction of the gate. A man in black walked beside each. They advanced slowly, studying each platoon. A review. Exile's men down to give the raggedy-ass militia the once-over . . .

Smeds stomach sank. They acted more like they were looking for somebody.

But they passed Fish's platoon without pausing. Maybe it would be all right after all.

The black riders passed the next platoon and started across the face of Smeds's outfit. . . .

The lead rider halted. One arm thrust out, pointing. Fingers danced. The footman beside the rider pushed in among the men.

Smeds nearly messed himself.

The dark soldier grabbed Green.

Smeds sighed. Green! Of course! The shit had to come down, didn't it?

He was so turned inward he missed the arm pointing again, did not notice the two footmen coming till they were almost to him.

His blood turned to ice.

They took hold and dragged him out of ranks.

The riders headed for the gate. Smeds trudged along behind Green, a horseman on his left and a foot soldier on his right. After the first overwhelming shock he began to take control. He'd gotten out of a couple tight places already. He just had to stay calm and alert and move fast when his moment came.

A minute after they were in among buildings, masked from watchers in the camp, Green burst out laughing. "You guys got more balls than brains!" He punched one of the riders in the thigh. "Thanks."

"Don't thank me. I figured you belonged in there. This was Darling's idea."

"Yeah?" Green laughed again. "I'll remember that

when your turn in the barrel comes. Why'd you grab my buddy Ken?''

"She says he's one of the men who stole the spike.''

Green looked at him. "No shit?''

Smeds clamped down hard. Panic would not get him out of this one.

LXIV

Fish understood what was happening the moment he glimpsed Exile's soldiers pulling Smeds out of formation. He didn't really think, he just reacted. Everybody was intent on what the blacks were doing.

He took a few steps back, turned, hoisted himself over the low stockade. A few of his neighbors in the platoon noticed but did not holler. Better, none got the bright idea of joining him.

He dropped to the ground, ran, softly cursing his body for having aged well past the point where this made any sense for him. He was all aches and stiffness from the day's drills and he doubted if he'd ever loosen up.

But by damn he wasn't going to give in, to those imperial vampires or to the weakness of his flesh.

He reached the uncleared ruins facing the stockade gate minutes before the riders came out. He crouched in darkness, waiting, and took stock.

He had two knives. Because he had come in as a volunteer the grays had not searched and disarmed him the way they had the conscripts. But two knives weren't going to be much use against that gang.

Craft was the answer. Like hunting and trapping and surviving in the Great Forest. Craft and stealth and surprise.

There were possibilities he rejected, like doing Smeds the way Smeds had done Tully. Smeds did not deserve that. It would do no good now because they knew who they were looking for anyway. Besides, Smeds was the only one who knew where the damned spike was hidden.

He watched the silhouettes of the blacks come out.

Before they left the cleared area he was sure there was some game running. They weren't headed toward Exile's setup in the goddess's temple uptown. Unless they were planning on going the long way.

What now?

Since he had expected them to streak straight to Exile he was set near their most direct route. He would have to move fast if he wasn't going to lose them.

He flitted through the ruins like a filthy ghost, making less noise than most haunts. He was very good at sneaking. One worry, not quite facetious, was that his quarry would smell him. For days before volunteering he had been too pressed to clean up and the days in the stockade had just been time to ripen.

In the Great Forest, to survive where the savages prowled, you paid attention to how you smelled.

He caught up quickly, was watching from twenty yards away when a couple of them started congratulating each other.

The key word trumpeted: Darling.

He was thunderstruck.

He hadn't really expected the White Rose bunch to be scared off by his threats but he hadn't figured them for so bold they'd take uniforms from Exile's people so they could ride into the training camp to spring one of their own, either.

This changed a few things. This made time less critical. This meant the odds were not nearly as bad. There couldn't be many of them left after the purges that had begun last week. Maybe, once they went to ground, he could pick them off. The big worry would be how aggressively they would press Smeds.

He followed them so closely he might have been an extra shadow, and so carefully none of them got that chill-on-the-neck sense of being watched. And, wonder of wonders, they led him to a place he knew.

He'd only been in and out of the Gartsen stable a few times, back during his flirtation with the Rebel cause. But knowing anything about the lie of the land was better than going in blind.

He had one scare shortly before the Rebels reached their hideout.

A big bird dropped out of nowhere and landed on the shoulder of one of the horsemen. The rider cursed and swatted at it. It laughed and started talking about how Exile was in a tizzy because he couldn't find some of his guards.

Fish recalled that the White Rose called the Plain of Fear home and talking creatures supposedly infested the place.

His luck was with him still. He had to consider the bird's advent a good omen.

Not so the man it had selected as its perch. He wanted the bird gone. The bird did not want to go. "I'm riding from here," it said. "I can't see diddle-shit in the dark."

Fish recalled the zoo they had been carrying the day he had seen them outside the Skull and Crossbones. There would be that to consider, too.

After they went into the stableyard Fish circled the place once, carefully. He did not spot any sentries but that didn't mean they weren't there, hidden from the cold.

It was getting chillier faster. And if that overcast was what he thought, it would snow before morning. A snow cover would make getting around unnoticed a real pain in the ass.

He faded into the shadows and went looking for a crawl-in entrance that used to be around back, where a lean-to junk shed had had the fence as its rear wall.

It was there, still, after all those years, and looked like it hadn't been used since the olden days. He opened it very carefully. It did not make half the noise he feared but what it did make sent chills scampering along his spine. He went in smoothly as a stalking snake.

Something cat size, that was not, started awake. He reacted first, his hand closing around its throat.

There was another thing, like a mouse or chipmunk, that he stomped as he was stealing toward the main stable, where a ladder nailed outside led to the hayloft. It died without a sound. He went up the ladder like a syrupy shadow.

The loft doors were secured only by a latch inside. He slipped a knife between, lifted it, eased inside. He dropped the latch into place.

There was a little light from below. There were voices down there, too.

And not ten feet from him were a man and woman, bound and gagged. The woman was looking his way but not at him. He eased closer. . . .

By the gods! These people had their brass! That was Brigadier Wildbrand herself. And that corporal from the Skull and Crossbones. It fell into place. The imperials and these people knew the names but not the faces. That corporal would be about the best witness available.

Down below, somebody started yelling at Smeds. Smeds didn't say anything back. Somebody else said keep it down or the neighbors would think there was cholera here.

Fish eased forward some more. "Corporal," he breathed, staying behind a bale. The soldier jumped, then grunted. Wildbrand looked for the source of the whisper. He might have been a ghost for all the luck she had. "You want to get out of here?"

Another grunt, affirmative.

"They're going to ask you to look at a man and tell them who he is. Tell them his name is Ken something. You stick to that, when they bring you back up here you're out of this. You don't stick to it, it's good-bye, Brigadier."

The man glanced at his commander. She nodded, do it.

Fish wormed his way into loose straw, out of the way, to wait. He had it all scoped out now.

LXV

Raven and Bomanz ragged my old tentmate Ken and each other. He sat in a chair—the only one we had—and didn't say nothing. He was totally pissed off, but in a way so stubborn I don't think they could have got a squeak out of him with a hot poker. He just looked at them like he figured on cutting their throats in about one minute. He even refused a meal.

I didn't. I stood around stuffing food in my face and wondering what the hell was going on since nobody bothered explaining anything to me.

Darling stomped, got everybody's attention, signed, "Get the soldier."

Now what?

Raven and Silent went climbing into the hayloft. In a minute they came back with a Nightstalker who was gagged and, from the way he chafed his wrists, had been tied. They brought him over. He glanced indifferently at Ken. Ken didn't react at all.

Silent took the gag off. Raven asked, "Do you know the man in the chair?"

"Yeah," the Nightstalker croaked. He worked some spit back into his throat. "Yeah. Name's Ken something. He used to come around the place I was billeted sometimes, drink a few beers with us."

Silent and Raven looked at each other and had a frowning contest. Raven asked, "You sure his name isn't Smeds Stahl?"

"Nah . . ."

Silent corked him one up side the head and knocked him

down. Raven asked, "You sure? This man here and the woman over there were at Queen's Bridge. They still have grudges."

The Nightstalker looked up at him and said, "Man, I'll call him Tommy Tucker, King Thrushbeard, or Smeds Stahl if that's going to make you happy. But that ain't going to turn him into Smeds Stahl."

"He fits the description."

The soldier looked at Ken. "Maybe. A little. But Smeds Stahl has got to be at least ten years older than this guy."

Raven said, "Shit!" I don't think I ever heard him use the word before.

It was not the right time but I couldn't help it. "There we was, headed into the last turn in the inside lane, leading by a neck as we headed toward the stretch. And the damned horse pulled up lame."

They appreciated it. For a second I thought Silent might actually say something. Probably something I didn't want to hear.

Darling stomped, asked what was going on. She read lips some but could not keep up with all that.

Raven and Silent signed like hell. She made a gesture she hadn't taught me, probably cussing, then told them to put the Nightstalker back in the loft. Raven and Silent dragged him off like it was his fault things didn't work out the way they wanted. Darling signed at anybody who would pay attention that it was all her fault for jumping to conclusions about some guys she saw on a porch one day. I didn't know what the hell she was going on about. When Silent and Raven came back we had us a big woe-is-me session. Bomanz's buzzard pal damned near got strangled by everybody.

A banging up in the loft broke that up. Everybody went charging up to see what the racket was.

The loft doors, where they hoisted the hay bales up and brought them inside, were banging in the wind. The Nightstalker and Brigadier Wildbrand, that they hadn't told me about before, were gone. Silent and Raven looked at the discarded ropes and gags and got into it over whose fault it was the Nightstalker didn't get tied up tight enough.

I dropped back down and told Darling. She had me yell at them to knock off the crap and get out there and catch them. They came, still bickering. She started giving orders aimed at stopping the Nightstalkers before they could get back to their own. "Paddlefoot stays here. He is in no shape." The Torque was crapped out in one of the horse stalls and had been since I'd come in. "Case. You stay and keep track of our guest."

That went over big. Raven and Silent gave me their famous deadly looks, like maybe I'd arranged the whole damned thing just so I could get her alone. Hell. After three days in that camp I didn't feel like doing anything anyway.

We were in a spot. From what Darling signed I gathered we was out of places to run. We couldn't even go back to the temple because Wildbrand and the corporal probably heard them talk about how we hid out right in Exile's pocket.

Even that buzzard got out to do some aerial scouting. I was glad. He hadn't started in on me yet but I was up to my ears with him nagging Bomanz. The old boy was all right.

I never saw Darling rattled before. She paced and stomped and made incomplete gestures and signed at me without ever finishing a thought. She wasn't afraid, just worried about what would become of the rest of us and the movement if the guys didn't catch the Nightstalkers in time.

I don't know what I thought we might get up to but at the time it seemed a good idea to tie old Ken up. Then I stood behind his chair, conversing with Darling, like I suddenly needed something to hide behind.

I don't know how much later it was, probably only a couple minutes, when I saw somebody move behind Darling and thought it was Paddlefoot Torque finally waking up. I went to work on me for being too damned chickenshit to have grabbed an opportunity when it was there. . . .

That wasn't Torque! That was somebody else. . . .

The second I realized that, before I could give her any warning, the guy laid a knife across her throat. "Turn him loose," he told me. And when I just stood there gawking he drew a little blood. "Do it!"

I started fumbling with knots.

Torque did decide to wake up then.

I don't think the poor silly sack ever knew what was going on. He stumbled out rubbing his eyes and mumbling. The guy holding Darling turned around and stuck him with a knife he had in his left hand, came back and got Darling in the side with the same knife as she was turning toward him, and in almost the same motion threw the knife with which he had threatened her.

It hit me in the hip. I felt it go deep and hit bone. Then the grungy stable floor opened its arms and jumped up to meet me. The guy yanked his knife out of Darling and bounced over to cut our guest loose. Then he got set to cut my throat.

"Hey!" our guest yelled. "Knock it off! They weren't going to croak me."

"This is the second time they shoved their faces in our business. They want to clean us out. I warned them last time. . . ."

"Let's just find my pack and get the hell out before the rest of them come back."

I could have kissed him if I could have done anything at all. I wasn't too spry right then.

The other one looked down at me. "You tell the bitch this was her last free chance. Next time, *skitch*!" He flashed his bloody knife past his throat. Then Ken found the pack I'd found in that alley. He put it on and they went away.

When the stable door closed behind them I ground my teeth and yanked the damned knife out of me. I didn't bleed to death on the spot, so I knew it didn't get any big veins. I crawled over to Darling. She was pale and she was hurting but she wanted me to check on Torque first.

He was still alive but I didn't think there was a whole

lot that could be done to keep him that way. I told Darling. She signed we had to do something.

Of course we did. But I didn't know the hell what.

Raven busted in. "We caught them! We're safe for . . . What the hell happened, Case?"

By then they were all inside, recaptured prisoners included. I told it. While I was, one of our little spies came in from the temple to report that Exile had ordered an all-out search for Brigadier Wildbrand and persons unknown masquerading as his guards.

Bomanz and Silent did what they could for us casualties, then everybody that could hit the street again. It was starting to snow out there.

"Some fun, eh?" I asked the Nightstalkers. They didn't see the humor.

Frankly, neither did I.

LXVI

"What the shit are we going to do?" Smeds growled at Fish when they stopped running to catch their breaths. "There ain't no safe places left."

Fish said, "I don't know. I used up all my ideas just getting you out."

"They know our names, Fish. And that bunch knows our faces."

"You're the one wouldn't let me take them out. You end up paying for that, don't whine at me."

"There's been enough killing and hurting. All I want is out." He tried to get his pack settled more comfortably. "I don't even give a damn about selling the spike anymore. I just want to wake up from the nightmare."

Snowflakes had begun to swirl around them. Fish grumbled about leaving tracks, then asked, "You know of anywhere to lay up even for a little while? Twelve hours would do. Twenty-four would be better. The Limper would be here and there wouldn't be any more ducking and slinking because the soldiers would be busy."

The only thing Smeds could think of was a drainage system that had been built when he was a kid, to carry water away from the neighborhood when it rained. Before the system there'd always been little local floods when it stormed. Some of the ditching was covered over. They had played and hidden out in there. But he hadn't paid any attention in ten years. Public works which did not serve the rich and powerful had a way of dying of neglect.

It was no place he wanted to spend any time. It would be cold and damp and infested with rats and, these days, probably, human vermin. But he could think of nowhere else to get out of sight, even for an hour.

"When I was a kid we used to—"

"Don't tell me. If I don't know I can't tell anybody. Just tell me where's a good place for you to see me without me or anybody watching me seeing you."

Smeds thought about it and mentioned a place he did know was there because his labor battalion had passed that way every morning and evening when he was doing time. He described it, asked, "What are we up to?"

"I'm going to see if Exile will talk deal."

"Oh, shit, man! He'll take you apart."

"He might," Fish admitted. "But we know somebody's going to do that real soon anyway. He's the only one who's offered any serious deal."

"I think if I had my druthers I'd rather the Rebels got the damned thing. The imperials are nasty enough without it."

Fish grunted. "Maybe. But they don't want to pay for it. They want you to do it for love. I'm a whore too old and set in her ways not to want to get paid for my trouble."

Smeds said, "I guess for guys like us it don't matter who's running things anyway. Whoever it is they're going to try to stick it to us."

The heavens had cut loose now, dumping snow so heavily it had become their ally.

Fish started explaining what he wanted Smeds to do.

LXVII

The gang came smashing in out of the blizzard. Raven snarled, "We lost them."

Stubby Torque said, "You can't see your hand in front of your face out there."

"You tracked Raker down in a snowstorm in Roses, didn't you?" I asked Raven.

"Different circumstances." He was double-pissed now because of what he thought he saw when he busted through the door. As if we could have done anything about it carved up the way we were.

Darling shut them up. She made it clear she'd had her mind on business because she told them what we were going to do if those guys told the gray boys where to find us again. She felt almost sorry for those two.

She overdid the empathy sometimes. I don't have any for guys who stick knives in me.

The excitement started a few hours later when a couple of our little spies from the temple came charging in to tell us how a guy who sounded like the one who stabbed me had dropped in on Exile to see if he could cut a deal. As a good-faith gesture he'd told Exile where he could find us and Brigadier Wildbrand. He'd also told Exile his headquarters was so riddled with spies he couldn't sneeze without some Plain creature reporting it.

That meant big excitement over there. A bunch of our little allies didn't get the word in time to get out. Gossamer and Spidersilk led the exterminator squads. Meantime, they were throwing together a gang to come after us. They figured we'd hear they were coming but counted on us getting caught being on the move in a city alert for us.

I thought they were a little optimistic there, considering Bomanz and Silent had done a good job keeping us from being noticed before. But Exile probably wouldn't know we had those kinds of resources. Not about Bomanz, at least. I figured his big panic would come when he started wondering what resources Darling could call up out of the Plain.

She did have something cooked up with the tree god. What I didn't know. It wouldn't be anything small.

Nothing like being nailed down on the bull's-eye of history in the making without a fool's notion of what was going on. Nothing personal, Case, old buddy, but they can't make you tell what you don't know.

Darling told Silent and the Torques to get the horses out so they could not be recaptured. They were going to hide them on an empty lot nearby. Yeah? What would they do about tracks? Something wizardly, I guess.

Horses were part of her plans. Whatever they were. I had caught part of an argument with Silent where she told him she wanted to steal a bunch more.

One heroic little rock monkey hung in the temple till the last moment, near getting himself fried by the twins so he could find out as much as possible about Exile's deal for the spike.

There was a deal. The monkey said Exile was going to play it straight and keep his end of the bargain if the guys with the spike kept theirs. The monkey said the guy dealing for them had no idea where the spike was nor any idea where the guy who did know was hiding.

Made sense to me. And to Exile, I guess. He didn't waste no time jacking the guy around, just asked the go-between how they wanted to make the exchange.

We'd had the guy who knew! I'd lived in the same damned tent with him for days! I wanted to kick some Nightstalkers around for lying to us.

Raven got the wind up, too. "How the hell are we supposed to con people into fighting the empire if the bastards go honest on us? Whoever heard of a wizard dealing straight?''

Bomanz gave him some dirty looks but never got no chance to argue because right then we got word that Exile's boys were closing in.

When they busted in all they saw was Brigadier Wildbrand and her buddy sitting on the floor by our runt menhir. The rest of us were still there but Bomanz had disguised us as heaps of manure and whatnot while we gave the Nightstalkers the idea we were sneaking out.

The talking stone boomed out, "Hi, guys! You're too late again. You're always going to be too late. Why don't you wake up and come on over to the winning side? The White Rose don't hold no grudges.''

The raiders were all Exile's personal guards, unlikely recruits, but the stone kept nagging them.

They spread out. Some rushed into the loft where nobody was hiding. Some went to work to get the Nightstalkers loose. And some went to work trying to figure how to silence that bigmouth stone.

The menhir vanished. And just when their eyes stopped popping, here it came back. "You boys better get your hearts and heads right fast. It's almost dawn now and before sunset tomorrow the White Rose is going to cure this berg of the imperial disease.'' Away it went again.

That crack rattled them some.

Here it came, spewing more mockery. They got so pissed they stopped doing a thorough job of searching.

There was some noise outside. Three of them charged out into the blizzard. There was a flash, a scream. A guy staggered inside. "They're all dead out there. They took the horses.''

That damned Silent was showing off for Darling. She would be pissed at him for wasting them when he didn't have to. I didn't blame him, though. He'd been keeping a lot bottled up. These guys were some he could make pay.

A bunch more went charging off to avenge their buddies. The talking stone whooped and laughed and carried on.

They never caught Silent, of course. But he got some more of them. They finally took Brigadier Wildbrand and got out of there while there were some of them left to get.

A little later Silent brought ten horses in. Him and the Torques were real pleased with themselves. I think maybe Darling was the only one who wasn't pleased with them.

LXVIII

The snowfall had ended. The sky had cleared. The world had grown almost intolerably bright by the time the Limper topped the rise that gave him his first glimpse of his destination. The silence troubled him some. There should have been birds out if nothing else. And why was there so much smoke drifting downwind from Oar, more than could be explained by all the city's hearth and heating fires?

No matter. No matter at all. He could feel that piece of haunted silver calling him as though he had been born to wield it and it had been wrought for him and him alone. His destiny lay there, ahead, and all the mousy scrabbling around by those who would deny him would not prevent him taking that power that was rightfully his.

He strode forward, walking now, no longer rushed, confident yet still ill at ease with the silence and a lingering suspicion that all the horizons were masks being worn by his enemies.

LXIX

Toadkiller Dog was only one of a varied pack of monsters running on the Limper's trail. But he was out in front, their leader, the only one of the crowd not carrying some dread lord or lady out of the Tower. He was the scout, the champion, and before this day was through he hoped to be entered in the annals of history as the destroyer of the last of the Ten Who Were Taken, as the closer of the door on the olden times.

He topped a low ridge line, saw Oar for the first time. He saw, from disturbances in the snow, that the Limper had paused there, too. There he was now, a remote speck tramping a lonely track across the pristine snowscape.

He dropped down onto his belly to lower his profile, listened to the silence. He watched the smoke drift from the city, noted that everything that had stood outside the walls last time had been cleared away, leaving nothing but a flat white surround. Uneasily for a moment, he surveyed the horizons, feeling almost as if distant groves were the massed helmets and spears of legions waiting in tight array.

His companions crowded up behind him. They waited till the speck that was the Limper vanished against the dark loom of the city's walls. Then they all moved forward, marching toward doom or destiny in a gradually widening line abreast.

LXX

Smeds sat in the icy shadows shivering, unable to stop. His stomach felt hollow. It ached. He was scared. He hoped it was the cold and hunger but was afraid it was the first bite of cholera.

The air was filled with smoke and the stench of bodies being burned. Death had reaped a rich harvest during the night. Few who were not soldiers had eaten well in days. Disease made easy headway in bodies already weakened.

He watched the bridge up the ditch and wondered if Fish would ever come, and what he would do if Fish didn't. Then he sat there and gradually convinced himself that he was the last of the four of them, possessed of the greatest treasure in the world and so poor he was forced to live in a sewer like a rat.

He scavenged through his pack for the dozenth time, looking for some scrap of food that might have gotten into it somehow. Again he found nothing but the gold and silver he had brought out of the Barrowland. A fortune, and he would have given it all for a good meal, a warm bed, and confidence that the great terrors of the world had forgotten his name.

He started. Daydreaming, he had not noticed the two men come onto the bridge. One looked like Fish. He made the signal he was supposed to make before he walked away from the other, who stayed where he was.

Smeds shoved his pack into a gap in the culvert wall, where some of the building stone had fallen away and high water had washed out some of the earth behind. Then he ran toward the light at the nether end, a hundred yards away.

Midway he stumbled over a corpse that the rats had been at for a while. He had become so inured to horror that he just went on, giving it hardly a thought.

He rushed out the other end, floundered through drifted snow, and hurried around to where he was supposed to meet Fish, masked from the man on the bridge by a hump of earth six feet high. Fish was carrying a sizable blue canvas bag. "Is it safe?" Smeds croaked.

"Looks like they'll play square. This is the first third, along with some food and clothes and blankets and stuff I thought you could use."

Smeds's mouth watered. But he asked, "What now?"

"You go out on the bridge, get the second third, tell him where to find the spike. I watch from cover. He messes with you, I hunt him down and kill him. Go on. Let's get it done."

Smeds looked at the old man a moment, shrugged, went off to meet the man on the bridge. He was calmer than he had expected to be. Maybe he was getting used to the pressure. He was still pleased with himself for not having bent for a moment while the Rebels had him.

The man on the bridge leaned on the rail, staring at nothing. He glanced at Smeds incuriously as he approached. Another blue bag leaned against his leg. Smeds sidled up and planted his forearms on the rail on the other side of the bag.

The man was younger than Smeds had expected and of a race he'd never before seen. Easy to see why he had taken the name Exile.

"Smeds Stahl?"

"Yes. How come you're playing this square?"

"I've found honesty and fair play productive over the long term. The second third is in the bag. Do you have something for me?"

"In the city wall. One hundred eighty-two paces east of the North Gate, below the twenty-sixth archer's embrasure, in the mortar behind the block recessed to take the support brace of a timber hording."

"Understood. Thank you. Good day."

Smeds hoisted the bag and got the hell out of there.

"Go all right?" Fish asked.

"Yeah. Now what?"

"Now I join up with him to go see if you told the truth. If you did he gives me the final third. If not he kills me and comes looking for you."

"Shit. Why not head out now? What we got ought to be enough."

"He's played straight. I figure it would be smart to play it that way with him. We aren't going to get out of Oar for a while. Be nice to know there was somebody who wasn't out to get us. You go back wherever you was hiding. I'll come back to the bridge."

"Right."

Smeds was just about to drop back into the ditch when alarm horns began blowing all over the city.

The Limper had come.

LXXI

Raven got him a wild hair. He'd go snag the spike and that would be a big foot in the door with Darling. The guy's head was getting a little bent. He didn't tell nobody but Brother Bear Torque, who he conned into going along with him.

He started out lucky. They hit no gray patrols. As they got into the heart of the city, here came Exile and an older guy just like they had timed it for Raven's benefit. They followed the two.

Exile and his companion ended up leaning on the rail of a footbridge over a big drainage ditch. Raven and Torque watched from a distance. The area around the ditch was clear. They couldn't get as close as Raven wanted.

"What the hell are they doing?" Torque asked.

"Waiting, looks like."

The older man resumed moving, went on, and vanished among tenements beyond the ditch. Five minutes later another man came out to the bridge, talked to Exile a little, walked away with a bag.

"That tears it," Torque said. "Time to bend over and kiss our asses good-bye."

"He hasn't got hold of it yet," Raven growled. "We stick and see what turns up. Look here." The older man was coming out to rejoin Exile.

They just stood there.

"Look!" Raven pointed.

The covert from which they watched was about ten feet higher than the bridge. Just enough of an elevation to reveal the head and shoulders of a man crossing the snow north of the bridge, behind a mound that would mask him from the men on the bridge. He carried two blue bags.

Alarm horns tore the guts out of the quiet.

The men on the bridge took off.

Torque said, "We better get back. . . ."

"Wait!" There was a nasty gleam in Raven's eyes. "Exile will be busy with the Limper. We get that man to tell us where the spike is, maybe we can get to it first."

LXXII

Smeds had gotten back to his starting point. He put the two bags into hiding with his pack, except for a couple of army blankets, a heavy coat, a knife, food, and a bottle of brandy. He stuffed, warmed his veins, listened to the horns. They were going berserk up there.

A noise from down the culvert shocked him. He listened closely, figured it had come from about where the corpse lay, and had been made by something a lot bigger than a rat.

He rose carefully, filled his coat pockets with food, laid his blankets in atop the treasure—and froze.

A man stood silhouetted in the nearer end of the culvert. One of those Rebels. Fish had been right. The bastards just wouldn't let up.

The man was coming in.

Smeds lifted himself into the hole with his plunder. It was a tight fit and a pathetic attempt at concealment but he was counting on the man's vision needing a long while to adjust from the brightness outside.

Absolutely.

The man was still moving tentatively when he came abreast of Smeds. Smeds reached out and cut his throat.

The man made an injured-rabbit noise and started thrashing around. Smeds climbed down and walked to the mouth of the culvert. He paid no attention to the noise made by someone stumbling toward him from behind. He looked out into the glare, his eyes smarting. He moved out carefully, ready for anything. And found himself alone.

The ditch bank was almost vertical there, faced with

stone, twelve feet high, spotted with ice. A lot of snow had blown into the ditch. Smeds floundered through it.

An angry bellow from inside the culvert gave him added incentive to make sure of his hand and toe-holds as he climbed.

He heard the man come out as he rolled over the lip of the ditch. He got to his feet and waited.

An angry face rose above the brink. Smeds kicked as hard as he could, caught the man square in the center of the forehead. He pitched backward. Smeds stepped to the edge, looked down at the figure almost buried in the snow. He caressed the knife in his coat pocket, thought better of going down there because two women and several children had paused near the footbridge, watching. "I hope you freeze to death, you son of a bitch." He kicked loose snow down, turned, and walked away.

He felt better than he had in a week and right then did not much give a damn *what* the future held.

LXXIII

Darling was foaming at the mouth when the alarm horns brayed. She had discovered Raven and Bear missing and was as thoroughly pissed off as I could imagine her getting. Whatever she had in mind, whatever she was making us get dressed up for, she had counted on having more bodies backing her.

Right then she had me and Silent and Bomanz and Stubby Torque. Paddlefoot Torque had died a half hour earlier. She stomped her feet and signed, "I do not need him. I survived without him before. Get moving. Get those horses ready." She pulled a knee-length shirt of mail over her head, followed that with a white tabard. As she buckled on a very unfeminine sword she snarled and grimaced so nobody argued.

Bomanz helped us both mount up. Stubby Torque handed her a lance he'd jury-rigged from junk from around the stable. She had her banner tied to it, furled. If her wound bothered her she didn't show it.

Silent finally got his balance enough to try arguing with the whirlwind. The whirlwind almost rode him down and there was nothing for him to do but jump onto his own animal and try to keep up.

Darling paused once, in the street outside. She looked at the sky, seemed pleased with what she saw. When I looked up all I saw was a gliding hawk, very high, or an eagle, higher still.

She took off. She hadn't bothered to tell any of us what she was going to do, probably because she figured we would have tied her up to stop her.

She was right.

We kept busy now keeping up and sorting ourselves out so the two wizards were closest to her, able to guard her with their skills.

She headed in the direction the alarms said the threat lay. The madwoman.

The imperials had several minutes' jump on us but we made most of that up. As we moved into that part of the city near the southeast wall we overtook hundreds of hurrying soldiers. Silent or Bomanz conjured an ugly sound and set it running ahead of us, to scare everybody out of our way. We burst out into the cleared space behind the wall. Darling headed straight for a long ramp that had been put up so heavy engines could be dragged to the ramparts. She headed up it, making soldiers jump to get out of her way.

I told myself it had been an exciting past year and now it was time to die.

Soldiers scampered away as we hit the rampart. I glimpsed Limper walking toward Oar, all by his lonesome.

Darling made her mount rear and scream. She unfurled her vermilion banner with the white rose embroidered in silk.

Utter silence. The imperials gawked, petrified. Even the Limper stopped his implacable advance and stared.

Then the shriek of the eagle—it *was* an eagle!—ripped the air. The raptor came screaming down. Before it lighted on Darling's shoulder, with what had to be bone-rattling impact, she pointed out at the land beyond the walls.

All heads turned. Three, five, six, seven, eight! The windwhales rose into the sky. Squadrons, troops, battalions of centaurs came cantering out of hiding, the drum of their hooves a continuous thunder despite the muting effect of the snow. Whole sections of woods started moving toward the city. Mantas began to slip off the backs of the windwhales, scouting for updrafts. More glided over the city from behind us, just to let the world know the place was surrounded.

Darling rose in her stirrups and surveyed her surroundings, searching for someone who did not agree that this was the day of the White Rose.

The snowfields erupted and talking stones began appearing, assuming posts along predetermined lines, forming the skeleton of a wall that would close the Limper in.

Damn me! The tree god must have started on the buildup clear back when we first hit Oar.

Darling settled into her saddle. She was pleased with herself. Everybody watched her for a cue, even the Limper.

Bomanz faced north, a resolute sentinel, never letting events behind him distract him from his watch for trouble. Silent remained as fixed on the wall to the south while Torque and I tried to keep a lookout everywhere at once. Bomanz said, "Case, tell her Exile is coming."

I backed my horse till Darling could see my hands without having to surrender her attention for the Limper and her continuing dispositions. She nodded. I told her I had spotted Gossamer and Spidersilk sneaking around north and south of us, respectively. She nodded again, unperturbed.

Exile approached us at a normal walk, careful not to give offense before he understood the full scope of his predicament. I was surprised that he looked so young despite the fact that I had seen the Lady, who was at least four hundred and looked a well preserved twenty. I noticed the old guy who stuck me and Darling drifting along in Exile's shadow.

Exile came up and looked the situation over. He showed no special response except to look at Gossamer and Spidersilk as if warning them to behave themselves.

He came to us. "Most impressive." He did not look impressed. "You quite took me by surprise. I am Exile. Who are you, and who speaks for you?" Just a stranger chance met, making casual introductions.

Bomanz and Silent were busy. Torque still didn't have the lingo so good. That left old Case. I was elected. "I'll do the talking." I indicated Darling. "The White Rose."

"So I see."

I didn't figure on naming anybody else, but Bomanz decided I should. He said, "Bomanz. The Wakener."

Exile showed a little surprise at that. Bomanz had a reputation. He was also supposed to be dead.

I indicated Silent. "Silent. Formerly of the Black Company. I'm Philodendron." I didn't name Torque. Seemed a good idea to leave something to nag on Exile's imagination.

"I suppose you're here for the same reason everyone else is?" He kept one eye on the Limper, I noticed. Right then the Limper was eyeballing the situation and counting up his options.

I signed at Darling. She signed back. I told Exile, "The silver spike. The tree god will not allow it to fall into the hands of anyone who wants its power. Whatever the cost."

"So I see," said Exile. It did look like the Plain had belched up all of every one of its weirdnesses. I wondered who was at home keeping the shop spooky. "That thing out there might have something to say about that to all of us."

Darling signed some more. I said, "We will destroy it if you can't. The tree has concluded that it has tormented itself and the world long enough. It will be destroyed."

Exile started to say something but never got the chance. I reckon Limper heard us well enough to get pissed because everybody wanted to put him into the past tense.

He had something all ready to go. But as he was about to cut loose, Spidersilk beat him to the punch, hit him from the side and knocked him ass over appetite. His spell went screaming straight up, making a sound like the biggest bullroarer in the universe. Gossamer hit him from the other side. A missile storm pounded away at him. Glowing red balls arced in from the fields to the south and for the first time I noticed a group of black riders down there, all mounted on the nastiest-looking critters I've ever seen. I thought I recognized our old buddy Toadkiller Dog. When the red balls came down they hit the ground like a giant stomping, leaving steaming black holes pounded into the snow and the earth beneath.

Exile just stood there with his hands in his pockets, watching.

None of my bunch did anything either.

The Nightstalkers came marching into the cleared area

behind the wall, all spit and polish, neatly in step, their band playing. They began taking over positions as though this was nothing more than a changing of the guard. Brigadier Wildbrand, all squeaky-clean, came marching up to report to Exile.

The uproar died down. Nobody had done much damage to the Limper. He hadn't done any either.

Wildbrand glanced at us. I winked. That startled her, so I tried another trick, pixie that I am. "What you doing after work sweetie?"

She snubbed me. Not good enough for her, I guess. Just as well. She was too old for me.

A shadow fell on us all as she and Exile talked tactics. A granddaddy windwhale had moved into position overhead, not all that high up. I was impressed.

Exile and Wildbrand checked it out. He seemed the more perturbed. They went back to tactics. I glanced at the world outside. Limper was getting set to try something. The black riders had dismounted. Their steeds had disappeared. Toadkiller Dog was among the missing, too. The riders were walking closer. I noticed that talking stones, walking trees, and centaurs had gotten in behind them.

Limper charged the wall, a dark cloud forming around him. Everything cut loose again. And didn't bother him at all. He jumped up and kicked the wall—and knocked a hole in it fifty feet wide. Exile joined the party, somehow pouring on an endless, torrential shower of fire.

Limper hadn't much liked fire last time we saw him. He didn't mind it now, except he had trouble seeing straight. He wanted to knock down the wall where we were. He hit it two more times, once to either side of us, then backed off to think about what to do next. Exile gave up with the flames. They hadn't done much.

The Nightstalkers were busy repairing the gaps already.

I knew what I'd do next if I was the Limper. I'd prance through one of those breaches and start taking out my top enemies.

Being almost as smart as me, he figured it that way himself.

The snow was pretty torn up out there now but he strayed onto some virgin stuff while he was making up his mind which breach to charge. About fifty slimy green tentacles shot up out of it, glommed on to him, and started trying to pull him apart. The snow all around erupted. A whole pride of monsters piled on Limper. Toadkiller Dog got his head in his jaws and tried to bite it off. Something else shoved a hoof in his mouth so he couldn't do no hollering. The people who had ridden those monsters ran toward the excitement.

Exile and the twins paid no attention. They faced the city now, making concerted, complex come-hither gestures. What looked like a flock of birds rose from deep in the city and headed our way. Close up I saw it wasn't birds at all but lots of chunks of wood.

The flock settled outside the wall, neatly building a monumental pyre. Did they think they were going to roast Limper? They'd tried fire already.

No.

A giant pot followed the wood, sloshing, settled amidst the pyre. A big lid followed. It just hung around in the air, waiting.

The black riders got in on the fun down below. Everybody and everything was trying to cut the Limper up or tear him apart. I asked Torque, "You got an onion we can toss in?"

Brigadier Wildbrand said, "That's the spirit." She winked when I looked at her.

The spirit? I didn't have no spirit left. This wasn't even my fight, when I thought about it. And my hip was hurting so bad I expected to fall off everything in a minute.

The Limper bit the hoof off the thing that had one in his mouth, spit it out, let out a howl like the world's death scream. Bodies and pieces of body flew. Only Toadkiller Dog hung on. He and the Limper rolled around growling and screaming while the others tried to get back into it.

Exile assessed the damage. He looked at me. "He's too strong for us. It wasn't a great hope, anyway. Will you contribute?"

I signed to Darling, "He wants help."

She nodded, fixed on the action. For a moment I thought she wasn't going to answer. Then she made a complicated series of hand gestures. The eagle plunged off her shoulder, went flapping off and up.

I saw what Exile meant about Limper being too strong. One of the monsters was doing the foot-in-mouth trick to keep his sorceries silent. Toadkiller Dog was on his back, hanging on with all four limbs, his jaws still locked on the Limper's head, which he had almost completely turned around. But the others could not keep his limbs pinned. He used those to devastating effect.

The shadow of the windwhale grew more and more deep. It was coming down. Already I could smell it.

It dropped tentacles into the fray, grabbed Limper without any care to avoid getting anyone or anything else. Toadkiller Dog was in that mess, a couple other monsters, and a couple of human beings too squished to scream. A windwhale has the strength to snap five-hundred-year-old royal oaks. The Limper did not. The windwhale tore the whole mess into bitty pieces and dumped it into the giant pot.

Something to be said for brute strength sometimes.

The pot lid slammed down. Clasps clanked. The pyre roared to life.

I wondered how the Limper would get out of this one. He'd survived the worst so many times before.

I looked at Exile. "What about the silver spike?"

He was not happy.

"You couldn't take the Limper, you can't take us."

He checked the windwhales, the talking stones, the walking trees, the centaurs and mantas, said, "You have a point. On the other hand, why surrender a tool you can use to knock the empire down? I have good soldiers here. The chances of battle look no worse than those of not fighting."

I couldn't answer that. I took it to Darling. Everyone in sight was watching, waiting for a clue to their next move.

Tension was not down a bit because the Limper was out of the game.

I signed. Darling had me hold the standard so she would have both hands free to answer. I felt funny doing that, like I was making a commitment to a cause I still did not truly support. She signed at me for a long time.

I told Exile, "The spike will not be used at all, by anyone, whatever the cost. A place has been prepared by the tree god, in the abyss between universes, where only a power greater and more evil can retrieve it." Which meant, I guess, that anybody bad enough to get the damned thing back would be bad enough not to need it in the first place.

Exile looked around, shrugged, said, "That's good enough for me. We planned to isolate it, too, but our method would have been less certain."

A flash and crash trampled his last word.

Bomanz had stirred himself. Up the way, Gossamer took a couple drunken steps and walked right off the rampart. The old wizard said, "She disagreed with the decision."

Exile stared at Spidersilk, frozen in midmotion. She relaxed slowly, lowered her gaze, after a minute went to check on her sister.

I checked Bomanz. The old boy looked real pleased with himself.

Speaking of old men. Where the hell was that guy who'd been following Exile around?

Gone. And I never noticed him go.

That old bastard was half-spook.

LXXIV

Raven came to slowly, shaky and disoriented. Memory of a flashing boot and savage impact. Realization that he had a ferocious headache. That his hip had begun to ache. That he was so cold he had begun to feel warm in his extremities.

A moment of panic. He tried to thrash around, found his limbs only vaguely cooperative. Worse panic before the onset of reason.

He wriggled his way out of the snow, got to his feet carefully. He felt himself over, scraped frozen blood off his face. The bastard had got him good. Almost had to admire those guys, the way they were hanging in there against the whole world.

Painfully, he dragged himself out of the ditch, stood on wobbly legs looking around, the old hip wound gnawing. Things had changed. There were monsters in the sky and witch fires flaring in the distance.

The Limper had come. Darling would be in the middle of it. And he wasn't there.

She would think he had run out again.

Raven reached the center of excitement in time to witness Gossamer's fall. Everyone seemed to relax after the incident. The Limper must not be a threat right now.

The crowd came down off the wall. Soldiers brought horses for Exile and Brigadier Wildbrand. A platoon of Nightstalkers fell in around them and they started moving north. Raven wondered what the hell was happening. It looked like Darling and Exile had cut a deal.

He could not catch them now, wobbly as he was.

The twins had their heads together. They threw dark looks after the departing company. They radiated a stench of wickedness about to break loose.

Better stick with them.

LXXV

When the monsters began sliding across the sky Smeds suffered an attack of caution. Able to think of nowhere else to run, he headed back to the ditch.

The guy he had kicked was still there, twitching once in a while. He backed off and watched, waiting to see what the guy would do. After a while the guy woke up, dragged himself out, and tottered off. Good. Now he had a place to wait for Fish. He went over and around and entered the culvert from the northern end, passed through, and sat down to wait.

Fish showed up a forever later, standing over there on the footbridge. . . . He didn't have the other blue bag. Damn. Smeds whistled just loud enough to carry to Fish, waved cautiously.

"What happened?" he asked when Fish arrived. "Where's the other bag?"

Fish explained.

Smeds told his story.

Fish said, "We need to get out of here, then. Let's get the stuff. We might be able to get out one of the breaches if there's any more excitement. With the spike up for grabs we can count on that."

They got the blue bags, which they rubbed up with dirt, and Smeds's pack, and headed for the area where the wall had been breached. The city was a place of ghosts. The living cowered behind locked doors and barred windows, praying their gods would keep them safe from the terrors without and the cholera within.

The occasional cry of a cholera victim made Smeds think more of haunts bedamned than of the living in pain.

LXXVI

Exile wouldn't say where the spike was hid. He didn't act like he wanted to pull something, just like he wanted to be in on the whole thing. Like he wanted a look at the cause for all the fuss. Can't say I blame him. I saw it back when it was just a big nail. I wanted to see how it had changed.

He led us up toward Oar's North Gate, got up on the wall, and started marching back and forth. We stuck tight. Outside, the friendly troops had begun a shift to the north. Exile took inspiration, told Brigadier Wildbrand to seal off the area inside the wall. We'd had enough trouble over that hunk of metal already. He asked for masons and heavy lifting equipment to be brought, too.

The damned spike was in the wall! No wonder nobody ever found it.

Wildbrand sent messages. Nightstalkers moved in. I was concerned. I would've been more concerned if the sky wasn't filled with monsters.

It took two hours to assemble machinery and workmen, and another for them to get set up to start pulling the wall apart. Nobody could stay tense all that time.

Sometime during the wait Bomanz asked Exile, "What arrangements did you make to keep your fire fueled? Rendering the Limper was a good idea but you'll have to pressure-cook him for days. The fire seems to be failing."

Exile looked down south. Bomanz was right. Exile frowned, muttered, grumbled at Brigadier Wildbrand. Next time I looked some of my scabrous old buddies from the militia were running firewood to the pot. And not doing a very good job.

Once everything was set and the spike's hiding place was sealed off inside the city and out, Exile asked Darling if she was ready to see it brought to light. She told him to get on with it.

There was a new kind of tension around, like everyone's temper was short and we were all waiting for somebody to do something inexcusable so we could let off steam by kicking his butt.

Guys started banging away with sledges and wedges and pry bars and ten minutes later the first stone rose out of its setting.

The day got on into late afternoon before the workmen exposed the layer of mortar supposed to contain the spike. For a moment everyone forgot enmities and allegiances and crowded up to stare at the blackened half of the spike that lay exposed. Darling told Silent to go get it.

He borrowed a mason's hammer, put on heavy leather gloves, took along a lined leather sack and somebody's old shirt to wrap and pack it in. He wasn't going to take any chances with the damned thing.

Darling readied a small wooden chest.

About the time Silent chopped the spike loose I glanced toward that giant pot. So I missed the beginning of the excitement around me but not its start at the pot, where the men feeding the fire suddenly scattered, like a school of minnows when a large hungry fish appears.

The top blew off the pot.

Something made of pieces of all the things that had gone into the pot, with way too many limbs and those in all the wrong places, crawled over the pot's lip, fell into the fire.

Someone screamed behind me. I whirled.

One slight Nightstalker had knocked Brigadier Wildbrand off the back of the wall. Another had stuck a knife into Exile. The first was hurtling toward Bomanz.

Gossamer and Spidersilk!

Bomanz went over backward, flailing the air, and plunged headfirst into the snow that had drifted against the wall.

Only Darling retained any presence of mind. She let go the White Rose banner, yanked out her sword, gave

Bomanz's attacker a hearty chop, and followed him over the edge.

The one after Exile screeched.

That screech plain demolished everybody. We all just collapsed.

She jumped down and started hacking and slashing at Silent. She took the spike away, climbed back up, raised it overhead, and howled triumphantly.

Raven appeared out of nowhere, stuck her in the brisket, tried to knock the spike away, failed on his first try but got it his second. It tumbled down into the snow outside. Raven and whichever twin followed it a moment later, Raven grinding his knife into her belly while she screamed and tried to strangle him.

And outside the wall the thing from the pot humped and waddled and dragged itself toward us, oblivious to the resistance of the Plain creatures.

LXXVII

"Time to go," Fish told Smeds.

They stepped out of hiding and strode toward the nearest breach like they were on a mission from the gods. Men wild-eyed with panic paid them no heed. They scrambled over rubble, dropped down outside, and started moving southward.

Smeds expected disaster every step. Not till they crossed the first low ridge and Oar disappeared did he begin to feel at all positive. "We did it! Goddamn! We really got out!"

"It could still go to hell on us," Fish cautioned. Then he grinned. "But I'll tell you, the future looks brighter than it has for months."

LXXVIII

Impressions swirled as Raven toppled from the wall with the screaming sorceress: ground turning and rushing upward, a windwhale making its booming protest as its attempt to grab the thing from the pot was rebuffed.

Impact! He felt his blade reach her spine, going between vertebrae. He felt his right leg twist beneath her and snap. They screamed at one another as their faces smashed together.

He got the better of it. He retained consciousness and even a fragment of will. He dragged himself away, a few feet, started trying to guess the damage to his leg. Didn't feel like a compound fracture. Hurt bad enough, though.

Bodies lay all around him. Only Bomanz seemed to be breathing.

Packing snow around the leg helped numb it a little.

People were yelling above. He saw Case jumping around, waving, pointing. He looked.

The thing from the pot was coming. It wasn't a hundred yards away. And nothing seemed able to stop it. Mantas pounded it with their lightnings. It didn't pay them any attention. It had only one thought: the silver spike.

Case was trying to get him to get the spike and get it up top before the thing got hold of it.

Bomanz rolled over, got to his hands and knees, shook his head, looked around dumbly, spotted the thing, turned almost as pale as the snow. He croaked, "I'll try to hold it off. Find the spike. Get it up to Darling."

He staggered to his feet, tottered toward the thing.

Raven supposed it really could not be called the Limper

anymore, though the Taken's insanity, ambition, and rage drove it.

He looked for some sign of the spike. The pain in his leg was the worst he had felt since Croaker had got him with the Lady's arrow.

LXXIX

Raven finally seemed to get it through his skull what we wanted. I'd already volunteered to go down. Darling wouldn't let me. Now I signed, "Looks like his leg is broke."

She nodded.

Bomanz hit the thing from the pot with a grandpa power spell. It stopped the thing in its tracks. It went down on its belly, lay there glowing biliously, making a nasty whining noise.

A couple of Nightstalkers brought Brigadier Wildbrand back up. She had a busted arm and some busted ribs and looked like death on a stick but she was ready to fight. I told her, "I think you're the top imperial left."

She looked at the mess, said, "Yes," but seemed fresh out of ideas.

A talking stone dropped out of the sky, hit the rampart. It was my old buddy with the scar. He wanted orders from the White Rose. The White Rose didn't have any orders.

Raven scrabbled around in the snow. The thing from the pot started moving again. Centaurs raced around it, throwing javelins. Bomanz's spell had softened its protection. Most of the javelins got through. The thing looked like a porcupine. But it didn't seem to notice or care about the missiles.

Talk about your single-minded obsessions!

Bomanz popped it again.

Stopped it in its tracks again, too. It smoldered. The javelins burned. But it was not out of the game, it was just stalled. Bomanz looked up, shrugged. What more could he do?

Raven kept digging in the snow, dragging his broken leg. He didn't bother looking around to see what was gaining on him. He'd find it in time or he wouldn't.

I told Wildbrand, "Long as we're standing around not doing anything, why don't we get some ropes down there so we can hoist my buddies up?" Silent was on his feet now but looked like he was only maybe ten percent in this world. In fact, he looked like a lunatic, foaming at the mouth.

Wildbrand looked at me like I had brain fever if I thought she was going to lift a finger to save any Rebel. I reminded her, "We got a whole gang of hungry windwhales up there." Scar flashed away to cue the nearest. It started dropping. Scar reappeared, chuckling.

Wildbrand gave me a classic dirty look, put some of her boys to work on one of the cranes that had been used to pull the wall apart.

I yelled at Silent, "Get ready to come up!" He ignored me. He was getting ready to give the Limper thing some kind of surprise.

Old man Bomanz yelled, cut loose with his best shot, and tried to dive out of the way all at the same time. None of it did him any good.

The thing smashed into him, flowed over him. He screamed once, more in outrage than pain or terror, then tried to fight.

Silent looked up at Darling, smiling through tears. He sort of bowed with just his head . . . and jumped.

Goddamned madman!

He hit the thing's back. Flesh splashed like water and burned like naphtha, though the flame was green. The thing started rolling over and over and over, leaving pieces of itself behind.

Raven kept on looking for the spike.

Darling started hammering stone with her fist, shedding silent tears. I was afraid she'd break something she was so violent. . . . She stopped, whirled, signed, "Have the windwhale take it now. It will never be weaker."

I didn't have to tell Scar. He read sign. He flashed away. By the time he got back the windwhale was pulling the thing apart again.

I asked Wildbrand, "You think you can keep the pot boiling this time, if we put the pieces back in?"

She got a face like a fishwife looking for a fight. "You do your part, I'll take care of mine. How do you plan to get the lid back on?"

That was easy. "Scar, have one of the big guys put the top back on the pot. Maybe carry a few hundred tons of firewood, too."

Wildbrand gave me the look, checked her temper, said "Maybe you aren't stupid," and had her men help her down to the street.

Down south, where the breaches were, there was mass confusion. People were heading out, a flood the grays could not stem if they were bothering to try.

The thing tumbled into the pot. The lid went on with a big, final clang.

Raven screamed.

He had found the silver spike. Or it had found him.

By the time I looked at her Darling was hammering the wall again, both fists bloody.

He had gotten hold of the thing with his naked hand.

He got to his feet. On a broken leg! He held the spike up toward us. I yelled.

He looked at me. I did not know him. A terrible change had come over him. He laughed horribly. "It's mine!"

His eyes were the Dominator's eyes. Eyes of insanity and power, that I had seen in the Barrowland the day the Lady had brought her husband down. They were the eyes of the Limper, ready to be entertained by the agony of a world that had given him nothing but pain. They were the eyes of everyone who ever nursed a grudge and suddenly found it within their power to do whatever they wanted, without fear of reprisal.

"Mine!" He laughed.

I looked at Darling, as sour with despair as ever I'd been.

She turned off the water, started signing. She was as pale as a sheet of paper. I shook my head. "I can't do that."

"We have to." Tears streaked her face. She didn't want to do it, either. But it had to be done or the hell we'd put ourselves through would have been time and pain utterly wasted.

Raven had studied sorcery long ago. Just enough to blot his soul, a taint the spike could rip into and use as a channel for its evil.

"Do it!" she signed.

Damn her! He was my best friend. Damn that rock Scar. He could have given the order anytime, but he waited and made us do it so we couldn't lay off the blame on his precious tree god.

"Kill him," I said. "Before it possesses him completely."

Near as I could tell Scar didn't do a damned thing.

But down there a centaur's arm shot forward. A javelin flashed. The shaft smashed in through one of Raven's temples and out the other.

This time he would not be back from the dead. This time he wasn't faking.

I sat down and turned inside myself, wondering if I hadn't dragged my feet so much while we were headed south would we have caught up with Croaker and so maybe never have gotten into this spot. This monster was going to be riding my shoulders for the rest of my life.

Darling did her own version of going into a pout.

Only Torque kept his mind on the job. He got the wooden chest from Darling, shinnied down the crane rope, got the spike away from Raven. He climbed back up, set the box down by Darling, came over to me and said, "Tell her I'm out of it, Case. Tell her I just couldn't take it no more." He walked away, maybe going looking for the brother who had left with Raven and hadn't come back.

I didn't much blame him for going.

LXXX

Smeds laid the last stone on the old man's cairn. The tears were gone. The anger was quiet. It was not right that Fish should have fallen to cholera after taking the worst that could be thrown by the world's nastiest villains. But there was no justice in this existence.

It there was, Timmy Locan would be here, not Smeds Stahl.

Smeds went on, into the city Roses. A year later he was a respected member of the community, owner of a struggling brewery. He lived well but without ostentation that would excite unwanted curiosity. He never told his story to a soul.

EPILOGUE

No matter how many times I walked around it, the hole into the tree god's "abyss" still looked like a piece of black silk suspended a yard above the ground. It refused to have more than two dimensions.

Darling brought the little chest containing the silver spike, threw it through. It took both of us to do the coffin that contained all that had been left in the big pot when, after a week of cooking, it had been allowed to boil dry. The black circle vanished as though a stage magician had sucked the cloth up his sleeve.

We went and got clean for what seemed like the first time in years, then Darling showed me around the rabbit warren that had been home for the Black Company and Rebel movement for so many years. Fascinating. And repellent. That people should put themselves through such hell . . . I wished them better times than mine, wherever they were.

Somehow we ended up doing what men and women seem unable to avoid. Afterward, she dressed in the clothing of a peasant woman, without a hint of mail or a single hidden blade.

"What goes?" I asked.

She signed, "The White Rose is dead. There is no place for her anymore. No need."

I didn't argue. I never was on that side.

For want of anything better to do we got Old Father Tree to give us a ride to where we could check out the progress of the potato industry.

It hadn't changed a whole lot, except the people I knew had got older.

The grandkids wouldn't believe a word of our stories but they'd fight anybody who didn't agree that we told the most exciting lies in the world.